How NOT to be Popular

Also by Jennifer Ziegler

Alpha Dog

How **NOT** to be Popular

Jennifer Ziegler

Delacorte Press

1 - 5164

Published by Delacorte Press
an imprint of Random House Children's Books
a division of Random House, Inc.
New York

Visit us on the Web! www.randomhouse.com/teens

Educators and librarians, for a variety of teaching tools,
visit us at www.randomhouse.com/teachers

Library of Congress Cataloging-in-Publication Data

Ziegler, Jennifer.
How not to be popular / by Jennifer Ziegler.
p. cm.
Summary: Seventeen-year-old Sugar Magnolia Dempsey is tired of leaving friends behind every time her hippie parents decide to move, but her plan to be unpopular at her new Austin, Texas, school backfires when other students join her on the path to "supreme dorkdom."
ISBN 978-0-385-73465-3 (trade) ISBN 978-0-385-90463-6 (lib. ed.) [1. Popularity—Fiction. 2. High schools—Fiction. 3. Schools—Fiction. 4. Moving, Household—Fiction. 5. Family life—Texas—Fiction. 6. Hippies—Fiction. 7. Austin (Tex.)—Fiction.] I. Title.
PZ7.Z4945How 2008
[Fic]—dc22
2007027603

The text of this book is set in 12-point Goudy.

Printed in the United States of America

10 9 8 7 6 5 4 3

First Edition

For Christy

Acknowledgments

A big thanks to the following people for all of their advice, inspiration, and assistance: Stephanie Lane, Christy Cerreto, the Bevill family (Jimmy, Will, Lynn, and Midgi), Julie Carolan, Lisa Holden, Jessica Arellano, Gina McFarlen, Cynthia Leitich Smith, Owen Ziegler, Donovan Gullion, and Allan Amaya.

And thanks forever to my family.

It was the best of times, it was the worst of times. . . .
—Charles Dickens, *A Tale of Two Cities*

Fair is foul and foul is fair. . . .
—William Shakespeare, *Macbeth*

Prologue: Constant Change

OH CRAP. WHAT did I just do? My right hand hovers over my phone, fingertips tingling like the sparking ends of live wires.

Now that I think about it, I probably shouldn't have sent that text message calling Trevor a faithless, crap-smeared ape. I'd been reading a lot of Jane Goodall lately and hit Send without really thinking it through.

Should I text him again? Maybe. Yeah. Yeah, I'll do that. But . . . what do I say?

"Tra-la-la-la . . . keep your smile on!" goes the song on the car stereo. The singer sounds like he's on helium. "Tra-la-la-la!"

I can't take it anymore.

"Rosie, Les, can you turn that music down, *please*?" I yell from the back of the car.

Les turns around in the passenger seat. "Really?" he says, his eyebrows arched in surprise. "It's not that loud."

"No. But it's not that good either," I mutter.

He and Rosie exchange one of their many mind-melding smiles. It's the one that silently communicates *Ah, our daughter. We love her. But she so needs to get in touch with the Universe.*

Rosie lets out a little giggle and turns her attention back to the road. "Such negative energy," she says, shaking her head. She continues driving along the interstate at fifty miles per hour while humming with the music, oblivious to the traffic zooming past us at twice the speed.

My heart gives a little guilty thump. I know she's trying to come up with reasons why I've been weirding out today. She has no idea my world imploded an hour ago, when I opened Trevor's message. First I pretended to be sleeping, so that I could blame my puffy, postcry face on the nap. Then, after I "woke up," they started playing their Joan Baez tape. I grumbled and pleaded with them to stop, telling them it was putting me back to sleep, when in fact it was just way too depressing. Now they're listening to some New Age band with lots of high, breathy vocals and tinkly background sounds. For the last five miles, I've been picturing fairies frolicking on lily pads and unicorns sliding down rainbows. And hanging out in an animated Smurfiverse is not what I want to be doing right now.

Les lowers the volume; then he turns around and

studies me, stroking his wiry reddish brown goatee. "Why so glum? Come on. Let me see you smile, Sugar."

It's not a term of endearment. It's my actual name. Sugar Magnolia Dempsey. Yes, I'm named after a Grateful Dead song. Yes, it's weird. No, I don't particularly love it, but I just go by Maggie and bribe or threaten teachers never to read my full name aloud.

"I don't feel like smiling," I say from my flat-on-my-back position. From this altitude I can see up his nostrils. Even his nose hairs are wavy. No wonder my hair is the way it is.

"Well, what do you want to listen to?" he asks.

"I don't know. Can we just . . . be quiet?" I ask, holding back a sob. If they sense how fragile I feel, it'll be all group hugs and chamomile tea.

Les nods. "You're right, Shug. Let's all just meditate awhile."

I close my eyes and listen for the squeaking of the old bucket seat as he turns to face forward. Then I flop onto my left side and stare at the small screen of my Nokia again, scrolling through Trevor's e-mail for the sixtieth time in as many minutes.

Hey Sugar-Mags,
I'm sorry to do this in an e-mail . . .

Why didn't I realize at this point? Any message that starts this way is *not good*.

I'm sorry to do this in an e-mail
but I don't know where you are
and I need to get this over with.
I don't think I can do this long-
distance thing. I'm sorry. I suck, I
know. I thought I could, but I was
wrong.

I like you a lot. But this is stupid if
I can't ever see you. My dad says I
should be a free spirit right now
anyway. And I know you'll be meeting
lots of new guys. . . .

What does that mean? Does he think I'm going to go all nympho the minute I start at the new school? I was going to stay loyal to him! I *was*! I was going to save up money and visit him over spring break! And he couldn't even last *three weeks*?

I'll bet anything that Candace Jacobi made a move on him. We used to make fun of how pathetic she was. He'd barely look at her when we were together, but it's hard to compete with a girl when you aren't there.

Stupid simian! I'm sure that's what happened. I'm glad I called him names!

Of course . . . it's probably not the best way to win him back.

Anyway, I'm sorry. At least I tried.
Good luck with your new scool and
stuff.
        Trev

"Scool." He didn't even bother to spell-check.

I consider texting him again but I feel too mashed up, like the remains of that skunk we passed on the road a little while ago. Instead I lay my head down and completely stretch out in the back of our family car—which, I should mention, is a '75 Cadillac hearse. We bought it while we were in Santa Monica from a really stoned surfer who called himself Ethan Foam. It's canary yellow with two black stripes down its sides and I've already nicknamed it the Bumblebee. It's old and clanky and uglier than donkey poo (and I should know—I saw lots of donkey poo when we lived on that farm in Oklahoma), but the one good thing about it is that if you want to lie down in the back, you can *really* lie down. We've even camped in it several nights. We're among the few people who can claim they've ever woken up in the back of a hearse.

It's also pretty damn appropriate for how I feel right now.

We're moving again. This time from Portland, Oregon, to Austin, Texas. You'd think I'd be used to it. In my entire seventeen years, we haven't lived anywhere for more than eight months. For the longest time, I really didn't mind it. I even liked it. I thought it was fun and adventurous to set off for a brand-new destination and start over. But once I turned twelve, it began getting harder. Every time we left a place, I would leave behind good friends and fun school groups. I felt so . . . *interrupted*. And yet whenever I try to explain this to Les and Rosie, they say the same things over and over: "Life is short, so why not see as much as possible?" "Humans aren't meant to stay in one place. If we were, we'd be plants." I sort of understand what they're saying, but I sort of don't. How can they say it's our normal state to wander when I sure don't feel normal?

This time is the worst of all. Not only did I have to say goodbye to my best friend, Lorraine, I also had to leave behind a boyfriend. Trevor and I had gotten together soon after we'd moved to Portland, so we were a couple for almost six months. Things were just starting to get really serious between us when my parents announced we were packing up and heading to Texas. Now I guess I'll never know what we could have been.

My crying restarts and I muffle myself with my green sweater coat (which I haven't needed since we got as far south as Tucson). I really don't want my parents to see me like this. They wouldn't understand. Rosie would hug me and say that Trevor and I just aren't meant to be—that the Universe has other plans for us. And Les would talk about how great it's going to be in Austin.

But he's wrong. It won't be great. Nothing will ever be as great as Portland and what I have there.

Correction: *had* there.

Eventually the sobs peter out and that empty, wasted feeling returns. I secretly wipe my eyes on the sweater sleeve and pitch it and my cell phone back into my bag. Maybe I really should take a nap. I need to shut down my brain or do something other than think about Trevor. Of course, I'll probably just dream about him.

"Look! A sign!" Rosie suddenly calls out. I push myself up onto my elbows and glance out the windshield. When Rosie sees a "sign," it could be anything from a list of gas stations at the next exit to a boulder shaped like a heart. This time it's an actual road sign.

" 'Austin . . . three hundred miles,' " Les reads aloud. "We'll be there just after sunset."

"Joy," I mumble, and flop back down again.

We were supposed to have made it to Austin from Portland in a week. But traveling cross-country with my parents is like entering a time vortex. They aren't very good with schedules and fixed destinations. In California they heard about a Renaissance festival and just had to stop. So for three days I watched my dad in tights and my mom in a push-up bustier run around a plywood facsimile of an old English village, saying things like "forsooth" and "zounds!" Finally we made it to Arizona, where we picked up a really skinny hitchhiker named Turin. He claimed to be investigating UFOs and talked

Les and Rosie into driving seventy miles off course to the middle of some desert so that we could drop him off at a point he called the pickup spot. It took us three more days to make it through New Mexico, since Les kept stopping at Indian pueblos. He loves showing off his knowledge of Zuni and Laguna culture by leading around groups of tourists, with his big sun hat and walking stick, looking like a redheaded hippie wizard.

You'd never know it by looking at him, but my dad is sort of a genius. He has two PhDs from two different schools: one in theater and one in medieval studies. He's forty-four years old and still doesn't know what he wants to be when he grows up. Rosie is a forty-year-old flower child. She doesn't do hallucinogenic drugs (at least anymore) or sleep with everyone she feels a karmic bond with (that I know of), but she's big on dancing—anywhere, anytime. Like at my junior choir concert last year. While all the other parents sat in their chairs, smiling and looking proud, she leaped to her feet and began an interpretive dance to our rendition of "Can You Feel the Love Tonight." At least she knows what she wants to do with her life. That's why we're moving to Austin. She got accepted into this really famous massage school. She'll finish her course work in four months and then . . . who knows where we'll end up?

And me? Your guess is as good as mine. Sometimes I think I don't know myself well enough to figure out

what I should be. Last summer I started seriously thinking about becoming a cultural anthropologist, like Margaret Mead. The great thing about it is that when you're
doing a study, you stay in one place for a really long time,
observing and interviewing. You can't just take off and
leave things half finished. If you do, all the hard work
you've done up till then will be worthless.

Of course, last summer I started picturing Trevor in
my future too. And look how that ended up.

I stare out the rear window in the direction we
came from—toward Portland and Trevor. A dark shape
rolls across the road, followed by a second, smaller one.
Tumbleweeds, Les calls them. Uprooted bushes that go
wherever the wind takes them.

Just like us.

My lips go all wiggly again, so I press them together
to make them stop. I need to crawl away somewhere and
have a good cry, maybe even call Lorraine. It would
make me feel better to hear her cursing Trevor's name in
one of her filthy rants. But then, maybe it wouldn't.
After all, I miss her too.

If you were to look through my address book and see
the hundred-odd entries, you'd assume I was one of
those rich teen starlets who carry around hamster-sized
dogs in designer sweaters and attend parties every night.
But the truth is I don't have many friends.

Oh sure, those address-book contacts all *start out* as
my friends. Right before we leave a place, they hug me

tearfully and promise to write and call. I get a few e-mails, maybe a phone call or two, in the first couple of months. Gradually the letters get shorter and less frequent. The phone calls become awkward and boring. And then everything just stops. In a matter of months, I go from one of their best friends, to a long-distance buddy, to "this girl I used to know."

And now Trevor. *Damn! He didn't even try!*

It isn't fair. I don't want to go to Austin. It's not like there's anything there for me. Rosie will finish up her certification. Les will run the thrift store of his friend Satya. And me? I just get to repeat this misery all over again—only in a new place and with new people.

Knowing this makes me mad-sad-scared. I can't do the new-school drill anymore. If I'm going to leave in a few months, why even bother trying to fit in? I should probably just give up on friends this time around and be one of those creepy loner types.

Wait. . . .

Actually . . . now that I think about it, that's not such a bad idea.

I struggle upright, feeling energized. I've never considered it that way before. It really *doesn't* make sense to find a new crowd of pals if we're not even going to stay past the holidays. So . . . what if I just avoided that altogether? What if I kept to myself and did nothing but schoolwork—steering clear of all the social stuff?

Of course, it would *really* suck. No one to talk to

(except Les and Rosie). No parties. No one to hang out with. Basically no fun at all. School has always been a place where I could feel normal. Could I stand *not* being one of the "normal" kids? I've always been popular, at least a little bit, and I've never, *ever* been a complete loser. So if I wanted to become one on purpose . . . could I even pull it off?

Four months of solitude would be better than how I feel right now. If no one likes me and I don't like anyone, then I won't have anyone to lose.

It's a crazy idea, but I have to admit, it's also kind of brilliant. No friends, no fun clubs, and *definitely* no boyfriends. Then, when it comes time to move, it won't hurt at all. Maybe I'll even look forward to it!

I reach for my woven Guatemalan tote and rummage through the contents for a pen and the notepad I keep to remind me of stuff. The frantic, ripped-up feeling that came over me after reading Trevor's message has eased a bit, replaced by a fierce energy.

All I need is a plan of action. I've never tried anything this bizarre, so I could use a set of rules to make sure I know what I'm doing. Shouldn't be difficult to think of some. I know how to be popular, and I've read tons of magazine articles on the subject, so it seems to me that I should do the exact *opposite* of what they advised in those handy tips.

And really, how hard can that be?

Chapter One: Act Naturally

TIP: Popular girls never go anywhere by themselves. Thus, it must also stand to reason that the unpopular are always alone.

First days of school always make me feel extra alive. My senses just seem magically improved. It's like I can fully live in the moment and simultaneously float along beside myself, carefully recording everything for later viewing. And this, I know, will become a treasured memory. The kind that replays in full color and digital surround sound, with credits rolling at the end. This will be the day I finally figure out my life. The day I overcome the burden of being a Traveling Dempsey. Today I begin Operation Avoid Friends (OAF?).

Knowing I have nothing to lose this time around makes me feel better about the whole situation. To tell the truth, I'm even a little excited about it.

Of course, this is the first day of school only for me. Everyone else has been here for over two weeks. That's another thing about my parents: they can't be on time for anything. First they took their own sweet hippie time making it to Austin; then yesterday they had the entire day to officially enroll me at Lakewood High, but when did we walk in the door? At a quarter to five. The registrar was just about to shut down her computers—something she reminded us of several times as she raced through the enrollment process. Of course Les and Rosie didn't seem to notice. As Les slowly filled out forms in his ornate handwriting, the lady kept tapping her car keys against her desk. But Rosie just hummed along with the rhythm.

So here I am, getting my first glimpse of Lakewood's teen population. The students don't look all that different from Portland kids. Or Seattle or Berkeley or Boulder or Madison or Santa Fe kids, for that matter. All the typical groupings are here. This is my tenth high school, so as you can imagine, I've gotten really good at figuring out the cliques and the power rankings, just by noticing the way kids dress and act.

Hanging at the edge of the parking lot, under a cloud of cigarette smoke, are the Thugs, aka Burnouts, Stoners, or Fry-Boys. Rockers and Skaters are subsets of this group, and they overlap like Venn diagrams for partying purposes. Trevor was a part of this group in Portland; shaggy-haired Skaters were the dominant breed there, but it's obviously different in Austin. Here they seem to be of skinnier, squirrelier stock and they aren't surrounded by a gaggle of admiring girls.

Sitting at a couple of picnic tables on the front lawn are the Brains. Or Nerds, Honor Roll Dweebs, Debate Club Dorks, or Goobers. Judging by all the big black instrument cases, I'd say most of them take band, which is typical. At other schools I've learned that almost all superbrain students take band or orchestra, but not all band or orchestra students are superbrains. Band as phylum, Brains as genus.

Swarming around a stone wall that separates the parking lot from the school is what I guess to be the art and/or theater crowd. A guy in camo pants and a T-shirt with something ironic on it (I'm too far away to read it) is reenacting some outrageous sketch with a bad British accent. Meanwhile his peers cheer him on. A Goth couple in the front is really cracking up, which makes me smile. It's always funny to see Goths laugh.

And finally, scattered about the covered walkway leading to the school's front doors are the heads of the high school ecosystem. This category differs slightly from school to school, but usually it includes perfect poser types with an overabundance of money and power. In this case, preppy jocks appear to be the ruling class—mainly guys with football-player builds, spiky flattop hairdos, and urban designer clothes.

There are a few pretty girls sprinkled in with them, but mainly as accessories. I haven't yet spotted the school's ruling females, the crowd I typically try to integrate with.

Being part of the power clique means you're automatically protected to a degree. You get access to the best clubs and parties and sometimes have more privileges at school. Everything is just easier. I've never made top tier, but I've almost always been part of that scene—until this time, that is. Under the rules of my antipopularity plan, I can't associate with any friendworthy people. Instead I'm going to be one of those weird outsider types—the ones who are always by themselves and give off lots of keep-away vibes. The kind of person no one notices after a while.

"Hey! New girl!" One of the alpha guys calls out to me. He's cute. Real cute, in fact. Dark blond hair, strong jaw, dimples. I know I'm trying to avoid people, but this guy is so gorgeous it's hard to look away. "Where're you from?" he drawls, adding extra emphasis to "you."

I hear my response in my head. *All over the place.* It's a struggle, but I don't let it out. Instead I tear my gaze off him and fiddle with my messenger bag, hoping he'll lose interest. Just being near a guy reminds me of Trevor.

"Hey, you! I'm talking to you!" He raises his voice, and out of the corner of my eye, I notice that his pals all turn their heads simultaneously. Even a couple of passersby slow down to watch.

I wish he'd just declare me a weirdo and move on, but instead he hops down off his perch and walks up next to me. His cohorts pivot around, their faces gleaming expectantly.

"Didn't you hear me?" the guy asks. He leans forward, hovering his face over mine as if to give the best possible view of his perfect cheekbones and navel-sized dimples.

A warm sensation trickles through me—probably hormones. This is the type of guy girls embarrass themselves for, a guy who could possibly help me get over Trevor . . . but even on the bizarro chance we hooked up (which isn't likely), who would help me get over *him* when we move in four months?

As I stand there, sifting through my jumbled thoughts, the guy's face slowly flattens. "Man, what's wrong with you?" he asks. "Just trying to be friendly here."

"Blow her off, Miles," calls out one of his guy pals. "She's probably got someone else giving it to her." Denied any entertainment, the crowd turns back toward the other approaching students.

The guy gives me a final once-over, shakes his head as if confused, and lopes back to his crowd. I feel simultaneously let down and relieved—mainly relieved. I could have messed up my antipopularity strategy five minutes after arriving at school, but I didn't. And if a TV star–handsome guy doesn't throw me off, nothing will.

I push through the double glass doors, and the mystery of the missing queen bees is solved. As I cross the foyer and enter the wide-open student-center area, I find a swarm of cheerleader and dance-squad types. All of them are thin and pretty and wearing the trendiest fashions—no doubt copied from whatever bad-girl starlet has made the tabloid covers lately. No one takes any notice of me. They're all too busy practicing routines or painting spirit posters or gossiping.

In the past I would have tried to join this crowd as a hanger-on—you know, those celebrity-assistant types who get to share in the spoils. But I won't do that here. Instead I make myself look away, and wander off to find my locker assignment.

So far I've seen nothing that makes this school seem any better or worse than the others I've been to—which is fine. Since I'll know exactly what to expect, it should be no problem to stay out of everyone's way for four months.

Then, when I leave, it will be like I was never here at all.

After wandering in a complete circle, I finally find my homeroom. Room 117 is an offshoot of the middle hallway, coming right after a succession of supply closets, restrooms, and stairwells.

I'm already late by a minute or two, but it doesn't seem to matter. Most of the students are out of their seats and talking loudly. A couple of girls in the corner are singing a hip-hop song.

I walk up to the obvious teacher—a small skinny woman with a 1950s-style hairdo—who my schedule identifies as Mrs. Minnow. She's standing near the blackboard, facing the room and muttering something. It's not until I'm right beside her that I realize she's addressing the class.

"Everyone quiet. Please take your seats. Sit down, please," she rasps.

She doesn't notice me until I wave the office forms in front of her.

"Oh! Hello, dear. I didn't see you there. New student? How nice."

She takes one of the forms and returns the rest to me.

"You may sit wherever you wish. Although . . ." She pushes her glasses up on her nose and peers out at the assembled mob. The hip-hop girls are teaching each other dance moves now. And a couple of doofus-looking guys are playing some game in which they slap each other on the back of the head. "I'm not sure what seats are available."

She shuffles forward a few steps. "Class? Sit down now. . . . Class?"

No response. The glasses of one of the slap-happy guys go whizzing past us.

"All right now." She tentatively waves her arms as if trying to stop an approaching truck. "Be quiet now. Take your seats."

"Hey!" A booming voice cuts through the noise, making everyone freeze. Mrs. Minnow drops the paper she took from me and I quickly retrieve it.

"Y'all sit down and be quiet!"

A tall guy is standing in the middle of the desks with his hands cupped around his mouth for better amplification. He seems like a total Young Republican, with his pressed navy slacks and powder blue button-down. His hair is neatly parted and combed, probably with some sort of mousse or gel in it. He reminds me of the Mormon missionary kids Rosie and Les are always inviting inside for tea and a talk on the Bhagavad Gita.

The students grumble and roll their eyes as they gradually take their chairs.

"Better do what Super Boy Scout says before he calls the police," mutters one girl. She's pretty in a waxy way. An orangey salon tan clashes with her red cami . . . too much eye makeup . . . hair the color of candlelight. A textbook example of high school female perfection, right down to the constant look of disgust. This is the type of girl I'd normally kiss up to—but not today.

The princess and her two friends are the last to sink down into the crowd, except for the loud do-gooder. As soon as the room is quiet, he lowers himself into his seat and smiles back up at us. At first I assume he's waiting for Mrs. Minnow to pat him on the head, but then I realize he's looking at me. I stare right back. He has a long face that matches his tall, lanky body, and his features sit lazily on it. His dark eyes are perpetually sleepy-looking, his lips are a little too thick, and his prominent nose bends down at the tip. Still, he's cute in a door-to-door salesman sort of way.

"Thank you, Jack," says Mrs. Minnow in her crackly voice. I realize I can still barely hear her, even with the room quiet. "Boys and girls . . . I'd like to introduce a brand-new student, Miss . . . uh . . ." She frowns down at the paper. "Miss . . . Sugar—"

"Maggie," I interrupt hurriedly. "I go by Maggie." I try not to smile or make eye contact with anyone, but my first-day superpowers still pick up everyone's stares—especially the one of the khaki-wearing teacher's pet.

"Please welcome Maggie Dempsey and help her feel at home," Mrs. Minnow continues. She leans toward me, lowering her weak voice to an almost nonexistent level. "Go ahead and find a seat wherever you like."

Without taking too much time to consider, I walk to the first vacant desk I see and plunk into the blue plastic chair.

"Oh my god. I hate you." A voice comes from behind me.

I'm so shocked that my head automatically whips around. I've sat down in front of the blond Bratz doll.

"I hate you," she says again, this time to my face.

At first I'm stunned, then hurt, then panicked. I've run afoul of a school's ruling class before, but never this badly or quickly. Then I remember . . . I don't want to be liked here. This shouldn't matter.

"Your hair is so pretty. I just hate you," she continues.

I start breathing again. "Oh," I respond, unsure of what else to say.

"Do you get it permed?" she asks between chews of pink gum.

"Uh . . . no."

Her perfectly plucked eyebrows rise to reveal her first expression beyond deadpan boredom: disbelief.

"Really?" She's the kind of girl who pronounces the word "rully" and probably says it a lot. "But you do color it, right?" she asks suspiciously.

I shake my head. "Nope." I consider mentioning that highlights can come from spending time in the sun, but I decide not to.

"I hate you," she says for the fourth time.

My right hand reflexively grips a lock of my hair. I wave the end at her and say, "No, really. It's a bitch to deal with."

"Rully?" The girl still looks doubtful.

"Who cares?" says one of the blond girl's friends from the next row over. She has short brown hair and sharp, scrunched-together features that make her look mean. "Most girls would kill to have hair like that. Am I right?" She turns toward the girl on the other side of the blonde.

Friend number two just nods. She has immaculately styled brown hair, bright pink lipstick, and a wide-eyed, dumb expression.

"I'm Caitlyn," the blonde says.

"I'm Maggie."

"Uh, yeah. We know. Duh," says the mean-faced one. "I'm Sharla." She motions to the dumb-looking one. "That's Shanna."

Shanna and Sharla?

"So where are you from?" asks Sharla.

"Oh, uh . . ." I'm always slow to answer this. Sometimes because I truly can't remember. But mainly because it implies that wherever you lived before, you were established there, with friends, neighbors, and a favorite hangout or two. The places I name are more like pit stops on a never-ending road trip. "Oregon," I say finally. "But we weren't there very long. Before that we were in California."

"Cool!" exclaims Caitlyn. "Did you meet any movie stars?"

I try not to roll my eyes. People were always asking me this in Portland too. For some reason, they equate the entire state of California with Hollywood. (We lived in Berkeley.) And they seem to think the place is crawling with celebrities—as if they line the highways, waving to their fans.

"I once met Ashton Kutcher at an Animal Rescue League benefit," I tell them truthfully.

"Cool!" Caitlyn and Sharla squeal in unison.

I smile somewhat guiltily. No need to tell them I was one of maybe four hundred people he shook hands with that day.

"You know . . ." Caitlyn cocks her head at me, apprising me with her light brown eyes (which also have an orangish hue that matches her overly tanned face). "You rully should join our club. Don't you think she should be a Belle?" She pivots her head between Shanna and Sharla.

They nod in agreement.

"A Belle?" I repeat, confused.

"Oh yeah. The Austin Belles. It's rully cool. We have all the best parties and all the best people, you know."

A tickly sensation sweeps up the back of my neck. *Oh no, no, no, no. What are you doing, Maggie? You aren't supposed to be making friends! Remember?* School's been in session only a few minutes and already I've forgotten my big plan. I just automatically started copying these girls' body language and rhythm of speech, the way I always do when I try to worm into the power group.

Now what?

I start tugging the fingers of my left hand. "Um . . . I don't know. I don't think so."

Caitlyn's nose twitches slightly and her heavily mascaraed eyes seem to ice over. "What do you mean

23

you 'don't think so'?" she asks, mimicking me in a snotty little mouse voice.

"I just . . . can't," I answer. "Sorry."

I watch her exchange looks with her posse. Shanna seems completely stunned, while Sharla just glowers at me. But then, maybe she always looks that way.

"Whatever. Your loss. And I mean *rully*." Caitlyn sits back in her seat, signaling the end of our conversation. A second later Shanna and Sharla lean in and they all bow their heads together for a whisper session.

I face the front of the room, feeling heavy. It's obvious I've just made a big-time mistake—at least in their minds. For a moment or two, I rehearse different ways of undoing it, pretending I was joking with them, or claiming to have misunderstood their offer. But I know it's too late for that. Besides, this is what I want, right? Score one for Operation Avoid Friends.

It's better if it hurts a little now than a lot later, when I move.

Lunchrooms are all the same. Hundreds of students' voices jacked up to an earsplitting level. The dizzy aroma of rancid grease and pine-scented cleaner. A sticky film on every surface. Tables like torture devices, with their sharp metal runners at knee level and those crooked plastic lily pads for seats.

Lunch at a new school is like the SAT of social tests. It determines your immediate standing. Whomever you choose to sit with tells people who you are, or who you see yourself as. Choose a crowd too low on the social scale and you'll forever be associated with that power level. Aim too high and end up getting rejected—that's even worse. Then you have to pick all over again and the rest of the groups will know you viewed them as second best.

Today, for the first time ever, I don't have to worry about all that. I'm just going to eat by myself.

Only . . . it's not so easy.

I pause at the entrance to the cafeteria. To the casual observer, I'm simply stopping to let past a custodian who's pushing one of those giant rubber trash cans with the word "inedible" stenciled on the side. (And may I just add: *Duh!* Don't see many kids mistaking them for vending machines.) But as I wait, I secretly check out the dynamics of the lunchroom.

The Stoners are over by the window. A group of Spanish-speaking kids are sitting near the exit. A few artsy types are congregated in the back corner. And the jocks are sitting at the table in front of the small stage. In fact, some of them are sitting on the stage itself. Judging by their level of volume and activity, I'd guess the in-group routinely gets away with rowdy behavior— something that's true at most schools. I spot Caitlyn, Shanna, Sharla, and the other popular girls. I also check for the cute guy from this morning—Miles, I think. He isn't around, but I do see his posse.

I have to find a place soon, before I end up looking so obviously lost I get some pity-induced invitations.

And then . . . I see it: a small section of about eight empty seats at the end of one table. As soon as the lady and her garbage can move by, I head for the spot and settle into the next-to-last chair.

My first-day powers sense dozens of eyes on me, and my ears pick up a few snickers and whispers. *"That's the girl who . . . mumble mumble . . ."* I dig my food out of my lead-free rainbow-colored bag and line it up in front of me, acting as if I'm deaf, mute, and eternally happy.

I figure I have to endure only about five minutes of intense curiosity before they lose interest. But that's a downside to my first-day ESP: five minutes can feel like five life cycles . . . of a sea turtle . . . in a really toxic ocean.

I do some deep, yogic breathing and try to concentrate on my ABC sandwich. It's my own invention— avocado, bean sprouts, and cheese on two slices of lightly buttered pumpernickel. Normally it's one of my favorite things to eat, but this time it has all the flavor and texture of dryer lint. Guess taste is the only one of my senses that *isn't* enhanced today.

Eventually the whispers die out. I've made it through. But it's hard to feel triumphant knowing I have four months of this ahead of me.

In Portland, on a sunny day like today, Trevor and I would be sharing a bench outside on the quad. We ate together all last spring, only I ended up losing a couple of pounds since we did more kissing than eating. Plus I avoided anything that would give me bad breath or leave food in my teeth—which, when you're a vegetarian, is half your diet. Salad, celery, corn, beans, fruit—they all love to hang around in your dental work.

I wonder where Trevor's eating today, and who he's with. . . .

The table suddenly wobbles and I glance up from my tangerine to see a girl sitting across from me. She's chubby, with straight brown hair parted right down the middle and held back by two metal clips. Her white blouse is buttoned all the way up to the lacy collar at her neck, and she's wearing a gold strand with a pendant in the shape of a capital letter *P*.

"They were supposed to have a nondairy option for the mashed potatoes, but they forgot," she says, scooting her cafeteria tray toward her. "So they gave me two apple crisps instead."

Her voice is rather low, and when she talks, she hyperextends her lips, like a pouty little kid. A new round of whispering wells up around us.

"Uh . . ." I want to say something, but I'm not sure what magic words would get rid of her. When I thought up my plan, it never occurred to me that someone might just choose to sit with me.

As I watch her slice through her chicken breast with her plastic knife, I get a brilliant idea.

I grimace at the meat and start packing up my lunch bag. "Hey, um . . . I'm sorry but I'm vege—"

"Oh poopy doo," she grumbles suddenly as her plastic fork breaks.

Poopy doo?

"Excuse me, please, while I go and get another," she says, rising to her feet. "You can have one of my apple crisps if you like."

"Oh . . . thanks, but I . . ." Before I can get out a coherent sentence, she's already ambled off toward the condiment table.

Now I have no idea what to do. Should I just get up and leave while she's gone? Maybe I could eat not only her crisp but her whole lunch. *That* would drive her away. Of course, there's no way I could force down the chicken.

As I sit there debating myself and ripping my tangerine into wedges, the light dims slightly and I realize someone is standing behind me. I turn to find the guy from this morning, Miles, grinning at me like a toothpaste model. At my level I have the perfect view of his chiseled jaw and the faint cleft mark at the tip of his nose. I'm also close enough to pick up the wet, treelike aroma of his cologne.

"I see that thing leeched on to you," he says, nodding toward my new tablemate. "Why are you over here, anyway? Come sit with us." He points his cleft in the direction of the stage and widens his smile.

I feel a little fraction of me following him, as if I'm a set of nesting dolls and the teeniest one in the very center is stuffing things into her lunch bag and leaping up to join him. But the rest of me stays put.

"Aw, come on," he says. "Are you mad about this morning? The guys were just having fun."

Once again, I'm struck dumb by how cute he is—and yet he also seems like the type of guy who wears his looks like a weapon.

"Uh . . . shouldn't you be glad to see me?" he goes on. "I'm here to rescue you. To take you back to the land of normal people."

Another doll inside me joins up with her sister, and together they beg me to listen to the guy and do whatever he says I should do. But I can't. What if I start really liking him? What if I find a bunch of friends at the new table?

"Um, hello?" he continues, somewhat impatiently. "Did you hear what I said?"

Right at this moment my lumpy tablemate reappears. She slowly sinks into her seat, keeping a wary gaze on the Miles guy. She looks like a gazelle at a watering hole trying to figure out if the nearby lion is there to hunt . . . or just drink.

Miles heaves an annoyed sigh. "Are you coming with me or not?"

"Not," I blurt to a chorus of doll gasps inside me. "I already have a place to sit."

Miles's eyebrows stretch up and under his bangs. He's so obviously shocked he loses all attitude. For a couple of seconds, he looks less like a perfect pinup boy and more like a completely real guy—a Trevor-like guy. My mind starts conjuring up pictures of us taking walks and riding bikes and doing all sorts of Maggie-and-Trevor things. . . .

And then his brows come down and hang over his eyes in a seriously peeved expression. He mumbles something like "What's her problem?" and lopes back toward the popular table.

The girl across from me and several kids within earshot are all frozen in place. Most have big round Japanese-cartoon eyes that radiate panic and curiosity. But the weird girl just gives me a slack-jawed stare—attentive but not all that animated.

As Miles's shadow passes, movement and conversation start up again. The strange girl continues to gape at me in that spacey way—as if *I'm* the one who plunked down across from *her* and started talking about my dietary problems.

"You just turned down Miles Larson," she says, her tone all hushed and churchy.

"Uh . . . yeah. I guess so." I try to sound all la-di-da, as if I blow off movie star–looking guys on a daily basis, but my knees are really shaking and my voice comes out quivery. I can't help wondering if I made a big mistake.

"Nobody does that," the girl continues in her awed

way. "He can be bossy sometimes, but he's the cutest of all the Bippies."

"Bippies?"

She nods. "It's short for 'beautiful people.' "

I stare across the lunchroom and watch Miles rejoin his pals. He straddles his seat, and the others automatically slant forward as if magnetized. His face is all scrunched in disgust and I can tell he's bad-mouthing me—especially when he turns and points a dimple in our direction. Score two for Operation Avoid Friends.

My weird lunch mate follows my gaze to Miles and back again—her expression never wavering from that limp, openmouthed state.

Finally she spears a piece of chicken with her new fork and pushes it between her parted lips. "I'm Penny," she says between bites.

"Maggie," I reply.

"How was school today, Sugar?" Les asks as he slides a battered-looking cardboard box out of the back of the Bumblebee.

"It sucked." I can tell I'm still all mad about the move, because every time I get near my parents, these little pains pierce my gut from all directions. . . . I call them the Stabbies. Right now they're doing a saber dance through my small intestine.

"Oh? How so?" he asks.

"It just did. The kids are shallow. The classes are

boring. Even the food is fattier here. Plus it's so damn hot all the time." I seize the moment and look him right in the eye. "I wish we could go back to Portland."

Les hands me the box and grabs another for himself. "Every place has its own beauty. You know that."

I blow out my breath extra slowly, trying to soothe that carved-up feeling in my midsection. I don't know what made me think my father would hear me *this* time when he hasn't the last few thousand. To Les and Rosie, complaints are nothing but negative energy that needs to be thwarted by sunshiny statements and bear hugs.

"Don't worry, Shug," Les adds, kissing me on the temple. "Before you even realize it, you'll love it here."

Not if I can help it.

He closes up the back of the hearse and we carry our packages through the rear door of the shop, which is also our new home. On the first floor is the funky thrift/vintage-clothing shop Les is running for his pal Satya while the guy goes on some spiritual retreat to India. In the back, next to the rear door, is a set of rickety wooden stairs that leads up to our second-floor apartment. As we pass the stairwell, I hear Rosie sweeping up after dinner, humming a Joni Mitchell song. I can still smell the curry-pumpkin soup we ate, along with other things, like mildew and mouse pee.

I've learned from experience that it takes at least a month before a place stops smelling like someone else's home.

Our new apartment isn't that bad. It's small and stifling and it seems kind of neglected, but it has charm. Cinder block walls painted the color of butter, scuffed wooden floors, little shelves and nooks—including one for the phone (which we have yet to buy). When you turn on a faucet, the water spurts out different shades of brown before eventually running clear. And when you open the windows, you can hear the sounds of the traffic on the street below and sometimes catch a whiff of the Greek restaurant on the corner.

But compared to other places we've called home, this is a royal hall. Over the years we've lived in tiki huts, earth lodges, yurts, various trailers and shacks, modified buses, rat-infested rental homes, slummy apartments and even a tent. In Portland we stayed in some rich guy's tree house. Les did some landscaping for him and helped maintain his grounds, and in exchange we stayed in this massive playhouse he had built for his daughter when she was young. It had electricity, three large rooms, a working toilet, and a full kitchen—but no bathroom. So every day I'd head up to the main house with my towel and a bottle of herbal shampoo to use their guest bath.

I remember wandering around their posh designer home and thinking how nice it would be to have a place you could make all your own. It wasn't so much the luxury stuff I envied but the hominess. Their photos were framed and hung on the walls instead of stuck in easy-to-transport scrap albums. They had paintings and African figurines and beautiful groupings of shells and sea stones. I imagined them picking out furniture and rugs to match their art and discussing which rooms to enlarge for family gatherings.

It made me think of birds and how some migrate and others, like cardinals, bulk up for the winter and stay put. Those people were definitely cardinals, whereas we're wild geese. I wondered what it would be like to set up a real nest and stay put for a while.

Les and I set our boxes in the middle of the shop, atop the industrial blue carpeting. Dudz looks like your typical thrift store, with chrome-finished clothing racks and shelves stuffed with shoes. In the back are three wooden stalls with thick nubby curtains and a large cheval mirror. And along the side wall, near the entrance, is a green boomerang-patterned laminate counter holding up an ancient cash register.

Les walks up to the counter and grabs a box cutter. Then he slits the tape on the first box and pushes back the flaps. I reach in and pull out the first item: a beautiful beaded top. Next come a couple of black velvet skirts, followed by a linen suit.

After a while we fall into a rhythm, unpacking clothes and hanging them on the rolling garment rack for Les to steam (if necessary) and price. The whole time I think about school and how my genius plan didn't work out the way I'd hoped it would. For some reason, it just isn't enough to keep to yourself. People still make assumptions about you and try to be friends anyway—like that bizarre girl in the lunchroom, Penny. What's her deal? And there were other students in my classes who insisted on being friendly. Plus if that cute Miles guy continues being nice to me, I'm not sure I can stay strong and keep ignoring him.

Maybe I just had the wrong plan. I should have pretended to be an exchange student from some tiny Slavic nation and spoken in broken, heavily accented English. Or I could have turned mute for these four months.

Whatevs. Too late now.

"Is that the last of them?" Les asks, lisping slightly from the clothespin in his mouth.

"Just one more thing." I snatch the last garment out of the final box and hold it up, letting gravity unfold it. "Oh my god!" I exclaim, cracking up. "Don't tell me you're going to try to sell this thing. Who'd buy it?"

Les looks it over and smiles. It still amazes me that he's running a clothing store. Him. A man who's worn the same outfits since I was born.

"Satya sells all kinds of stuff," Les explains. "Says people always come looking for costumes for Halloween or local plays or for acting out sexual fantasies."

This makes me laugh harder. "Who'd find this thing sexy?" I press the outfit up against me and swing back and forth in front of the cheval mirror. It is, without exaggeration, the ugliest dress I've ever seen. A chintzy, flower-patterned number with short sleeves that poof up to my ears, a big bow that ties in the back, and a layered skirt that reaches to the middle of my shins and ends in an eyelet ruffle.

Unless Laura Ingalls Wilder herself comes in looking for a prom dress, no one would dare buy this thing. Not even Penny. Just being seen in it would mean instant, incurable loser-ship.

I stop laughing and hold the dress out at arm's length, studying it closely.

Hmmm . . .

Chapter Two: Pretty Ugly

TIP: In order to be unpopular, you must look the part. Remember four words: "plastic flowered swim cap."

Never in my worst cold sweat nightmares did I ever think I would go to school looking like a pimped-up Little Bo Peep. But here I am, setting phase two of Operation Avoid Friends in motion. I realized yesterday that it's not enough to *not seek* popularity. I have to actively pursue *un*popularity. And dressing like a loser is the quickest and easiest way to make people keep their distance.

Crossing the school's front lawn this morning, I instantly see the results of my new plan. Everyone is staring at me. Some point, some cup their hands to whisper to nearby friends, and some (like the happy Goth couple) burst out laughing.

Even though my mind is totally sold on this strategy, my body isn't. My legs are literally shaking in my lace-up boots, which are also borrowed from the shop. (Les, who's all about bending rules in the name of free expression, didn't even lift a brow when I asked if I could borrow the dress. Nor did he question my sanity—something I'm doing this very second.)

I keep propelling myself forward, concentrating on the light clopping of my heels and the rustle of my bag brushing against the big bow on my butt. Eventually I near the front entrance. I instinctively clamp my molars together, readying myself for the final gauntlet: Miles and his cronies.

"Holy . . . !" cries one of the lesser jocks, too stunned to finish.

The others turn in unison. I straighten my spine, lift my chin, and keep my eyes on the double glass doors, which seem absurdly far even though I'm only a few steps away.

"Jesus!" exclaims Miles, his Texas drawl stretching the word into three syllables. He busts out in staccato laughter, his friends' guffaws adding a jarring harmony.

All at once, I want to take it back. I'd wanted my plan to work, but not this effectively. I'm really not sure I can handle a whole day of this. Already my heart is pumping so fast I can't make out individual beats.

I suddenly get an image of me lying unconscious on the floor, EMTs zapping my chest through the Holly

Hobbie dress. . . . Maybe you really can die of humil-
iation?

Somehow my feet keep working and I find myself at
the glass doors. All I want to do is scurry to my locker
and hide until first bell. Unfortunately I'm a little too
vigorous in my movements, and as I swing my arm forward to pull the handle, my big Guatemalan bag goes
flying off onto the ground below. More chuckles follow.
Now I have to break my momentum to retrieve my stupid purse.

I bend over, having to lift my skirt a little to perform
the movement successfully, and reach for my bag. But
before I can grab hold of it, it's snatched away. I look up
and find Miles crouched beside me. His eyes are all
sparkly—no doubt from his hearty laughing fit—and his
mouth hangs in a lopsided smirk.

Like the proverbial deer, I freeze. Being this near to
him makes me a little breathless. I can't help imagining
what it would be like to get even closer. Would kissing
him be like kissing Trevor?

"That is one butt-ugly dress," Miles says. "But you
know, you totally make it work."

He hands me my satchel and we rise simultaneously.

"Thanks," I mumble. It's a preprogrammed response—
triggered entirely by his fetching my purse for me. But as
soon as my sound waves enter the atmosphere, I realize
he thinks I'm grateful for his crude and rather back-
handed compliment.

Miles's grin widens. "Knew you'd talk to me eventually." He lopes back over to his friends and mutters something I can't hear. They immediately start laughing like a pack of howler monkeys.

My mind fills with curse words. *Way to play it cool, Maggie.* I reshoulder my bag, yank open the door, and enter the student center, as dignified as a clompy, skirt-swirling, butt-bowed creature can be.

Which is not very.

It almost becomes worth it when I enter Mrs. Minnow's homeroom. As soon as she sees me, she looks me up and down, pushes her glasses up on her nose, and then looks me over again.

"Yes?" she says, taking a couple of tentative steps forward. "May I help you?"

"Uh . . . I'm new. Remember? From yesterday?"

She continues to frown and blink until a flash of recognition rekindles her features. "Oh yes! Mary!"

"Maggie."

"Please take your seat, Mary. Announcements will begin soon."

Caitlyn and her ladies-in-waiting are all huddled together for a gossip session, so they don't catch sight of me until I'm heading down the aisle toward them.

Shanna is the first to react. Her eyes grow alarmingly wide and I hear her suck in her breath. Sharla follows her gaze to me, and her whole face seems to drop an inch: her brows lower, her nose stretches downward, and her jaw falls open, revealing a giant wad of purple gum.

Caitlyn, who had been the one talking, first gives an angry huff at having lost her audience. But the instant she spies me, her scowl washes away.

"Oh . . . *my* . . . god!" she exclaims. I can't help noticing the emphasis on "my." Seems she lays claim to absolutely everything.

As I take my seat, Caitlyn lets out a cackling laugh. Taking their cue, the other girls join in.

"Nice dress," Sharla says between giggles.

I decide to play it dumb. "Thanks!" I reply, flashing her a big clueless smile. As soon as I face forward again, I hear the sizzly hisses of their whispering.

This is exactly what I figured would happen. Yesterday these girls wanted to be my friends. But now that I've dared to wear something outrageous, I've gone from potential pal to "total loser we can't be seen with." As much as I don't like it, I do understand. I've done the catty, behind-your-back talk myself at other schools. It's sort of standard behavior if you want to be part of the in-crowd—a way of constantly reminding people that you're on top.

I lean forward, straining to hear Mrs. Minnow, who's jerking her arms and trying unsuccessfully to get the class's attention.

"God! Look at that bow!" A loud whisper comes

from behind me (Sharla, I think), followed by a mocking laugh (Caitlyn, I think).

I petrify my body so that they won't get the satisfaction of any response. Still, my face feels all electrified. *You wanted this*, I remind myself.

I guess I still have some residual effects of yesterday's ESP, because I'm suddenly aware that I'm being watched. This is not as amazing as it sounds, since most of the class is gawking at my dress. But when I turn around, I notice Jack gazing right at me. Me. My face. Not my outfit. Unlike yesterday, though, there's no friendly grin. And as soon as he sees me staring back at him, he looks away.

Guess my new clothes have changed Jack's mind about me too. Ironic, really, since the guy always looks as if he just stepped out of a courtroom. Like today. His gray pants seem starched and carefully ironed. His dress shirt is a brighter white where it covers his wife beater. And his thick brown hair is slightly wet and separated into neat furrows by a comb—except for one little doinky piece in back. I have a weird urge to reach over and pat it into place.

As I watch, Jack and his flappy lock of hair rise. "Come on, guys! Keep it down!" he hollers. "Let's get quiet." He pauses, waiting for everyone to stop talking before he sinks back into his chair.

Behind me, Caitlyn lets out a sarcastic snort. "What a spaz," she whispers. "Who named him high king ass-kisser?"

"For real," I want to reply.

But then I remember: I'm not one of them. Not this time.

At lunchtime that Penny girl plunks down across from me again. Today she's wearing big plastic flowery clips in her hair and a pink smocked blouse, also with puffed sleeves—not exactly like mine (which graze my earlobes) but somewhat similar.

I wonder if people will think we planned this.

"I brought my lunch today, too, because the cafeteria has taco salad and that always gives me gas." She chats away while unloading plastic-wrapped items from a paper sack. One of these she holds out to me. "You want one of my pigs in a blanket? I have tons. I made them last night while watching that game show on TV. The guy lost. I felt bad for him."

"No, thanks," I say with a little wave. "I'm vegetarian."

Penny stops unpacking and watches me awhile, breathing through her mouth. "Really? Why?"

I haven't been asked this in a long time; people always just accept it. So it takes me a moment to frame a response. "Because . . . I don't believe in murdering animals for food," I finally reply.

"Oh." She watches me bite into my tomato-and-Muenster-cheese sandwich. "I guess I do. Although I wouldn't call it murder like I hate them or anything. I just think they taste good."

She's so unapologetic and matter-of-fact that I have to smile. It amazes me how blank faced she is about *everything*. Not once has she seemed to pick up on the stares and the snickers being lobbed at me in the lunchroom. Makes me wonder, is she clueless? Or does she simply not care?

Penny takes a huge bite out of a pig in a blanket, making her pudgy cheeks puff out even more. "Mmmm," she exclaims, sounding more scientific than passionate. A couple of seconds later, she swallows the glob and claps the crumbs off her hands. "This brand of weenies is better than the last one I bought. These are good by themselves, too. You can make a great dipping sauce by mixing grape jelly and mustard and cooking it in the microwave awhile." A thoughtful look comes over her face. "If you want to quit being vegetarian, I mean," she adds.

I eat my strawberries and try to ignore the group of cowboy-looking kids at the next table who are pointing at me and laughing.

"So did you think he'd win?" Penny asks, opening a bottle of chocolate soy milk.

"Who?"

"The man on the game show. He was from Illinois, I think."

I shake my head. "No. I mean . . . I didn't watch it. We don't have a TV."

It surprises me a little to hear myself say this aloud.

Normally I try to avoid confessing this for as long as possible, since it automatically marks me as an oddball greenie freak. But that doesn't seem to be a big worry for me anymore. At least, not with Penny.

"Oh," she says. "My parents let me watch one hour a day as long as I've finished my homework, done all my chores, and practiced the harp."

"You play the harp?" I blurt out in amazement. "Are you in the band?"

She shakes her head, and her hair skims her puff-ball sleeves. "Uh-uh. I was in orchestra but dropped out. This school is all about marching band and it's real hard to march with a harp."

Again I have to grin. The way she used "real hard" instead of "impossible" makes me wonder if she might have actually tried it.

"Besides, band kids have B lunch. This is A."

I wonder if this is why she has no one else to eat with. I consider asking but don't.

"I do private harp lessons now," she adds.

I notice her staring at my strawberries. "Want some?" I ask, pushing the container toward her.

"No, thank you," she replies, still gazing at them somewhat longingly. "I love them, but they give me hives."

"Oh. Sorry."

"That's okay," she says with a shrug. "Did you know that King Richard the Third was allergic to berries? He was mad at this guy and ate strawberries on purpose right before giving a speech to people. When he broke out in bad hives, he said the guy was a demon and had put a curse on him. So they chopped off the guy's head." She bites off half of a pig in a blanket and chews it thoughtfully awhile before swallowing. "Did you know you can stay alive for four minutes after getting beheaded?"

"Um . . . no." I find myself trying to imagine it. Would you feel excruciating pain? Would you know what was going on? Or would you just zonk out from the shock of it all?

How does she know all this stuff, anyway?

I'm lost in thought, absently rubbing the high collar of my dress, when Penny grumbles, "Oh pooper scoop!" She's staring at her watch, her sparse brows wavy with panic. "I'm on this new asthma medicine and I was supposed to go take it ten minutes ago."

"Aw, well, I wouldn't worry." I try to reassure her as she hurriedly tosses her food back into her bag. "Ten minutes isn't that lo—"

"Bye!" she cries as she leaps from her seat and bolts down the aisle. I'm left saying "—ng" to an empty space.

With Penny gone, I feel suddenly open and vulnerable in the loud, crazy lunchroom. I can't help hunching over, all forlorn-like. The plan is working. I'm alone and friendless.

And that's when it occurs to me: Penny never once mentioned my weird outfit.

• • •

Midway between the school and our new home, on a curvy creek-side avenue, stands a building with a big hourglass out front. The sign above it reads Gym-Perfection: for Ladies in pink script lettering.

I noticed it yesterday, and today decided to treat myself to a nice stress release. So after racing home for a snack and a quick change into workout wear, I pack up a bag with a towel and a bottle of water and jog out to the place.

Over the past five years, I've gotten really good at yoga. I like the way it steadies me and shushes up my mind. I'm still a little wobbly in the pretzel poses, but my strength and balance have improved, and Rosie says it's turned my aura a deeper shade of indigo.

At the front counter I'm greeted by a lady with a ponytail gathered at the exact top of her head. She hands me a couple of forms to fill out, along with a list of classes and a temporary membership card.

"Your-first-week-is-free-and-after-that-there's-a-monthly-fee-but-you-get-unlimited-classes-and-time-on-the-equipment," she says, her mouth moving like hummingbird wings. "My-name's-Gayla-come-get-me-if-you-need-me." She gives a little twinkle of a smile and flounces off in the direction of the treadmills.

I wonder what her hurry is if they're so big on unlimited time.

I finish filling out the forms and glance over the class schedule. Luckily I've brought along my faded tankini, so I can at least do a few laps in the pool if there's nothing going on today that I like.

Let's see. . . . Step class? No. Too spastic. Kickboxing? Nope. Getting my ass kicked is not my preferred way of working out. There's no yoga anywhere on the schedule, but there is a Pilates class that starts in ten minutes.

That will do. Pilates is sort of like yoga, only with less focus on meditation and breathing and more on body shaping. I'm pretty sure it was invented by yoga fanatics who said, "Screw inner peace. I just want killer glutes."

I hear a rush of sounds as the front door opens behind me.

"Oh god. Look," mutters someone in a snippy female voice.

I turn around and find Caitlyn, Shanna, and Sharla standing on the pink hourglass welcome rug.

"Hi, there," Caitlyn says in a phony, sticky-sweet voice. "What are you doing here?"

I want to say "Getting an oil change," but I don't. "I just joined."

Sharla gives me one of those up-and-down looks that popular girls have a patent on, taking in my yoga pants, baby tee, and worn-out walking shoes. I can almost hear her thoughts, all slow and snide-sounding. So it's no surprise when she asks, "Are you taking the Pilates class?"

I feel rattly inside. Obviously if they're just showing up, they're here for the same class. *Damn!* I need exercise more than air right now, but spending an hour with them could very well make me explode in a shower of half-absorbed strawberries and kinky brown hair. They'll probably make fun of my every move. And if not, what if I forget again and start acting like one of them?

"Nuh-uh," I say, shaking my head.

Surprise smooths out Sharla's frowny features for a second. "So what are you taking?"

My eyes quickly flit around the gym as if searching for a Bright Idea sign . . . and then I see it: an actual sign. There's a paper taped to the wall reading Water Aerobics This Way.

"That one," I say, motioning toward the notice. Already a couple of elderly women in skirted swimsuits are heading down the hallway in the direction of the arrow.

"Water aerobics?" Caitlyn exclaims, not even attempting to disguise her revulsion. Sharla breaks out in high-pitched bleating. Shanna, of course, just stares.

"That's right," I say. Hoisting my gym bag, I race into the nearby locker room.

Once inside I sit down on a wooden bench and close my eyes. The heavy air is spiked with the competing scents of hair spray and BO, but I go ahead and fill my lungs in some cleansing yoga breaths.

So it's come to this. I am now supposed to hang out with the support-hose-and-hip-replacement crowd. If I didn't want to like Austin, I'm certainly succeeding.

"Hi."

A familiar throaty voice yanks me out of my thoughts. I open my eyes and see my self-appointed lunch mate, Penny, standing in front of me. She's wearing an orange swimsuit with yellow polka dots, piping, and a peplum skirt. On her head is a plastic swim cap with flappy butterflies all over. Her body is pale and freckled, with a major case of knock-knees. And even though her thighs and upper arms are rather widish, and her long curved belly sticks out farther than her breasts, she really isn't as heavy as her chubby face would have you believe. In fact, she looks sort of . . . strong.

I suddenly realize I'm giving her the once-over, just like the Bippies did me. "Hi," I reply, snapping my gaze to her eyes.

"Are you here for the water workout?" she asks, pointing in the direction the sign indicated. Funny how she doesn't seem at all surprised to see me here. For that matter, I'm really not that shocked either. Guess I'm getting used to her popping up all the time.

"Yeah," I answer, unzipping my bag and pulling out my swimsuit. *I guess I am.*

"Here. You'll need to wear this. It's required."

I glance back up and see that she's holding out another rubbery swim cap. Light pink with little flappy flower thingies stuck all over it.

"We need to hurry," Penny says, pointing to a clock hanging from the ceiling. "The class starts in one minute and forty-five seconds."

I follow her as she heads down the gym corridor, her orange flip-flops making loud *swack*ing sounds. She has a strange, lumbering walk, as much sideways motion as forward momentum. And as she rocks from side to side, her arms swing far back, hands open and flailing—sort of like a toddler.

Her face is all crumpled up in worry, just like earlier in the cafeteria when she was late for her medicine. It's obvious she's really into being on time, and I feel a little guilty that she waited for me.

As we pass a room to our left, I catch sight of Caitlyn, Shanna, and Sharla all folded over in a spine stretch. Shanna, who seems to be struggling a little, doesn't see us, but Caitlyn and Sharla both erupt into twittery giggles. I quicken my step. Penny doesn't even notice.

Finally we push through a squeaky glass door and head into a large natatorium with gray-green tiles, gray-green walls, and gray-green water. The only contrasting colors come from the bathing suits and swim caps worn by the four elderly women standing waist-deep in the pool.

"Oh, look! There she is," says a lady in a purple one-piece.

"Penelope, dear!" calls out a very tall, angular woman in hot pink, her voice echoing slightly. "We were worried you wouldn't make it."

Penny takes off her shoes, sets her towel on a metal bench, and wades down the steps into the water. "I was helping Maggie," she explains. "She forgot a swim cap."

All heads pivot toward me. Once again, I imagine their thoughts and see myself through their eyes: tallish, skinny, long-waisted girl whose coral tankini clashes with the skin pink bathing cap. Without all my hair hanging down, I feel extra gangly and awkward, and I wonder if they see me as another Penny. It upsets me a little to think so, especially since I'm not *trying* to be weird right now.

"Hello, dear. Please come join us," calls the lady in pink.

"Better hurry, Maggie," Penny shouts, cupping her hands around her mouth. "Class starts in less than a minute."

I toss my towel on the bench and ease myself into the pool. The water is bathtub warm and reeks of chemicals. I slowly make my way over to the others and stand beside Penny.

"Maggie, this is Helen," she says, pointing to the pink-clad woman, "that's Mabel"—she points to the one in purple—"and Doris and Barb." She points to the two at the end of the lineup—a tiny frail-looking lady in a tropical-patterned suit and a heavyset one in black "slimming" swimwear. Everyone smiles and nods.

"Are you from Penny's school?" Helen asks.

"Yes, ma'am. I just moved here from the West Coast."

The large woman, Barb, makes a harrumphing noise that bounces harshly off the walls. "All these folks moving here from California . . . they're the ones making traffic worse and driving up our property taxes!" Her voice is deep and braying, almost manly, and I instinctively shrink back out of her line of sight.

Helen laughs lightly and leans across Penny toward me. "Don't mind Barb," she says, her blue eyes glittering under the fluorescents. "She's not happy unless she's mad about something."

I smile and nod.

"Oh, and no need to call me ma'am. I'm really not that much older than you," she adds with a wink.

Barb makes another harrumphing sound.

Right at this moment the door squeals open and a muscular woman in a red racer-type swimsuit strides into the room.

"All right, ladies! Spread out and get ready for leg lifts!" she shouts at near-Barb volume.

For the next half hour, the teacher (she never gives her name or asks me for mine) commands us to do several reps of lifts, bends, kicks, and side stretches. The movements are tougher than they look and I find myself straining to keep up at times. Penny is a star student, Mabel whimpers, and Barb, of course, complains loudly—which makes Helen laugh and shake her head.

Occasionally Doris will slip and go underwater, requiring Barb to stop what she's doing, reach down, and lift her back onto her feet. "Whoopsie!" Doris says each time, with a tinkly laugh, followed by various grumblings from Barb.

I can feel some stress working its way out of my body. I can't believe I'm here, with these people, wearing a dorky rubber cap and moving like a marionette. If my cool friends from the past could see this, they'd disown me forever.

Only . . . they kind of already have. Except maybe Lorraine. And she hasn't replied to any of my messages since we left Portland three weeks ago.

"You're doing really well for your first time," Penny says to me as we stop for a quick breather.

"She sure is," Helen remarks. "You fit right in, Maggie."

"Thanks," I reply.

But her comment makes me feel sad.

By the time I walk back to our shop, my arms and legs feel all loose and floppy. Our upstairs apartment is completely empty. Judging by the silence, I figure Rosie and Les are probably working in the store. I head into the kitchen and open the refrigerator, hoping to claim the leftover avocado salad, but it's not there. I grab a carrot instead, shut the door, and immediately let out a yelp.

Rosie is suddenly standing there. Usually I know

she's around by the swishy sounds of her skirts, but not this time. Probably because I'm a little dopey and worn-out from water aerobics, but also because Rosie's naked.

"Rosie! You scared me!" I cry, clutching my chest in a mini CPR move.

"I'm sorry," she says with a giggle, which totally annoys me. I'm really tired of being laughed at today.

She slips past me and opens the fridge. "I was hoping we had another one of those mango sodas," she says, scanning the contents.

"There's one in the door shelf," I point out.

"Oooh yay!" she exclaims, doing a jiggly hop for joy. "The Universe loves me."

Yeah, you *maybe*, I think wearily.

"I hope you weren't downstairs like that," I say, sounding more snappish than I mean to.

"No, no." Rosie flicks away my comment with a hand flourish. "I was on the roof."

"What?" My hair whips around in a double take.

"You should go up there. It's nice." She opens up her bottled soda and sits down in one of the red vinyl dinette chairs.

"But . . . but . . ." My head is suddenly throbbing. I press my fingertips to my temples and take a long breath. "What were you doing on the roof completely nude?"

"Hanging out the clothes," she explains as if the answer should be obvious.

This is one of Rosie's things. She loves doing laundry—specifically, hanging it to dry in the open air. This is why I don't wear a lot of denim. Sunshine-dried blue jeans can practically stand up and walk around on their own.

"Everything takes longer to dry here because of the humidity," she goes on. "But at least it hardly ever rains. There's lots of sunshine. Les wants to fill a washtub with good soil and start an herb garden up there."

I shake my head. "Rosie, we aren't living off the land right now. We're in the middle of the city. You can't just stroll around naked on rooftops. They probably have laws against it. I mean . . . what if someone sees you?"

She shrugs. "How can they see me all the way up there?"

"We have neighbors."

"Don't be silly. No one else was on their roof."

By now I'm totally exasperated. "But the building across the street has a third story! All they'd have to do is look out the windows!"

She shrugs again and takes a big sip of mango soda.

It's no use. Trying to discuss the rules of society with my parents is like trying to talk about world economics with a couple of two-year-olds. When I started attending school, I began to realize just how different my home life is. Even though I agree with my parents on most things, I found myself constantly wishing that they'd try to fit in with the masses a little more—if only for me and the sake of my reputation. But they don't care about things like social rankings and respectability.

I suppose under my new antipopularity plan, it doesn't really matter if I seem like a freak. But I'd still rather not *feel* like one.

"Oh!" Rosie cries out suddenly, leaping to her feet. The vinyl seat sticks to her bare butt for a second before dropping back to the floor. I make a mental note not to use that chair for a while. "I almost forgot. You got a package today!"

"A package?" I repeat stupidly. Now it's my turn to do a little song-and-dance number. I bounce on my feet, going, "From who? Who? Who?"

Meanwhile the answer keeps echoing through my brain: *Trevor!* He's the only person who knows our new address! Did he change his mind about the breakup? Is he mailing me candy or jewelry or a manuscript-sized apology in the hopes that I'll forgive him?

As Rosie heads for a set of shelves, I rise on my toes and pitch toward her as far as possible without falling on my face. My hands are pressed against my chest, my right palm squeezing my left fist so hard my turquoise ring is digging into flesh.

"I know you've been expecting this," Rosie croons happily as she walks back toward me, holding out a giant padded envelope.

I eagerly snatch it up and catch sight of the

return address label—Westbank High School in Portland, Oregon.

Joy whooshes out of me, making me feel woozy. *Oh
yeah.* I forgot that Ms. Ritenour, my old guidance coun-
selor, promised to forward me some college materials.

"It's that stuff you've been waiting for, isn't it?" she
asks, a big oblivious grin pushing her cheeks into perfect
balls.

"Uh-huh."

"My baby's getting all grown up and ready for college," she croons, her eyes crinkled in a sappy look. "My
future anthropologist. My little Margaret Mead."

The squeak in her voice suggests she's about to cry,
which I really don't want—because I might cry too.
That sudden high of hopefulness about Trevor followed
by a bitter crash-and-burn disappointment has left me
shaky and jet-lagged. I just don't have any energy to play
it cool anymore, and sobs are right beneath the surface.
But I can't have Rosie fussing over me in all her mater-
nal glory.

"I think . . . I'll go up to the roof and open this," I
mumble, trying to figure out a way to get some alone
time.

"You should!" Rosie exclaims. "The sun's starting to
go down. It's pretty."

I tuck the packet under my left arm and make my
way up the steps.

And she's right. It is pretty. The sky is full of pinks

and lavenders, with puffy grayish purple clouds. The orange sun is straining through the oak trees behind our building, making a mottled camouflage pattern on the roof. I walk to the midpoint and sit cross-legged on the rough gravel-like surface.

Clothing flaps in the breeze on the line Rosie has stretched from the stairwell to the metal shack-thing that houses the attic fan unit. For several minutes I just sit there, dazed, turning the package over and over in my hands. The sobs that have been trapped inside my chest gradually make their way up, until I slump forward, crying. I think about Trevor and how his whole face snapped to attention when he saw me. How his smile would practically ding. And the way his eyes looked when he said he loved me. It was the first time I really felt like I was superimportant to someone other than my parents. It sounds corny, I know, but I thought maybe we were fated to meet.

What happened to that? Why did he give up hope that we would be together again someday? And what if no one ever looks at me that way again in my life? Trevor could have been my only chance to find my major "other" and I blew it.

I hear a whapping noise and lift my head. The breeze has picked up and the clothes are thrashing about on the make-do line. A whole row of my parents' shirts are facing me, their arms stretched out as if waiting for a hug. I abruptly turn away.

I love Rosie and Les, but I also can't help hating them a little. Really it's all their fault I was torn away from Trevor. Their fault I don't dare make friends this time around. Before we left Portland I really tried to explain to Rosie how much it hurt me to leave Trevor. I told her I thought I loved him. She hugged me and said that was wonderful; then she said that if it was real love, distance shouldn't matter, and that there was a whole world full of people to love just waiting for me to meet them. Then she handed me some condoms.

Trevor and I had discussed having sex, but in the end we never did. Now I wonder if it was the right decision. If we had gone all the way, I could be hurting much, much more. But maybe it would have made Trevor more committed.

A strong gust of wind sweeps over the rooftop, lifting my hair and whipping our clothes into a frenzy. One pair of Rosie's all-cotton undies is now hanging by a single clip. Fearing it might wrench itself free, flutter down onto some innocent motorist's windshield, and cause an accident, I set down the package, struggle to my feet, and go reattach it—adding a third clip for extra security.

Next to her panties is one of my tops—my favorite one, in fact. It's nothing special. Just a classic scoop-necked tee in a soft blue, made even lighter from several washings and air-dryings. But it's one of those shirts that seems to have been made just for me. You know? The kind that fits perfectly, seams hitting in all the proper places. And the color warms my skin and brightens my eyes. Or so I'm told. People always compliment me more when I wear it.

My lucky tee. The shirt I was wearing when Trevor first asked me out.

But I won't wear it here. I want the *opposite* of luck in this place. When the time comes to leave, I don't want to shed a single tear.

I unclip my T-shirt and shove it inside the elastic of my stretch pants. Then I grab the envelope and yank the exposed tab on the back. The red string-thing pulls open a wide slit and I peek inside to find a few university pamphlets, some color-coded forms, and other assorted papers all held together by a rubber band. A brief letter has been clipped to the front.

Miss Dempsey, the note begins. *Here is the information you requested, along with another copy of your transcript and a letter of recommendation from Mr. Whitmire.* I look over the glossy brochures for various universities and liberal arts colleges. Then I glance at the letter from my former English teacher—a brief, general, "Miss Dempsey is a hardworking student" sort of recommendation.

I still wish the package had been a tearstained note and a box of salt water taffy from Trevor, but it does lift my mood slightly. A year from now I'll be out on my own, studying anthropology or something, and making real, lasting friendships. No more moving around. And if Trevor and I end up at the same university, it's still possible we could finish what we started.

If only I could fast-forward the next several months.

I notice that many of the colleges you are interested in emphasize extracurricular involvement, the letter continues. *Although your grades are excellent, and I'm sure you will have no problem drafting a quality essay, you have very few school organizations listed on your record. Be sure to sign up for as many activities as your schedule allows at your new school. Also, you still need at least one more recommendation, perhaps from a club sponsor. Remember, the deadline for many of these applications is December 15. Best of luck, Diane Ritenour.*

What? My eyes back up to reread the last three sentences of her note: . . . *sign up for as many activities* . . .

Don't tell me. . . . Now I have to join a stupid club?

Chapter Three: Artificial Life

TIP: Only popular people join popular clubs. And . . . it always helps to be seen lugging around foliage.

After a long night of worrying about clubs and having a few sporadic, disturbing dreams about Trevor, I wake up with a major headache.

I shuffle into the kitchen, wearing the big poufy genie-type pants and high-collared silk shirt I picked out in the store yesterday evening. I originally planned to wear a ponytail (I seem to remember, among my few scattered memories of TV watching, a girl genie with a ponytail), but it hurts to pull my hair back.

"Good morning, Margaret."

I stop and stare at Les. I'm so zombified and my skull is throbbing so relentlessly that for a second I truly wonder if I could have been lobotomized during the night.

"Did you just call me Margaret?" I croak.

"Yes, I did," he replies, sharing a shifty grin with Rosie.

I blink at him, trying to pop-start my sore brain. After all these years, has my father decided to give me a normal name?

Les leans back and lets out his blaring Santa Claus laugh. I clutch my head to keep it from detonating.

"Rosie told me about your package, Ms. Margaret Mead," he says teasingly. "Almost time to pursue your big dream. You must be one thrilled monkey."

"Oh. Yeah, I am." I pull out one of the chairs I'm pretty sure was spared my mother's nakedness and drop gracelessly into it.

Rosie frowns at me. "You don't look like a thrilled monkey."

"I just have a headache," I explain, leaning forward to rest my forehead on my arms.

"Poor butterfly!" Rosie starts clucking over me with all her motherly superpowers. She rubs my shoulders and the back of my neck while humming a lullaby-sounding tune.

"I know what you need, Sugar," Les says. I hear him rummaging through the cabinets and opening and closing the fridge.

I sit motionless for a while, letting Rosie spoil me

with her soft voice and strong, professionally trained hands. "You're going to put me back to sleep," I mutter into the table.

Right then the blender starts whirring. Seconds later the noise stops, and I raise my head just as a glass of frothy pink liquid appears in front of me. One of Les's famous smoothies.

Normally I'd dive right in, but as soon as the smoothie's fruity scent hits my nostrils, my stomach runs whimpering behind my appendix.

"Sorry, guys," I rasp, rising carefully to my feet. "Don't think I can eat right now. I'll just grab a couple of aspirin and head out."

"I'm sorry, sweetness. We don't have aspirin," Rosie tells me. "But here. Use this." She grabs a rosemary plant off the windowsill and hands it to me. "Take deep whiffs until your head clears up," she instructs. "And you can crush up the needles, too."

"I can't carry around a potted plant all day," I protest, staring numbly at the small bush.

"Why not?" Rosie asks.

"Because I'll—" I break off. I'm about to say "I'll look stupid," when I suddenly remember . . .

Don't I want to?

My head still aches when I get to school, so I'm only vaguely aware of the pointing and giggling as I cross the lawn.

I see Miles at his usual post near the entrance. He's

talking so animatedly to his assembled group that I wonder if he charged admission. In fact, he's so busy holding court he doesn't even notice me until his audience starts snickering and looking in my direction.

He turns around, gives me a big once-over, and begins laughing so hard it throws him off balance. While he staggers around like a drunken idiot, I stroll past him as casually as possible. Just when I think I'll make it inside without incident, he runs in front of me.

"Nice pants," he says, his voice all vibrato from laughing. "What's in them? Can I see?" He glances back at his assembled pals, and like good trained doggies, they all crack up.

I want to say "How sweet. Do they fetch and roll in their own crap, too?" Instead I step around him and quicken my stride toward the doors.

I hear the pounding of feet and once again Miles is standing in my way.

"What's the Christmas tree for?" he asks. Now that we're out of earshot, he doesn't bother with his backup chorus.

When I don't reply, he takes a step forward, smiles crookedly, and says, "You want to sit on my lap and tell me what you want for Christmas?"

I stare right into his smirking face. Even now, annoyed as I am, I can't help going a little tingly. He's so crazy handsome.

Miles seems to pick up on this and amps up his power even more. He tilts forward, lips right next to my ear, his breath breezing across my neck. "Go ahead, tell me what you *really* want," he murmurs. He's so close, the sound vibrates through my body. "It's me, isn't it? Come on. Be honest."

Suddenly the heat I'm feeling turns into anger. I'm mad because he's all smug and blocking my way—but also because he's a little bit right. I *am* attracted to him. Or at least I would be if I could let myself. I know that this guy could single-handedly destroy my avoid-attachments plan, and I'm wearing myself out trying to avoid him. And yet he won't get a clue and give me a break!

I turn to face him. His smile is so sexy it's almost in-human.

Right then, my fuse burns up and it's like there's a di-rect line from my mouth to the primitive part of my brain. "Fine! You want to know what I really want?" I hear myself say, my voice hissy and sizzly. "A micro-scope. *And* surgical tools. So I can find and remove your teeny tiny manhood!"

Miles seems to freeze in place. His eyes widen and his smile falters, but otherwise there's no movement. I push past him and head into the building.

I'm not sure if it's the rosemary or what, but suddenly my head feels a lot clearer.

By lunchtime I'm completely starving. Luckily Les has packed one of my favorite sandwiches: a whole wheat pita filled with mushrooms, olives, leaf spinach, grilled peppers, and feta cheese. I've already scarfed half of it by the time Penny sits down with her tray.

"I like your plant," she says matter-of-factly, as if she were remarking on a new hairstyle.

"Thanks." Surprisingly, none of my teachers have objected to it. I suppose they assumed it was a gift or part of a science project or something. Only one teacher, a squat, pudgy guy with a bad comb-over, gave me a big bug-eyed stare in the hallway. But that was it.

On the other hand, the students have definitely reacted to my pants. Caitlyn and her pals had a massive whisper session in homeroom, and Jack gave me a horrified stare. Later, as I walked from class to class, several kids called me genie, and one of Miles's jock friends asked me to take him on a magic carpet ride.

Overall my plan is going extremely well. All the people who were nice to me on the first day now snicker along with the others or scurry away as if radioactive waste were oozing from my pores. Only Penny doesn't mind being seen with me.

Of course, being successfully unpopular is going to make it hard to join an extracurricular activity. In the past I would have signed up for show choir or drama club, and I would have eagerly accepted Caitlyn's offer to be a Belle. Now I'm totally stuck. I can't end up in a group of people I'll like. That will only make Operation Avoid Friends even tougher. In fact, that was how Trevor and I met. We were in an outdoor club called the Rangers. Every other weekend we went out camping or canoeing or walking through Forest Park.

I'll never forget that time we ducked off the trail and Trevor carved our names into a Douglas fir. *Trevor + Sugar-Mag.* He loved my real name. In fact, he was the first guy who didn't think my home life was weird—maybe because his parents were also ultraliberal. I thought that was a good sign, like we were custom-made for each other.

As I attempt to push a bite of pita past the clod of self-pity in my throat, Penny leans forward and studies my rosemary plant.

"Why did you bring this?" she asks, gently tapping the needles.

"I had a big headache this morning and its fragrance relieves that kind of stuff."

"Really?" she says, sounding interested rather than skeptical. "I get sinus headaches all the time. I was born with very narrow nasal passages, so the mucus gets trapped inside my forehead and becomes infected."

I'm starting to fully understand why no one else wants to eat with this girl.

And all of a sudden . . . I get it. The answer to my problem is right in front of me.

"Penny?" I say, leaning forward. "Do you belong to any clubs?"

At first she seems a bit startled. I realize I've never asked her a direct question before. Maybe no one has.

"Yeah," she replies, setting down her fork and sitting up straight. "I'm in the Helping Hands. We do fund-raisers and community-service projects. Last year we did this ten-mile hike for cancer research, only I got a bladder infection on the day of the walk and—"

"How do you join?" I interrupt. This sounds perfect. A whole group of Pennys and do-gooder types. It'll look great on my application but won't be so much fun that it'll mess up my big dislike-Austin plan.

"You just show up at the meetings," she explains. "Our first one is next Monday after school. You want to come?"

"Sure. That'd be great."

Penny's eyes spark up and a peach-colored tinge creeps across the tops of her cheeks. For a while she just sits there, gleaming like a freckled jack-o'-lantern. Then, suddenly, she leans toward me.

"Can I ask a favor?" she says in a timid-sounding voice.

"Sure."

"Can I sniff your plant?"

I'm sitting on the roof again, staring out at the surrounding buildings. The sky has that heavy metallic cast of late afternoon, and a male grackle is doing his hacking cough of a song in a nearby oak tree. Even though it's really muggy, I've found a shady patch near the downstairs door that makes it bearable.

We're all killing time before dinner. Les is working his last hour in the shop, and Rosie is standing a few yards in front of me, dripping with sweat as she fills a wood-and-steel planter with topsoil.

"What are you guys going to put in there?" I ask, faking an interest to be polite and feeling a little guilty that I won't budge from my cool spot to help out.

"Oh, I think Les wants to grow some herbs. Basil, coriander. I hear some mints do well here. I never could get that Corsican mint to grow in Oregon."

A thoughtful, faraway look comes over my mother's face, and I feel an opportunity presenting itself. "Rosie? Don't you ever miss our old home in Portland?"

"Miss? No."

"Why not? Didn't you like it?"

"Of course I did, butterfly! Just because I don't miss it doesn't mean I don't love it. I do! And who knows? Maybe my path will bring me back someday. But 'miss' implies ownership—that someone or some place has control over you, as if you're tied to it. And that's not real love. Real love is all positive and free."

"I don't think being tied to something is always a bad thing."

Rosie laughs and shakes her head. "You're so young. Young people think everything belongs to them."

Her laughter pisses me off. Every time I bring up the topic of feeling homesick, she acts like I'm a silly child.

"I don't get it," I grumble. "You're always saying stuff like 'We belong to the world but the world doesn't belong to us.' So . . . what's the point? I mean, why even bother planting herbs right now—especially if we're leaving in a few months?"

"We're not just doing it for us," she replies, still using that gentle, correcting tone. "Satya could use it when he comes back. Besides, this rooftop deserves a little patch of beauty. We like to leave a happy mark wherever we go."

I think about her answer as I fan myself with a paperback copy of *Gulliver's Travels* my new English teacher is making us read. *Leave a happy mark . . .*

Rosie's phrase makes my mind flip backward. I remember walking in the woods with Trevor, when he carved our names into the Douglas fir. At first I didn't want him to do it; I thought it would hurt the tree. But he assured me that Douglas firs were tough and could take it. Now I'm glad we did it. I guess we left our mark too. The trees were witness.

If I close my eyes and concentrate, I can remember the earthy, foresty smell and the feel of Trevor's long hair brushing against my cheeks as we kissed. Sometimes, in the privacy of my new room, I act out moments as if I'm still there. I pretend that I never left, and that I never got that awful message from him. And I tell him things I always wanted to say but couldn't because I ran out of time—or was too scared.

Suddenly I'm on my feet, brushing pebbly fragments off the backs of my legs. I have to call Trevor.

After he sent me that stupid text and I wrote him back, calling him all those names, I told myself that I would never contact him again—that he would have to make the next move. But I have to hear his voice again. Otherwise this whole breakup thing doesn't seem real. Besides, maybe he's had a chance to rethink things. Maybe he wants to talk but he's afraid I'll jump all over him. If I were to call him, it would give him a chance to apologize.

"It's hot. I'm going back in," I say as casually as possible. Then I pick up my paperback and race downstairs to my room.

My cell phone is exactly where I left it the day we arrived—atop the old, sticker-covered dresser. I haven't used it since I sent that scathing text to Trevor. I'd meant to call Lorraine and tell her we'd made it to Austin, but considering she hadn't responded to my previous two messages, I decided to wait. Besides, I just didn't want to go near the phone again.

I close the door, grab my cell, and press it against my sternum. The thwack of my heartbeat causes it to vibrate a little, making it seem as if the Nokia is coming to life. I take that as a sign.

My bedroom is barely big enough for its two pieces of

furniture. So as I turn away from the dresser, I don't even have to take another step to climb onto the mattress. I huddle in the corner, cross-legged, and press the phone's On button. It makes its chirpy powering-up tune and flashes me a menu screen, waiting for action.

I push the contacts list and select the very first entry that comes up—contact number one: Trevor's cell.

It rings once, then twice, and suddenly I hear his trademark answer. " 'Lo?"

It takes me a few seconds to reply. "Hey, Trevor?"

"Hey, babe."

A warm, gushy feeling spreads through my chest. He's glad to hear from me! Happy tears start slipping down from the outer corners of my eyes.

"God, I've missed you!" I squeal. "I'm so sorry about my last text. I was just angry. I'm better now. At least . . . I'm trying to understand. And I . . . I really wanted to hear your voice."

There's a brief pause. "Sugar-Mag?" he says, all hushed-sounding.

"Yeah." Didn't he already know that?

"I'm sorry. It's just . . . whoa. Time warp, you know?"

Not really. Instead I say, "Yeah."

"So . . . what's up?" He says it as if I were ringing him up from across town instead of midway across the country.

"Did you hear what I said? I said I was sorry about my last message."

"Yeah, I heard. It's no biggie. You were upset." Another pause follows. I'm glad he's not angry with me, but it still feels weird. Maybe he's just really surprised to hear from me. Or maybe he *is* mad but doesn't want to say anything.

"Look"—I take a big gulp of air—"I know you don't think we should be exclusive and stuff but . . . we can still stay in touch, right?"

"Of course. Just because we're not a couple anymore doesn't mean we hate each other."

I don't know how to react to this. I teeter back and forth between being thrilled that he wants to keep up with each other and feeling totally crushed by his emphasis that we're not a couple.

Silence sets in. I squirm in my corner, listening to the melancholy buzz of the cell connection.

"So . . . how are you doing?" I ask, just to make noise.

"Fine."

"How's school?"

"Aw, you know. Okay. How's Texas? How do you like your new place?"

"It's . . . fine."

Again, there's silence. It makes me ache.

I close my eyes and take a shaky breath. "Are you at all glad to hear from me?"

"Yeah! It's just, you know, a big surprise. Especially after your message."

"I said I was sorry about that!"

"Yeah, I know. Chill. I was just saying I was surprised."

Chill. He always used to say that to me whenever I got really happy or frustrated, basically anytime I veered out of the middle range of emotion. I hated hearing it, and I consider telling him so right now. But I don't want to start a fight. And besides, it doesn't make me mad anymore, just sad.

"I got a package from Ritenour with a Stanford application in it," I say, to change the subject. "I'm going to send it off as soon as I beef up my transcript and get another letter of recommendation. That's where you're going, right? You and I could be back together in less than a year."

He doesn't say anything.

A squeezy sensation passes through me, pushing tears out of my eyes and making my voice high and squeaky. "You're . . . still mad?"

"Don't do this. You already made your decision. You left."

"You know I didn't want to go! I hate it here! I miss you so much!" I'm really crying now.

"Look, just chill, okay? I'm not mad. It sucks here too."

"Really?" That I might not be alone in my suckage makes me feel a little better.

"Yeah."

"Just one more year, Trev. We can do that, right?"

He sighs, and it makes a long crackly sound. "You

know I think you're great. You know I'd like to see you again but . . . let's not make promises and stuff, okay?"

"Why not?"

"Because . . . it's so controlling, you know. We should just let things happen."

Great Gaia! He sounds like my freaking parents! I know that's one of the reasons I love him, because he is so easygoing and hippielike, but right now I want him to fight for us. He says it sucks there without me, but I need to hear him in a little bit of agony. I need to know he feels as gashed up inside as I do.

"Do you ever go see our tree?" I ask hoarsely.

"Sometimes." This time there's a trace of sadness in his voice, which comforts me. I wait for him to go on, but he doesn't.

"Well . . . tell it I said hi when you're there next."

"Sure."

I want to say more, but I can't transform my thoughts into words.

"Hey, Sugar-Mag . . . I'm sorry but . . . I have to get off the phone. I have to go to a Ranger meeting."

I almost say "Now?" but then I remember: he's two hours behind. He's just now getting out of school. For some reason, that makes the vast distance between us seem even more real.

"Okay," I mumble. "Will you write me sometime?"

"Sure. Yeah. When I get the chance. Senior year is a bitch."

"Yeah." Again I go all panicky. There's so much more I should be saying, only I'm not sure what exactly.

"Well . . . thanks for calling. Take care, okay?"

"I love you, Trev," I say. But it comes out so croaky, I don't think he understands me. And he doesn't say it back.

The line clicks and goes silent. He's gone.

Chapter Four: Alone Together

TIP: Never let them see you be cool—
even outside of school.
In case of emergency, flash your undies.

Les and Rosie have a new pet. His name is Norm. He's a forty-something-year-old man who lives in an abandoned chicken coop on someone's land.

Norm is nothing like his name. I've met some powerfully weird people in my life, but even I took a giant step backward when he appeared at the door three nights ago asking for my parents. Apparently they'd met him the day before at the farmers' market and told him to stop by. Since then he's showed up twice, usually around supper time.

Norm is supertall, with a big shaggy mane of hair, a beard so long it might very well house a family of gerbils, and the flat-eyed, startled expression of someone in the middle of a very unpleasant hallucination. If my first meeting with him had been on a dimly lit street, I would probably have used an entire can of Mace. Or maybe Raid.

In spite of his appearance, though, Norm is quite harmless. No matter where we go in the world, my parents have a way of attracting the Norms of a community. Rosie calls them wayward souls with "tortured karma" brought on by past-life situations, and she feels it's her duty to help them. Les mainly just gets a kick out of them and loves having a willing audience for all his stories.

Which brings me to tonight and why I have to get the hell out of here.

Norm is going to teach an astrology class. I love astrology—we Cancers are always looking for ways to solve the mysteries of the Universe—but Norm freaks me out too much. And not just because he looks like Bigfoot on a bad acid trip.

The first night he stopped by, while Rosie and Les were in the kitchen making chai, he stared at me hard, as if he'd just then realized I was there, and said, "She's sad. . . . Sad, sad, sad. . . . Don't be sad." It made me feel all ooky inside. So no way am I going to let him dissect my birth chart and start preaching about my so-called sadness. It's been hard enough keeping my nightly crying jags over Trevor a secret from my parents.

"Norm, my brother!" Les calls down as Norm's bushy head appears on the staircase.

"I brought the dead heads," Norm says in his booming Christopher Walken voice. He hands a bowl of fruit over to Les, who then hands it to me.

"Put this in the kitchen with the other snacks. Okay, Sugar?"

It's code. Les wants me to be sure to wash them thoroughly, since Norm likes to find free food. If he says he got something from Whole Foods, it probably means he dug it out of a Dumpster *behind* Whole Foods.

I give him a knowing nod and head to the sink to wash Norm's "dead heads." It's a snack he invented. He takes organic, migrant-friendly blueberries and tops them with organic, migrant-friendly raspberries so that they resemble faceless blue heads with fuchsia Afros. I spray the fruit with a special wash solution and dump it into a colander, then wash the bowl. After that I head into the living space, where Rosie is lighting candles and Norm is helping Les arrange pillows around the coffee table.

"Okay. I'm going now," I announce. I lean forward to kiss Rosie, carefully avoiding the lit fireplace match in her hand.

She looks surprised. "You're leaving? But you'll miss the class."

"Sorry," I say with a shrug. "I've got plans."

"The others will be here soon," Les points out. "They really wanted to meet you."

We've been in Austin less than a week and already my parents have so many new friends they're hosting a party. Meanwhile I'm hanging out with senior citizens and chronic-bladder-infection girl. But this does not sway me.

"Sorry," I say again. "Maybe next time."

Rosie still looks disappointed. "I guess we should have realized. Young people always have plans."

"Have fun, sugar bear," Les says, giving me a quick hug and kiss.

Norm claps his hands together in front of his Legal-ize Cannabis T-shirt and gives me a little bow. "Go find joy, indigo child."

"Yeah. Thanks."

As I grab my bag and head for the stairs, I hear Norm say, "Ah, those Cancers. So sensitive."

I walk ten blocks to the nearest theater, where a new James Bond movie is playing. As I stand in the ticket line, I pull a handkerchief out of my Guatemalan bag and dab my forehead, cheeks, nose, and neck. Texas is so damn humid, I might as well have worn my bathing suit. But I have to admit, it feels good to have on normal clothes—a bunchy white cotton blouse and a swingy blue skirt—instead of my crazy school attire.

Of course, I'm pretty sure I wore this exact ensemble

on a date with Trevor. Maybe even to the movies. Now here I am alone.

Ever since my surprise phone call to Trevor, I've careened back and forth between hope and despair. On one hand, he did seem to care still. But he also wasn't all that encouraging. If only I could have seen his face. If I could have been there, watching him, I'd know exactly where we stood.

As I wait in line, sweating and feeling sorry for myself, I'm suddenly aware of the person behind me. Maybe it's intuition. Or maybe it's that this doofus is standing just a smidgen too near. Whatever the reason, I feel compelled to turn around. And there in back of me, grinning like a politician, is the Young Republican from homeroom. Jack.

"Hey," he says.

He *is* rather close. I can see dark rims around the light brown color of his eyes and faint grooves on his front teeth. And I can practically feel the warmth coming off his body.

I dab my forehead some more. "Hey," I echo. Luckily the line starts moving, and I take a giant step back, safely out of heat range. I notice he's still decked out in dork wear—slacks, dress shirt, and loafers—even though it's a Friday night. No teachers around to give him gold stars.

"What are you here to see?" he asks, walking forward to close the distance between us.

Crap burger! I have no idea what to say. I figure he's

probably here to see the Bond film too, considering everything else is starchy, Academy Award–courting stuff. I scan the Now Showing posters for the most boring option, hoping to exchange my ticket for a later showing of 007. "That one," I reply, gesturing toward a poster for a very bleak-looking, subtitled Russian movie called *Heat of Winter*.

Jack's eyes grow enormous. "Really?"

"Yup," I say, silently congratulating myself.

"Me too!" he exclaims. "I thought I was the only person my age who liked Mironov. Man, he's cool, huh? Did you see his collection of shorts? You know, where women play all the men's parts and men play all the women?"

"N-no," I respond truthfully.

Jack starts rambling on excitedly about "tracking shots" and "monochrome cinematography," as if I've pressed some sort of On switch, while I just stand there liquefying in the humidity. It's one of those horrific moments when your mind is in complete conflict with your body. The kind when you smile and nod and by all outward appearances seem quite peaceful. Meanwhile your inner voice is letting out spine-tingling screams and praying to an unseen almighty to make you fall through a trapdoor.

Now what? I can't change my mind about the movie or it will be totally obvious that I tried to fool him. But do I care? It's not like I'm so concerned about being a friendworthy person these days.

And yet, it's not that easy. He's being nice to me right now—nicer than practically anyone has been so far. Still, I don't want to see some depressing foreign film, and I really don't want to see it with him, and I'd better make up my freaking mind fast because there're only two people in front of me. . . . Make that one. . . . *Ack!*

"Two for *Heat of Winter,*" Jack says, reaching past me to push a twenty through the hole in the ticket window.

"But . . . but . . . ," I sputter pitifully.

Jack smiles his best lead-candidate smile and says, "You can buy the popcorn."

Damn, damn, damn, damn, *damn!*

I bounce nervously in my theater seat, cursing inwardly on each downbeat. I can't believe this. I'm sitting in an itchy chair. I'm sitting in an itchy chair next to some Young Republican. I'm sitting in an itchy chair, next to some Young Republican, about to see some sleep-inducing foreign film. A movie so deadeningly dull we're the *only ones in the entire theater!*

I should have stayed home with Norm.

"He was really influenced by the French New Wave, especially Godard." Jack is still orating. "You've seen *Breathless,* right?" He's leaning forward, hanging over me again—his aura melding with mine. His eyes are all superfocused and he makes little waving motions with his hands as he talks.

"Nope," I reply truthfully.

"Really?" At first he looks shocked. Then he tilts his head sideways, reconsidering me. "I bet you're into the American mavericks, right? You a fan of Altman? Kubrick? Lynch?"

I shrug, hoping he'll just drop it.

Jack's forehead bunches into tiny folds. "Okay, so . . . who *do* you like?"

"I don't watch movies all that much."

"Why not?"

I blow out my breath, irritated that he won't just shut up. "I don't know. Maybe because we move around a lot, so I don't do much of *anything* regularly."

"That explains everything." He sits back in his seat, nodding.

"Explains what?" Now I'm the one tipping forward into his space. He just looks so damn pleased with himself I have to find out what he thinks he knows.

Jack's eyes swivel up toward the ceiling. "It explains a lot, actually. . . ." I can tell he's using some annoying debate-team strategy of rephrasing my question to buy time. "It explains why you don't know much about film . . . and why you aren't all that good at . . . fitting in." He meets my gaze and looks worried.

"Ah." I slowly sit back in my chair. A chain of reactions goes off inside me. I *am* slightly hurt and insulted that he would say something like that. Plus I'm surprised he's been paying that much attention to me. But I also feel a little like laughing. Because he's wrong. When you rove about as much as my family does, you get almost *scarily* good at fitting in. It's just that I've chosen *not* to this time. "Yeah . . . well . . . oh well," I mutter.

"That's got to be tough. Moving all the time," he mumbles, his head shaking pityingly.

A medley of Trevor-moments parades through my mind, bringing on sudden and severe Stabby pangs. I hunch forward slightly, folding my arms across my middle.

"It's not so bad." I wince as I hear myself. My tone is not at all convincing. "I've been to a lot of really cool places. . . ." *All too briefly.* "And met a lot of cool people. . . ." *Who have totally forgotten me by now.* "And I'm really close with my parents. . . ." *Even though I kind of hate them these days.* "And . . ." I try to come up with something else but can't. Instead my words just hang there lamely. "It's not so bad," I repeat, just for some sort of closure.

Jack nods and smiles. Not his ultraconfident campaign-trail grin, but a nice, warm, snug one. "Still," he says. "It's got to suck. At least a little."

"Yeah, okay. Maybe a little," I concede. Then I crack up. I don't know why; I just do.

I flop back against the itchy upholstery and turn toward him at the exact moment that he turns toward me. He's so near I have to focus on one eye at a time. First his right, then his left, and back again. My laughter slowly loses power, and I realize that this is the first real moment I've had with someone in Austin.

It also occurs to me that I'm still staring at him. And that he's staring at me. And that this close up he looks sort of sweet and gentle. Cute even. And his eyes have this optical illusion quality that makes it seem as if they go deeper than the diameter of his head. And when he smiles, the landscape of his face becomes soft and curvy. His hairstyle, with its severe part and too-tidy edges, doesn't seem to fit. I have a sudden urge to reach up and muss it.

And because I'm not real good at stifling my impulses, I sit on my hands.

"You know . . . I'm glad I ran into you," he says.

He's so earnest that I have to look away. I fidget on top of my hands while heat sizzles up my neck.

Fortunately, just when my cheeks start to feel like two enormous blisters, the lights go out.

Oh my god! The movie is actually *good*!

This lady wanders into a village. It's the middle of winter and the weather keeps the town totally isolated, so these people sort of take turns looking after her. She's absolutely gorgeous, but she can't talk. Because she doesn't say anything, people ramble on whenever they're alone with her, to fill up the silence. Before they know it, they're spilling out all this personal stuff. And there're all kinds of characters: this sweet old lady and this crazy guy and his wife and a supersmart kid and this guy who's falling in love with her . . .

What does she think she's doing? She can't go in there! *Stop!*

Damn it! This is horrible!

I just grabbed Jack!

There was this scene where the lady and the kid were lost in a snowdrift and all of a sudden they fell into a ravine. It scared me so much I let out an eagle shriek and yanked down on the thing closest to me—which happened to be Jack's right arm. I ended up pulling him toward me until we were practically cheek to cheek!

"It's okay," he said when I finally freed his arm.

Now we're sort of leaning toward each other, almost shoulder to shoulder. And you want to know the worst part? He smells really good.

The credits roll to some sappy violin music. I pretend to scratch the bridge of my nose so that I can secretly wipe the tears that built up. Otherwise, neither one of us moves.

I wonder if Jack feels as worn out as I do from all the comedy, drama, and sweaty sex. Watching it, I mean.

I should leave, but I want to be cool about it. If he realizes how awkward I feel, it might imply that his presence is having a strong effect on me. In other words, that I like him. Which I don't.

The music stops. I arch my back and stretch out my arms, trying to appear casual. Unfortunately it only makes it seem like I'm pushing my boobs to the foreground. Jack happens to glance at me right when they're at their zenith. He abruptly turns away and starts drumming his hands on his lap. I quickly straighten back up.

I want to say "I'm not flirting! Really!" but that would suggest the opposite. So instead I blurt, "Did you like it?" in an overly cheery voice.

"Huh?" He seems rather startled, almost guilty.

"The film," I clarify, my face going prickly as I realize what he might have thought I meant. "What did you think of the movie?"

"I liked it." His face relaxes and his mouth bends into a sideways smile. "You sure seemed to get into it. Especially during the scary part."

"Yeah." I can't help laughing a little, recalling how I almost dislocated his shoulder.

He laughs too and we lapse into another friendly face-off, our gazes bouncing from one eye to the next. And suddenly it hits me: I'm having fun.

Crap cakes!

This is awful. I can't let my guard down here! Especially with a *guy*! It's totally against the rules for me to be enjoying myself. And I haven't moped over Trevor in two hours! Of course, I am *now*—thoughts of him are practically dive-bombing me from all directions—but that's beside the point. I don't want to lose sight of the reason I began Operation Avoid Friends.

I just can't say goodbye to another friend—girl *or* boy. It would probably do irreparable damage to my impressionable young psyche, leaving me incapable of bonding with people later in life. And it could very likely be the finishing blow to my relationship with my parents.

Plus it hurts way too much.

What to do . . . what to do . . .

My smile must be slowly faltering, because Jack mirrors the expression back at me. "You okay?" he asks. "You look so . . . sad."

Great. Now he sounds like Norm.

I command the sides of my mouth to lift. "I'm fine. I was just . . . thinking about the movie. It was a real downer at the end. I don't get why she had to wander away again when spring came."

He toys with the straw in his empty cup. "It's symbolic," he says in his authoritative film-school-101 voice. "She's not really a person but a force of nature or something."

"Huh." For some reason, this makes me feel sadder.

Just then the lights come back on. Jack stands up and slowly rolls his head in a circle while rubbing his neck. Once again I sit on my hands, resisting the urge to give him a Rosie-style upper-body massage.

"So," he says, turning toward me and looking at his watch. "It's still real early. You want to do something?"

Oh no. Oh no. Oh no. This is exactly what I was

afraid of. He must think we're really hitting it off. Somehow I've got to remind him that I'm a loser. If only I'd dressed like a weirdo.

Wait . . . that's it! Even though I can't completely *look* weird right now, I can still *act* it!

"You know what I feel like?" I glance around the vacant theater. The place seems huge and grand with its speakers and spotlights and dark red carpet. "I feel like . . . turning cartwheels!"

"What?"

I don't look back at him. Instead I bounce out of my seat and head onto the wide carpeted aisle. I raise my arms, point my right toe forward, and do a perfect wheelaround, my hair whipping all over the place. Then I do another. And another.

Eventually I run out of room. "Ta-*da!*" I shout, ending in the classic Olympic-gymnast pose.

Jack looks so stunned his features seem to be sliding off his face.

"You try it!" I cry.

"No, no." He shakes his head and lets out a nervous-sounding chuckle.

I can tell this is really bothering him. So I do a few more. Now I'm getting into it, adding some roundoffs and arm flourishes. I've never been the most nimble of creatures, but it's fun to use your body and stretch your limbs. Strangely enough, the more I jump and flip, the less awkward I feel.

After a while I pause to take in Jack's reaction. His mouth has curled into a grin but his eyes are wide and spooked-looking.

Yes! I decide to do a couple more, just for insurance's sake, and then leave him in total shock.

Only . . . I must have put my cart before the horse, because I get completely thrown off on the next one. I realize this when I'm at the most upside-down part, but by then I've gotten up so much momentum there's nothing I can do. My left leg goes flying into the seats. I hear a popping sound and smell the syrupy odor of spilled fountain drink, and then the rest of me comes crashing down—limbs onto the seat cushions, ass on the gooey concrete floor.

"Aw crap!" I hear Jack's cry, followed by the pounding of feet. Suddenly his brown loafers are right in front of my face. "You okay?"

"I'm fine. I'm fine. Fine, fine, fine," I babble, as if saying it enough will make it so.

Jack grabs the body part closest to him (my right arm) and carefully helps me upright.

"See?" I say. "Totally fine." I try to prove it by throwing my arms up in another Mary Lou Retton pose, when a chill suddenly wafts up my legs. I glance down and see my skirt lying bunched around my ankles.

So here I am, frozen in place like some half-dressed superhero action figure, wishing some real force of nature would take me up, up, and away.

The only things that fly up are Jack's bushy eyebrows. He moves backward a small step, takes in my peasant-blouse-over-racer-striped-undies ensemble, and says, "Uh . . . I think the Italian judge just gave you a perfect ten."

At this point the blood flow returns to my extremities. I bend over, grab my skirt, and pull it up, only to have it whoosh back down the second I let go. "Whoopsie . . . uh . . . I guess I snapped the waistband. Ha, ha, ha," I blather as I retrieve it yet again.

"Here." Jack unbuttons his shirt and hands it to me. "Use this."

I tie the sleeves around my middle, just below the skirt's waistband, so that the shirt holds it up like a belt. "Thanks," I mumble.

"No big deal."

Jack looks almost rugged in his wife-beater undershirt, and I can't help noticing his well-toned arms and shoulders. Just in case I get any bizarre urges, I move my hands safely behind me, grabbing hold of a metal armrest.

"So . . ." He claps his hands and rubs them together. It's clear he wants me to fill in the rest.

"So . . . ," I echo, "see ya!" I quickly trot over to our abandoned seats and retrieve my purse.

"You're leaving?"

"Yep. Gotta go!" I reply without glancing back at him. As I head up the aisle toward the exit, I start to ache, and my gait is somewhat wobbly. When I approach the door, I almost collide with an usher pulling a large rubber trash can into the theater.

"Okay. Bye!" Jack calls.

I refuse to look at him. I race through the lobby and push through the glass doors into the steamy outside air. It's not until I'm two blocks away from the cinema that I start to breathe normally again.

Well, I wanted to look like a weirdo and totally turn him off. Check plus on that.

If only it hadn't been so damn painful.

When I reach our building, I hear several voices through the open upstairs windows, and the aroma of patchouli has traveled down to street level. I'm sore and cranky and the air is still suffocatingly humid. There's an evening breeze, but it feels like a blow-dryer on the high setting. I really don't want to go inside and have to hug strangers and talk about my rising sign while eating overripe fruit. So, making sure Jack's shirt is securely holding up my skirt, I continue walking down Rio Grande.

I pass a used-furniture store, a beauty salon, a lawyer's office, and a café/pastry bar. I consider going in for some tea, but it looks like a hangout for kids my age. Being in the most antisocial of moods, I just keep going.

As I usually do whenever I'm alone with my thoughts, I start obsessing about Trevor. I wonder what he's doing right now. Maybe he went to see the new James Bond. If he did, did he go with friends? Or a date? Or maybe the Rangers had a big picnic or campout. They must have been planning something to have had such an important meeting the other day. Unless . . . he lied about that just to get off the phone with me.

Just thinking about that conversation makes me feel tight and stomped on. I hated all those long pauses and the overabundance of the word "fine." That's not us—or at least not how we used to be.

Love is supposed to be forever, right? So how can it turn into something so awkward and bad in just a few weeks?

My nostrils start stinging and my vision goes all hazy. I can feel a big round of blubbering coming on, and I really don't want to do that on a sidewalk in the middle of a strange city. I have to make myself think about something else.

I try out a few general topics—college, the state of the world, the weird gunk that suddenly appears beneath my fingernails—but somehow, everything takes me back to Trevor. Finally I hit upon a definite non-Trevor-like subject: Jack.

I can't help smiling a little when I remember Jack's rapid-fire laugh, like the sound of whirring helicopter blades. Or that stupefied look on his face as I began my spur-of-the-moment tumbling routine. It was the first genuine fun I've had in this sauna of a city. Even though

I can never let it happen again, it was nice while it lasted.

It seems strange that I could share a moment with a guy like him—some rigid, bureaucratic type who bosses students as if he's been deputized by the principal. Maybe that's just it. Maybe we can be easygoing with each other because we know we could never seriously like each other. Like I could Trevor . . .

Crap-a-roni! I'm doing it again!

Is there no safe issue my sad, sore little mind can take on?

I come to a stop and glance around. As I've headed in the direction of downtown, the street has changed. Up ahead I see parking garages and office buildings instead of funky eateries and renovated Victorian homes. To my left, just across the street, is a small thrift shop. Naked vintage-looking mannequins stand in various poses in the display window—some holding knick-knacks, some perched on retro furniture. Repo Sessions reads the puffy 1960s-style lettering on the roof. Since I'm still not ready to head home, I decide to venture inside.

"Welcome!" calls a man sitting on a stool behind the cash register. He's supertall, with long sideburns and a mini pompadour. The sleeves of his Western shirt are rolled up to reveal a Betty Boop tattoo on his left arm. "Can I help you find something?"

"Just looking," I reply.

He gives me a nod and goes back to reading an issue of *Interview*. I heave a little sigh of relief. Seeing that I'm the only customer in here, I was afraid he'd want to engage in small talk. And I really don't want to converse with anyone right now.

Holding my big woven bag against me to keep it from bumping things, I wander around the various racks and displays. An old stereo console is playing synth-heavy 1980s music—Duran Duran, if the displayed album cover is correct. Beaded curtains and old posters cover the wall. I see one of Jane Fonda as Barbarella, all slinky in her silver halter and space boots. (It's one of the few movies I've seen. One of Les's favorites. Go figure.) Then there's one of a blonde in leggings and a white headband. Physical, it reads above her head. I start wondering if our shop has headbands like that.

If only I'd dressed weirdly today. Maybe then Jack wouldn't have even spoken to me and I wouldn't have had to resort to doing gymnastics in my underwear.

From now on, no more dropping the act—ever. It's too risky. I don't want to like anything about Austin. And if I remain in a superloser state, I can move about unbothered and unwelcome, like some enormous two-legged virus.

I cock my head as I hear the faint rhythm of girly chatter. Gradually it grows louder and louder, until two skinny, salon-chic females walk through the open doorway. I'm not sure, but I think they were with the group in the café.

Looking them over, I decide that they must be from some other high school, because these two are definitely dominant types. I can tell by the way they move, all languid and strutting. Two lionesses that know they're at the top of the food chain.

I pretend to look at a collection of Happy Meal toys while listening in on them.

"Oh my god. This stuff is so old."

"Yeah. Look at this. It's, like, from the eighties or something."

They both speak in that lazy drone specific to their breed, full of bubbles and pops and very little melody— as if they already have so much, they are now completely bored with life. I sometimes wonder if this is why I never cracked the top tier of popularity in any of my schools. I have a naturally bouncy, somewhat dramatic voice, probably from the Les half of my genetic makeup.

The taller one, with the white-gold hair, is clearly the leader. *Why are all power princesses blond?*

"Oh god. Is that supposed to be a clock?" She turns to her lady-in-waiting, her pug nose all wrinkled in disgust. "Can you believe they try to sell this stuff?"

I instinctively glance over at the clerk. He shoots me a tiny smile and rolls his eyes as if to say "Don't worry. I'm used to this sort of crap."

Just then the queen Barbie lets out a supersonic squeal. "Oh my god! Look at *this*!"

Her friend stands on her tiptoes to look over the

girl's shoulder. "No way!" she exclaims with a snort. "Would you be caught dead with that stuff?"

I strain to see what they're looking at, but their designer bags act as a shield.

"Uh-uh. No way. Might as well wear a sign that says 'major loser.' "

The queen's attendant quacks appreciatively. "Yeah, right."

As they move off toward the videotapes, I finally glimpse the objects of their scorn: a *Star Trek* backpack and a matching lunch box.

Sold.

Chapter Five: True Lies

TIP: You must worship all that is totally
and tragically unhip.
Disco is not dead.

It's working. Thank the Cosmic Forces, this is really working!

Just as I hoped, several of the students gathered on the front lawn of Lakewood High are pointing at me. The Goth girl is giggling so hard her black eye makeup is streaking down her cheeks.

Luckily it's sprinkling this morning, so in addition to my new *Star Trek* purchases, I'm carrying a green frog umbrella with two eyes on top. Plus yesterday I discovered a whole box of zippered jumpsuits—the kind car mechanics wear—in the shop's storeroom. So I'm also sporting a gray jumper with the name Wayne stenciled below my left collarbone and a pair of plain black galoshes that are only slightly too big for me.

I must look devastatingly weird. As I walked the eight blocks from our apartment to the school, a bunch of people in cars slowed down to gawk. Some lady at the bus stop caught sight of me and promptly choked on her venti coffee.

"Hey, loser!" shouts one of the thugs at the edge of the parking lot. He says that like it's a bad thing. This guy just made my morning.

I know how these things play out. Whenever a person does something highly embarrassing, anyone with style and status has to actively tease and then automatically avoid the guilty party for a couple of months. So this should get me at least halfway through my time here.

For some reason I'm not nearly as nervous as I was on the first day I dressed strangely. In fact, this is almost fun. I've worked hard for this, so I take pride in every single snicker and whispered dig. In a way, I feel like some anti–Miss America taking her victory walk down the runway. *There she is . . . Miss Most Hideous. . . .*

The only real challenge left is to get to the front door without being accosted by superstud sadists.

As soon as he spots me, Miles starts a hooting laugh.

"Damn, girl!" he drawls as he hops off his regular perch and falls into step beside me. "Your outfits get uglier every day."

I suck in my cheeks to stop myself from saying "thank you." It's funny. In all the other high schools I've been to, I would have given anything to get noticed by a guy like this. Now I've got the attention, without even really trying for it, and I don't want it at all. Everything is opposite here.

Miles looks me over, chuckling, as he accompanies me to the entrance. Through the glass I can make out a flock of short-skirted cheerleaders chatting on the other side of the door. They turn in unison, watching me approach. Then they all careen into each other, laughing hysterically.

Suddenly Miles leans in close, becoming my whole view. I can see the moisture on his lips and a faint crop of gold whiskers on his jawline. "Why do you do this?" he asks in a low voice. "Why do you hide that hot bod behind those lame clothes? You dress like crap."

This time I suck in my cheeks so hard the sides of my mouth disappear. If I'm so disgusting, why does he keep swooping in on me like this?

"You know you're sexy," he murmurs, inching even closer. "So why don't you dress it?"

I remain totally silent. My chest feels tightly packed—probably from all the trapped curse words. *Why won't this guy leave me alone?*

"Oh, so you're back to the not-speaking thing, huh? I liked it better when you talked dirty to me."

I turn and glance back at the gaggle of laughing cheerleaders, avoiding his deceptively gorgeous eyes.

Miles heaves a loud, frustrated sigh. "Man, what's *with* you? How come you won't even look at me? Are you some sort of snotty bitch?"

And just like that, the flirtation turns cruel—which I suppose it always was in disguise. I decide not to give him the satisfaction of an outburst. Instead I point my frog umbrella toward him and flap it open and shut to shake off the water. Miles jumps backward with a whiny-sounding "Hey!" followed by a mumbled curse.

Shouldering my closed umbrella, I head into the student center and find the assembled cheerleaders grinning at me treacherously.

"Hey, nerd-girl. Who beamed you in here?" sneers Sharla, her overplucked eyebrows doing weird wiggles on her face. The rest of them laugh demonically.

Well . . . *almost* all the rest. Standing in the back, Shanna watches me with her typically empty gaze, her big blue eyes all done up in silver glitter to match her uniform. She's not laughing. But then, she probably didn't get the lame joke. I have the feeling Shanna probably watches the fashion channels exclusively. In fact, the only reason I recognized the Trekkie stuff was that Les has a soft spot for ancient science fiction and let me watch reruns of the show with the community-school kids in Santa Fe.

As I continue to walk past, I realize that Shanna's not the only silent one. Usually Caitlyn's conducting the pack, but this time she's not even joining in the fun. Instead she's standing off to the side with her arms folded behind her back, making it look as if she has paper pom-pom wings. She's staring at me hard, her face all bunched up and twitchy.

Something tells me if we were on *Star Trek* right now, I'd have been phasered out of existence.

Fortunately, Caitlyn and her pals aren't in homeroom today since the cheer squad is leading an optional spirit rally in the gym. After roll call Mrs. Minnow excused everyone who wished to attend, which left behind just me and a few bookworms.

In another stroke of luck, Jack is absent today—a fact made glaringly obvious when Mrs. Minnow needed a full ten minutes to take attendance.

I'm so relieved. After what happened in the theater, it's going to be a while before I can face him. The more I think of it, though, the more I'm convinced that my little underwear-flashing episode saved me from a worse situation. Thanks to weak elastic, Jack will think twice about being sociable with me.

The whole experience also made me realize that if I want to completely avoid any friendly ties to this place,

I need to step things up a bit. Although I'm hoping that a couple of accessories with 1960s space adventurers on them will do the trick, so that I don't have to resort to stripping again.

I'm just getting into my battered copy of *Gulliver's Travels* when I hear a mumbling sound, followed by a familiar helicopter laugh. My head instantly snaps up. Sure enough, there's Jack talking to Mrs. Minnow. He hands her a pink tardy slip and she keeps smiling adoringly at him, not even bothering to look at it. She mutters something I can't hear and gestures toward the desks. That's when Jack turns and looks straight at me.

Crap cola! My face feels like it's been covered in a warm, sticky glaze.

He grins and raises his brows in a how're-we-doing sort of way. I produce a weak smile in return.

Suddenly he's striding down the aisle toward me. In a panic, I quickly bend back over my book.

"Hi," he says as he settles into the seat on my left and faces the front.

"Hi," I reply. I manage not to look up and instead concentrate hard on the word "Big-Endian," but I'm unable to stop myself from smiling.

"Have a good weekend?"

At this I bust out laughing. I try not to by pressing my lips together, but that just makes a loud snort flee through my nostrils. Mrs. Minnow and the other five or so students stare at us in annoyance. I clamp my hand over my mouth and try to refocus on page eighty-three.

As soon as everyone looks away, Jack tilts sideways and whispers, "Did you happen to bring my shirt?"

I shake my head, the gooeyness seeping back over my face.

"That's okay. No hurry. Feel free to use it if you need to."

My chuckles sputter to a stop. I don't like this. We've got this funny secret between us. It suggests a certain . . . chumminess. Something I never wanted. Come to think of it, why's he still being nice to me? Isn't he worried about his own reputation? Seems like he can't afford to lose cool points.

Jack slants toward me again. "You want to meet after school?" he asks. "There's this—"

"I can't."

He quickly straightens up. "Okay," he says, sounding a little taken aback. "Maybe later we—"

"Sorry. Got plans." I sing a silent song of praise to Penny for hooking me up with her club meeting today.

Jack nods briskly. "Right. Yeah, yeah, yeah."

Like a good teacher's pet, he learns quickly. For the rest of the period, he doesn't say another word.

"I like your lunch box."

Penny, once again, plops down across from me in the cafeteria. I'm starting to realize that she considers our sitting together to be some silently agreed-upon arrangement between us. I thought up various sneaky ways of getting rid of her ("My doctor says I'm not supposed to breathe in the vicinity of people"; "I need lots of space around me because of the projectile vomiting thing"; "I'm sorry, but that seat and the others around it are being saved for my imaginary friend Hubert and his eight fairy wives"), but then I realized that her presence could only help with my whole not-wanting-to-be-liked scheme. She's obviously one of the school's bottom-feeders. And besides, it's not like she could ever seriously be my friend.

She slowly turns my lunch box, examining each of the pictures stamped into the vinyl. "I used to have a Harry Potter one in middle school, but it got stolen."

I make a sympathetic noise as I dig in to my Thai noodles.

"Do you like Harry Potter?" she asks.

I nod. Even though I haven't seen the films, I have read most of the books.

"It's my favorite story," Penny says, becoming kind of quiet and wistful. "Do you believe in magic?"

I consider the question as I continue chewing my noodles. Do I? Rosie is a big advocate of all things psychic and miraculous, which I guess fall into the realm of magic. Les, on the other hand, exists on planet Earth a little more than my mother. Although he does believe in the healing powers of rocks, gemstones, and magnets, and he swears he once conversed with a dog.

But me? I don't know. Sometimes I think it's all wishful thinking—just crazy imaginations going under a new name. And yet I've seen too many bizarre things in my life to totally write it off as hogwash.

"Maybe," I say after swallowing. "I guess I believe in everything a little bit. Nothing totally."

"Yeah. There's no such thing as witches," she says, sounding disappointed.

"Actually, there is. I've met some."

Penny's eyes grow so wide her lids almost disappear. "Really?"

"Oh yeah. But it's nothing like Harry Potter," I explain. "They don't wear pointy hats or ride brooms or anything."

"What do they do?"

I chew another bite while trying to put it all into simple terms. "Mainly they watch the moon cycles a lot and carry around crystals. And they wear really cool ponchos."

"Oh." Penny goes back to studying my lunch box. She has this annoying habit of breathing through her mouth when she's deep in thought. "Do you think he's cute?"

My eyebrows mash against each other. "Who?" I ask, afraid she might have seen me with Jack or heard something from someone else.

Penny nods toward the lunch box, where Mr. Spock is making his weird peace sign at us.

"You mean . . . *Mr. Spock?*" I practically screech.

Penny's back goes rigid and she starts frantically

hoeing her taco salad with her spork. Her cheeks look like they're suddenly sunburned.

I instantly feel horrible. Here I am sounding just like those perky prima donnas at the thrift store. I'm not popular here, so there's no need to act snarky. Besides, *I'm* the one toting his image around.

"Of course he's cute," I add. "That's why I bought it."

"Right." She slips into another openmouthed reverie, gazing at the front panel of my lunch kit. "You can tell just by looking at him," she says softly. "You just know he's nice. And really smart."

"Uh . . . yeah. Great guy." *Except for his being fictional.*

Over Penny's shoulder I notice Miles perched on top of his table, staring our way. Not a slimy leer, just a really intent gaze—as if he's been told to draw a picture of me for a major test.

I'm about to turn away when I realize he's not the only one looking at me. Sitting at the same table—the one populated by the popular—is Caitlyn. She's just a few bodies down from Miles, flanked by Shanna and Sharla. Shanna is pondering her manicure and Sharla is chatting away, but Caitlyn doesn't seem to be listening. She's too busy giving me her patented bitch glare.

What the hell did I do to her?

"Do you know that girl Caitlyn? The cheerleader?" I ask Penny, who's still moony-eyed over the Mr. Spock picture.

"Caitlyn Ward?" She looks up and frowns. "Yeah. Everyone knows her. Why?"

I shrug. "I don't know. I think she's mad at me or something."

"She's a big meanie. In middle school she took one of my Ho Hos. And she was always making fun of my bad leg."

"You have a bad leg?"

Penny nods. "My right one. That's why I do water aerobics."

"I hadn't noticed."

Her mouth makes a small U shape, and another faint blush tints the tops of her cheeks. "Thanks. It's getting stronger. Now I only limp when I'm really tired."

I take a big bite of noodles and think back to my first sight of her in a swimsuit. I'd made fun of her too—only in the privacy of my own head.

"Caitlyn's probably just jealous of you," she says matter-of-factly.

I almost suck ramen down my windpipe. "What?" I croak. I cough a few times and sputter, "That's ridiculous."

"It's because Miles likes you," Penny goes on. "And she's been in love with him since ninth grade. Every year they're boyfriend and girlfriend for a little while, and then they stop. Right now they're broken up, but I can tell she's trying real hard to get back with him."

I sneak a glance at the Bippy table. My view of Miles is obstructed by a burly football player, but I can still see Caitlyn. She really is pretty, in spite of her cornea-frying expression and all the Vegas-showgirl makeup. In fact, all the girls at that table are beautiful—the products of salon merchandise and the select breeding of trophy people. Plus they just act like they're better—an attitude I usually try to copy.

"That's stupid. Why would he like me?" I ask, gesturing at my peanut sauce–stained jumpsuit and decades-old school supplies.

"Why not?" Penny replies with a shrug. I realize she truly doesn't seem to notice that I'm dressed like Sloppy Fidel Castro. Or she doesn't care. But then, it's pretty obvious she has no idea about the rules of popularity.

I make a few swipes at the sauce stain with a couple of napkins. I don't mind looking like a pig, but this is store merchandise. Unfortunately the napkins just seem to spread it around a little more.

"They have packets of wet wipes up at the condiment counter," Penny suggests.

"Thanks."

As I walk over to the far end of the room, I notice another glob of sauce in my hair. My table manners have taken a serious dive lately.

At the front counter, I grab a handful of wipes packets. Just as I'm wondering whether four will be enough, Caitlyn appears beside me.

"What are you doing up here?" she asks sternly.

I glance about, wondering if it's a trick question. The popular table is just a few feet away. I can't see Miles, but Sharla and Shanna are watching us closely.

"Is this one of your pathetic schemes to throw yourself at our guys?" Caitlyn continues.

Huh? What scheme? The one where I dress to do brake jobs? Or the one where I put peanut chunks in my hair?

Eventually my mouth reconnects with my brain. "What are you talking about?"

"You heard me. I'm on to you, freak. Stop flirting with people who are better than you."

I want to shout that there's no way someone like Miles is better than me, and besides I've been trying to *avoid* him and his pack. But before I can even form the words, Caitlyn goes prancing back to her yes-girls.

Static roars in my ears and I fight the temptation to toss ketchup packets at her rear end.

By the time I return to my seat, my molars are ready to crumble. Penny was right about Caitlyn. Too bad she missed the whole exchange, since she sits facing the other way. I consider telling her about it but decide to attack my stain instead.

What is with the divas at this school? Why is Caitlyn giving me a hard time when it's obvious I'm no threat? Are they just extra cruel here in Austin, or are they clueless about popularity rules too?

The more I think about it, the madder I get. I'm so busy grumbling inside my head and tearing open wetwipes packets with my teeth that I don't hear someone come up behind me.

"Excuse me?"

"What?" I snap, whirling around.

A girl is standing there, slightly off to the side. She's younger than me, probably a sophomore, and she's clutching a large notebook in both hands, holding it in front of her like a shield.

"Are you Maggie Dempsey?" she asks in a breathy voice.

I hesitate but, failing to sense anything sly about her, eventually say, "Yeah."

"I'm with the school newspaper," she says, venturing a step closer. "We have this column on new students called 'Welcome the New Wagoner,' and I was wondering if I could interview you for it."

"I've read that column," Penny says. "Last year they talked to a new boy from Minnesota. He collects trains."

My shoulders slump. Oh no. Not this stuff. I really hate these getting-to-know-you things. Like when teachers ask us to pair up and write each other's biographies. My life is so different, I can't help coming off like some homeless street urchin or a forgotten character in a Lemony Snicket book.

Then again . . . Suddenly I reinflate. Sounding like a weirdo can only help my cause.

"Sure," I say, facing the timid reporter girl. "What exactly would you like to know?"

She starts off with the basic stuff: my name, my age, where I've just moved from, whether I have brothers and sisters, et cetera. As I talk, she slowly relaxes.

"Some of us on the staff were wondering . . ." She stops and bites her lip.

"What? What were you wondering?" I prompt.

"About your clothes." Her limbs pull inward and her volume drops again. "We were wondering why you . . ."

"Dress like this?" I finish for her. I give a little shrug and decide to play dumb. "Why not?"

"Oh . . . uh . . . nothing. Just . . ." The girl trails off and glances past me at the popular table. I follow her gaze and catch sight of Caitlyn. She's still watching me, her face all wrinkled up in a menacing glare.

"Just . . . ," the girl says, restarting, "aren't you ever afraid you might look . . ."

"Stupid?" I finish for her again. "No! I'll tell you what's stupid. Being the way other people tell you to be. There are—what—over two thousand students in this school? Then there should be over two thousand different styles. Instead you have ten percent of the population telling the other ninety percent how they should dress and act! How stupid is that? It takes zero brains to get someone else's haircut. Real style is all about being yourself. It takes guts."

"Right . . . yeah . . . I guess," the girl says as she scribbles furiously.

"Here's a scoop. Popular people aren't any better than regular people; they just act like they are. And the thing is, we totally give them their power. If everyone stopped believing they owned us, they'd be nobodies. They'd have to eat each other."

The girl scrawls out another few lines and then stops and looks right at me. "Was it like that where you came from? In Portland?"

"Uh . . . yeah. People weren't scared to be themselves. To be real." It's completely untrue, but I figure there's no way she'll ever know.

"Sounds like it was great there."

"It was. . . ." My voice trails off. Once again I think about Trevor, and my throat gets that just-strangled feeling.

"So . . . is *Star Trek* your favorite show?"

At first I'm taken aback, and then I remember my mission to be strange for the article. "Oh totally," I lie. "I really love Mr. Spock and . . . that other guy."

The girl smirks ever so slightly as she writes it all down.

At least *she* knows the rules.

"Why did you lie to the school reporter?" Penny asks later as we walk to the Helping Hands Club meeting.

"I didn't lie," I protest.

"But you said you were a spy."

I smile as I remember the newspaper girl's startled expression. "No, I didn't. I said I could not confirm rumors that I was planted inside the school by the government to report on illegal activities. That's absolutely not a lie since I really can't confirm it."

"Oh." Penny frowns and breathes through her

mouth for a few steps. "And you really did used to live on an alpaca farm?"

"Yep."

"And you really do have a Pawnee Indian name?"

"Yes, I do."

"And you love disco music?"

"Okay. That might have been a lie."

She shoots me a look of shock. "Then why did you say it?"

"I don't know," I say with a lazy shrug. "I was just having fun with the girl."

There's just no way to explain that I consider that interview to be my masterpiece—my best and most efficient strategy yet to prevent people from liking me. Once the article is in print, it will cement my status as the school's biggest weirdo. Then no one—not Jack, not Miles, maybe not even Penny—will ever want to be seen with me.

As long as they let me stay in this club. I really need it for college.

"Well, here we are," Penny says in a formal voice, stopping in front an open classroom door. Classical piano music is playing and I hear a loud laugh.

As we enter, I see a large woman in a bright flowered dress sitting at the front of the room on top of the teacher's desk. Surrounding her are four students, all of them nerdy bookworm types.

Penny strides up to the group and clears her throat

for attention. "Hello, everyone. I brought us a new member." She gives a little arm flourish and everyone turns to look at me. For some reason, I feel a little nervous, which is weird considering they're all supreme dorks.

"Good for you, Penny," the woman says.

The others continue to stare at me, their jaws hanging open. I wonder if everyone in the club is a mouthbreather.

"Mrs. Pratt, this is Maggie," Penny continues, sounding all ceremonial. I have the feeling she doesn't get to be the center of attention all that often. "Maggie, this is Mrs. Pratt, our sponsor."

"Nice to meet you," I say.

"Likewise," she replies with a broad smile. "What brings you to the Helping Hands Club?"

"Oh, you know," I mumble. "Just like to help out." I feel an eensy bit ashamed. It would wipe that jolly smile right off Mrs. Pratt's face if she knew that I don't really want to be here, that I'm just hoping to fulfill an entrance requirement for college so I can get away from my parents and maybe get reunited with my ex-boyfriend. I do like to help people, but right now I need to help myself.

"Good. Welcome to my classroom and welcome to our little club," she says. "I'm glad to see you came dressed for hard work."

At first I'm confused; then I remember the jumpsuit. "Oh. Right," I say, laughing politely.

"All righty then." She raises her voice and glances at her watch. "Everyone find a seat. We'll get started as soon as our illustrious president arrives."

I figure Mrs. Pratt must be a history or world studies teacher, judging by the posters of the Sydney Opera House, African tribesmen, Chinese rice farmers, Guatemalan sheepherders, and that sand castle–looking building in Moscow. She also appears to be the type of teacher who believes in small-group work and lets students talk. In here there are no square desks arranged in neat rows. In fact, there are no desks at all. Instead she has five large circular tables, each with six chairs around it and a potted plant in its center.

"She seems fun," I whisper to Penny as we take two chairs at the table nearest the front. "Is she one of the real popular teachers?"

Penny shakes her head. "No. The Bippies all make fun of her. They call her Fat Pratt the Old Bat or Mrs. Claus. They don't like her because she doesn't give them special treatment like the other teachers do."

I've noticed that. At this school the primo popular get away with all sorts of stuff regular students can't— more so than at other places. They get out of their seats all the time, talk to each other, make wisecracks (or dumbcracks, as the case may be). And it seems all they have to do is mention the words "football" or "cheerleading" and they can come and go at will.

We're joined at our table by the four other members, three guys and a girl.

"Everyone, this is Maggie." Penny reintroduces me in that formal voice, complete with upward-palm gesture. I wish she wouldn't do that.

"Hi," the others say collectively.

"Maggie, this is Carter." Penny points to the person on my right, a tall, skinny, major geek of a guy whose thick bangs hang over his eyes.

"Hey," he says, tilting his head back to look at me.

"And this is Drip." Penny motions to Carter's right, where a very petite girl with short hair and dark freckles is sitting, her feet dangling a good two inches off the floor.

"Drip?" I repeat, unsure if I heard right.

"Yeah. My real name's Joanie Driffenbach, but everyone calls me Drip," she explains in a surprisingly husky voice.

"And over here are Hank and Frank." Penny sweeps her hand toward the two guys sitting between her and Drip. They are obviously twins. Both have bushy hair and faces that would be considered really cute—if they were eleven.

As soon as she introduces them, they start giggling and bumping each other's shoulders.

"You tell her," one of them says. Hank, I think.

"No! You tell her."

"You said it!"

"Whatever!"

"Fine!" Hank leans toward me and says, in a voice

wavery with suppressed giggles, "Frank thinks you look like Galadriel, only with darker hair."

"Oh . . ." I smile vaguely, unable to place the name, although it does sound familiar.

The twins notice my confusion. "You know," Frank prompts. "*Lady* Galadriel? Ruler of the Elves?"

"She didn't rule all the elves, dorkwad!" Hank snaps. "Only the ones in Lothlorien!"

Frank rolls his eyes. "Uh, doofus. She's *nobility*. That means wherever she goes, she rules."

I finally remember the Tolkien character and realize they're paying me a huge compliment. "Thanks," I call out. Only they're too busy arguing about the power rankings of Middle-earth dwellers to hear me.

"Either Hank or Frank is going to be our valedictorian," Penny explains.

"I am," the twins say simultaneously, cutting off their squabbling.

"Nuh-uh! You got a ninety-eight on that calculus quiz!" Hank snaps at Frank.

"So? My science scores are way higher. Remember when we did that diagram of the vocal tract and you labeled the uvula as the epiglottis?" Frank throws back his head and laughs.

"Shut up, guys!" Drip hollers.

"Aw, come on. It's just one of their *average* fights," Carter says. He lets out a slow, nasal-sounding chuckle. "Get it? 'Average'? As in grade point average?"

Everyone at the table groans.

"Try to be cool, dude. Or you'll scare off Galadriel," Drip grumbles.

"Hey. Just trying to entertain," Carter says, still smiling sneakily. "I'd do my Napoleon Dynamite, but I don't want to make a bad first impression."

Again everyone groans. Drip throws an eraser at him.

As excruciating as this is, I can't help grinning. This club is too perfect. *These* are the kind of losers I need to be with—the type I need to *be*. They're the ones people never see, even when they're right alongside them.

I can't believe I'm doing this; normally I can't stand being seen with kids so off the charts on the weirdo scale. But my school life isn't normal right now. And one thing's for sure: I'll definitely be able to spend time here without growing too attached.

"By the way," Frank says, leaning across the table toward me, "that's an awesome backpack and lunch box."

I almost say "Seriously?" but I catch myself just in time. "Thanks," I reply.

"All right, listen up!" Mrs. Pratt's voice hacks through the noise like a guillotine through cheese. Mrs. Minnow should make recordings of it. "Our president has *finally* arrived, so if you all will kindly shut your yaps, we'll get started."

We all fall silent. I turn my chair to face the front and instantly go stiff.

"We have a new member today," Mrs. Pratt says, pointing to me.

"Yeah, I see that." Jack smiles his salesman's grin and straightens his blue-flecked tie. "Welcome to the club, Maggie."

Is paisley print in fashion or out of fashion?

Rosie is at her late class, so I'm helping Les in the shop. The smell of Les's eggplant lasagna is wafting down the stairs, making me swallow and drool every few seconds.

I'm flipping through the racks, trying to find something weird to wear tomorrow, but unfortunately most of the stock in my size is very tasteful and flattering. Right now I'm wondering if a paisley quilted jacket is bizarre enough for my needs. I decide it has potential and put it on over the jumpsuit. Just a little big, but that could be a plus.

"How's school going, Sugar?" Les asks as he pulls a circular clothing rack several feet to the left. Lately he's convinced himself that the store has poor feng shui, and he's rearranging it for better energy flow.

"It's okay." I hold my breath, hoping the reply will be enough.

"So"—he grunts a bit as he pushes the rack into its new spot—"tell me about it."

I make a muffled groan as I exhale. That's another thing about my parents that makes them different from most. When they ask how I am, they really want to know, and they never accept safe answers like "fine" or "okay."

"It's just *going*, Les, whether I want it to or not. Not great. Not awful. School just . . . is." I'm sounding sort of snippy. I really don't want to restart the whole why'd-we-have-to-move fight, so I toss him a little nugget to throw him off track. "I joined a club today."

It works. The M-shaped worry lines on his forehead fade away and he breaks into a huge smile. "That's wonderful, Shug. Which one?"

"The Helping Hands. It's a community-service organization."

"Good for you. I'm sure they're happy to have you." Les points his nose upward and takes a couple of big sniffs. "You know, I think dinner smells about ready. Can you watch for customers while I go take it out of the oven?"

"Not a problem. Go. I'm starving."

He gives me a pat on the shoulder before charging up the stairs.

I heave a shaky breath and move on to search a new rack, trying to ignore my Stabby stomach. Lately I feel like I'm marinating in guilt. I'm hiding stuff from Les and Rosie. Not just my experiences at school and the details of my grand unpopularity plan—but all my feelings too. I've always told them everything—even stuff most teens wouldn't, like what guys I like, what kinds of stuff

I did or was tempted to do at a party, even my thoughts about sex. The thing is there's no reason to be sneaky with them because they don't forbid me to do anything. Their philosophy is to arm me with lots of facts and a few cautionary tales and then tell me how much they trust me to make good decisions. You'd think I'd be the most X-rated, extracurricular, drugged-up teenager on the continent, but I'm not. Maybe I'm too chicken to really go wild. Or maybe it's just not my style. But I also think maybe I don't want to destroy their faith in me.

I hate that I secretly hate my parents. I have this blimp-sized problem, and for the first time ever, I can't talk to them about it. Because *they're* the problem. Them and their endless national tour of life.

Will I ever forgive them for dragging me away from Trevor?

As I angrily flip through the rack, I think about the club and the unpleasant surprise of discovering Jack was president. For most of the meeting, I wasn't even paying attention. I was too busy mentally rehearsing ways to *un*-join the club. But then I realized I have no other choice. I have to sign up for something, and all the other organizations are probably full of potential friends or boyfriends, more so than this one. Besides, what am I afraid of? Jack isn't even my type. I mean, I know we sort of hit it off at the movies that day, and there are times I find him cute, but I'm just missing Trevor so damn much, it might not be long before I think Norm's sexy.

After thinking it through, I decided to stay put. I accepted their complimentary hand-shaped sticker and even agreed to work some big park cleanup this Saturday.

Note to self: find extra-weird outfit for Saturday.

The tinkling sounds of the front door zoom me back to the here and now. I blink a few times to readjust to my surroundings and then, remembering I'm by myself, head to the front to seek out our customer.

A girl is standing in front of the shoe display. I notice her hip jeans, cool wraparound top, and designer-looking print handbag. Good. Maybe we can make some real money tonight.

"Can I help you?" I ask, stepping forward.

The girl turns around and we both do a double take.

It's Shanna. As in *Caitlyn's* Shanna. Looking more clueless now than ever.

"You . . . ?" she says after a while.

"Yeah, me. I work here," I reply. "What are you doing here?"

"I . . . I . . ." Red blotches appear on her face and she glances around as if surprised to find herself in our shop.

"Well, I was right. It's done. But we need to give it ten minutes to cool off before we dig in." Les's voice grows louder as he tramps down the stairs and into the showroom. He spots Shanna and instantly zips right up to her. "Hello there!"

"Hi," she says, staring down at her sandals.

"I've got your stuff right here." Les walks behind the register, grabs a group of plastic-sheathed items off the mounted rod, and holds them out to her. "Here you go."

Shanna hesitates for a full second before snatching the bundle from his hands. She quietly hands him a couple of twenties and stands stock-still, blatantly avoiding my eyes as he rings up her change.

"Come back again soon, okay?" Les sings as he places a couple of bills and a few coins in her outstretched palm.

She mumbles something inaudible and then, without the slightest glance in my direction, practically runs out of the store.

"Do you know her?" I demand of Les.

He looks past me at the door. "That young woman? No. She came in here yesterday and asked to put some clothes on hold till today. Why? Do you know her?"

"Not really." I finger a nearby blouse and try to act casual. "She goes to my school, but I don't know her."

I must sound a little wistful, because Les comes over and hugs me. "Give it time, Sugar," he says. "You've only been there a few days." He squints toward the window. "Sun's going down. Why don't you close up while I make us a salad? I doubt we'll get any more customers tonight."

I nod silently, unable to speak.

As Les clomps back up the steps, I start walking around, turning off lights and picking up a couple of fallen items off the floor. I'm just reaching toward the front door when it suddenly opens wide and Shanna swirls in with the evening breeze.

"Don't tell anyone you saw me here, okay?" she blurts out.

I gape at her stupidly. I've never heard so many words come out of Shanna's mouth at once. I didn't even know what her voice sounded like—which is ironic considering she's a cheerleader.

I guess Shanna realizes how abrupt she was and mistakes my look of shock for insult. "Please," she adds, staring down at her pedicure.

Who, exactly, does she think I'll blab to? Penny? And for another thing . . .

"Why not?" I ask. "What's the big deal?"

Shanna's face contorts into a series of awkward expressions. "You won't understand," she says finally. She watches me long enough to recognize that I won't accept that as an answer and adds, "Look, if my friends find out I'm buying used designer clothes, they'll . . . she'll . . ." Again her face distorts this way and that. "Let's just say Caitlyn will throw a special pep rally just to give me shit."

I freeze up again, spellbound by her sudden display of personality. Apparently Shanna isn't the empty-headed snit I thought she was.

"It's just for a short time," she goes on. "My dad just made some bad investments recently. It'll get better."

Her pitch is low and somewhat disconnected—as if she's talking to herself more than to me.

I feel kind of bad for her. After all, I know what it's like to be at the mercy of your parents' actions. And I remember the fear of being targeted by the power crowd back before I purposefully tried to be unpopular.

"Don't worry," I tell her. "I won't say anything."

Shanna looks right at me, pupil to pupil, and I can tell she's afraid to trust me.

"Come on," I add. "Who'd listen to me, anyway? Look at who you are and look at who I am."

I watch her slowly relax. This she understands.

"Okay." She gives me a small smile. "Thanks."

"Yeah, sure."

Chapter Six: Planned Chaos

TIP: Unpopularity is a state of mind. Feel nerdy.
Think uncool thoughts.
It also helps to use the word "vaginal" a lot.

It took forever to get to school today. I had to take itty-bitty steps because the kimono I'm wearing is tied on way too tightly. Then, when I finally reached the front lawn, I saw something that—combined with the severe squeezing of my outfit—almost made me faint.

It was the Goth girl. As usual she was dressed all in black, but there was something very different (and yet jarringly familiar) about her look. As I got closer, I could see she had on an industrial jumpsuit, exactly like the one I wore the other day—only jet-black and without all the food stains.

What the hell?

For a moment I just stood there, gasping and staring, wondering if she was trying to go friends-free too. If so, it wasn't working. Her artsy crowd seemed completely indifferent to it.

Eventually the bell rang and I restarted my slow walk, telling myself it was probably a strange coincidence. Maybe she worked in a garage. Or maybe she just loved all the nifty pockets—the better to carry around extra eye makeup and femurs, or whatever. As it turns out, I really wish I'd thought to wear another jumpsuit.

There are no pockets in kimonos, and today the school is conducting some sort of testing. You know, the kind where you figure out what shape a flattened diagram would make if you folded it up. Anyway, everyone is supposed to test in homeroom and no one can bring backpacks. I'd forgotten this until I saw a big sign on the door reminding us to leave most of our stuff in our lockers.

Mine, by the way, is at the opposite end of campus from my homeroom. I swear I saw kids pass me both ways during the first leg of my journey. And the balding teacher-guy looked extra grumpy. Finally I limped into Mrs. Minnow's class, seconds before the bell, my arms loaded with paper, pencils, extra erasers, my lunch box, and a paperback.

I then had to sit down for three straight hours. Only it's really hard to bend the right way in this kimono, so I had to fold my body into about a 120-degree angle, perch my butt on the edge of the seat, and lean my shoulders against the top of the chair back. I can't imagine how this was ever standard dress for women in any culture. Maybe Japanese women learned to breathe from the very tip-tops of their lungs. That or they never sat down.

I'm just glad the test was easy, especially since I had to take it at arm's length. Now that it's over, I'm slouched way down in my seat, reading *Gulliver's Travels*.

I'm way ahead of where we're supposed to have stopped. That's one unintentional perk about Operation Avoid Friends: I've been extra good about doing schoolwork. Normally when we first move someplace and I don't have anyone I can hang out with yet, I spend lots of time with Les and Rosie. But I'm still all guilty-mad. And anyway, they keep inviting Norm over. If that kinky-haired orangutan asks me one more time why my Cancerian eyes are filled with sadness, I'll give him a good karmic kick in his Zang Fu organs.

I try to take a deep breath and turn the page. Gulliver is with the horses now. Trevor loved horses. . . .

I guess I'm sort of caught up in the book, because all of a sudden Jack's face materializes next to me, whispering, "Maggie."

I let out a James Brown–sounding squeal and almost pop the sash off my dress. Everyone around us starts laughing.

"What?" I snap, more embarrassed than annoyed.

"*Shhh.* A few people are still testing," he scolds.

"Mrs. Minnow has been trying to get your attention for about five minutes. She got a note saying to send you straight to the office." He's using that President Dweeb voice of his, the one that makes him seem to think I'm an irresponsible third grader.

"Sorry," I mumble. Then a new thought hits me. "Did it say why?"

He lifts his shoulders. "Don't know. Maybe they just need you to sign something." He gives an urgent nod toward the door. "You should hurry and go before they send another note."

"Yes, *sir*."

"And Mrs. Minnow says to take your things. It's almost time for lunch."

"Great," I grumble as I gather up pencils, lunch box, and battered paperback and try to hold them up against me.

I'm rising to my feet, moving extra slowly so I won't burst open my dress, when suddenly I get all wobbly. Jack catches me by the arm.

"You got it?" he whispers, steadying me with his strong hands.

"Yeah-huh," I say, feeling kind of dopey. The belt-thing must be cutting off blood flow to my head.

Jack smiles the same snug smile he gave me at the movie theater that day—right before I ended up flashing my panties. If it hadn't been for his quick reflexes, I might have accidentally done it again just now.

It occurs to me that I'm grinning back at him. "I should leave," I say, commanding the sides of my mouth to go down.

Remember the grouchy, heavyset man with the bad comb-over? The one who kept making vulture faces at me in the hallway? (No offense to vultures, which serve an important role in our ecosystems.)

Well, turns out he isn't some teacher burnout. He's the principal. His name is Dr. Wohman (which, in my mind, I see as Dr. *Whoa, man!*), and he's a real huffy puffy type.

I'm not so innocent that I've never been summoned to the principal before. I've dabbled in delinquency a few times. Never by myself, though—always with a group of new friends. The last time was with Lorraine in Oregon. We got yanked into Mrs. Everson's office for switching our English teacher's classical background music with one of Lorraine's rap CDs. Trevor was in that class too. I remember he laughed so hard he fell out of his chair.

So being here now dredges up a whole smorgasbord of emotions. Shock and frustration, fear and homesickness (or Trevorsickness). I'm not exactly sure why I've been called in, but I have a feeling this has something to do with all the scowly faces he makes at my outfits.

"Your mom and dad should be here any minute," Dr. Wohman announces almost gleefully while easing back in his seat to watch my reaction. I imagine most kids reward him with tears or spasms or pleas to reconsider, but not this delinquent. Threatening me with my parents is like threatening me with a cup of cocoa and a long bubble bath. But at least my look of annoyance seems to satisfy him.

I study the curlicue pattern on my satin slipper shoes while playing music in my mind, something I've gotten really good at over the years. Right now my mental boom box is spinning Radiohead's "Karma Police" for some reason.

"Karma police, arrest this girl,
Her Hitler hairdo is making me feel ill . . ."

It's obvious Dr. *Whoa, man!* is a little stoned on his own power. In fact, his office seems designed for maximum intimidation. He sits his extra-large frame in a gargantuan executive-style pleather chair, behind a desk the size of a Volvo. Meanwhile we visitors have to squeeze our heinies into square plastic seats, with nothing to hide behind and with no choice but to face his almighty massiveness. The walls are covered with diplomas and certificates and photos of him shaking some politician's hand. All that's missing is a buzzy purple neon sign that flashes "I'm important" in big script letters.

After a few restless minutes, I catch sight of the Bumblebee puttering past the rectangular window on my right. Soon after, Les and Rosie step into the principal's precinct.

"Hi, butterfly!" Rosie greets me as if she hasn't seen me in weeks. I thrash about and finally make it upright to give her a hug.

"Hey there, Sugar," Les says, throwing his arms around me.

After they finish fussing over me, my parents face Dr. Wohman.

"Hello there!" Rosie grabs his hand and pumps it up and down. "I'm Rosie Littlefield-Dempsey and this is my mate, Les." She motions to my father, who flashes the principal a peace sign.

"Uh . . . yes. Hello," Dr. Wohman says stiffly.

"You have a very lovely school," Rosie gushes, making upward flourishes with her hands. "So much natural light! Good for growing kids as well as plants. Isn't that right?" she adds with a giggle.

Dr. Wohman glances my parents over, taking in Rosie's handmade turquoise jewelry and Pakistani scarves and Les's woven tunic and Moses sandals.

"Yes. . . . Thank you," he finally says. "Won't you please have a seat?"

Rosie and Les settle into the chairs on either side of me. Rosie reaches over and squeezes my knee excitedly, as if we were all buckling ourselves in for a roller coaster ride.

"Mr. and Mrs. Dempsey, I'm afraid I—"

"Call us Les and Rosie," Les interrupts.

Dr. Wohman blinks a few times, his train of thought

obviously derailed. "Fine. Yes. . . . As I was saying . . . we have been having problems with your daughter, Sugar." He pauses, waiting for the news to trigger a response. My eyes pop wide with surprise, but Rosie and Les just smile back at him.

He clears his throat and continues. "It's her wardrobe. For several days now, I've noticed she has a tendency to dress . . . *inappropriately* for school." Dr. Wohman's voice gradually grows louder and bossier. "This blatant attention-seeking has gone on long enough. If it doesn't stop, she will be severely reprimanded. I'm sure you will do everything you can to assist me in this matter." At this Dr. Wohman frowns at me, signaling the end of his rant. I clench my jaw so hard my temples start throbbing.

Stupid, smug, self-important slave driver! I expected the other students to give me crap about my clothes. But the *principal?*

"I don't understand." Rosie turns to Les. "What rule has she broken?"

Les shrugs. "Please explain," he says to Dr. Wohman. "Exactly which part of the dress code has she gone against?"

Dr. Wohman rubs his forehead. "Well . . . *technically* she hasn't broken the dress code. But her manner of dress is very . . . distracting."

"Oh? Have the students been complaining?" Rosie asks.

"Well . . . no, but—"

"The teachers have?"

"Eh . . . not formally, but . . . but it's quite clear that she is dressing in a way meant to upset the status quo—for fame or maybe scandal, I'm not sure. In fact, a couple of ill-advised individuals have already begun imitating her. Such behavior could prove to be very disruptive and interfere with the educational process." He sits back and resumes his haughty expression.

Rosie and Les exchange one of their fleeting tele-pathic looks—one I've seen often enough to translate as *Poor, poor, misguided man.*

Les leans sideways and places his hand on my shoulder.

"Sugar bear, is that what you're doing? Are you try-ing to cause a scene and prevent people from learning?"

"No," I reply honestly.

"Can you tell us why you dress the way you do?"

I bite the inside of my cheek and mentally rehearse my reply before saying it. "I just . . . like it."

Rosie grabs my other shoulder. "You see, Dr. Wohman? She's not trying to cause any harm."

Dr. Wohman closes his eyes and pinches the skin be-tween his eyebrows. "Mr. and Mrs. Dempsey," he says, sounding sort of worn-out, "I realize this is not an obvi-ous case of deliberate wrongdoing, but I do have a PhD in education and I can assure you that—"

"You do?" Les brightens up. "From where?"

The principal pauses, once again yanked from his line of bull. "University of North Texas."

"Is that so?" Les nods while stroking his wavy beard. "That's a great school. I got mine from the University of Arizona. And the University of Wisconsin–Madison."

I try not to laugh as a look of shock flattens Dr. Wohman's features. He makes a few fishlike motions with his mouth before saying, "You have a PhD?"

"Oh sure. Two." Les leans forward and rests his elbows on his freckled knees. "Now, about this wardrobe business . . . Rosie and I have noticed that our daughter is going through a phase and, like all teenagers, is trying out different identities. In this case, by dressing the part. Wouldn't you agree that this seems to be the case?"

"Well . . . I don't—"

"And it appears in the absence of any formal complaints that the only person bothered by this is you," Les continues. "Now, I can see how you might take this as a personal affront, considering your obviously well-run school . . ."

"So lovely," Rosie adds. "Love all the big trees out front."

"But I don't see how you have a legal recourse— especially since there has been no real infraction of the rules. Now, Rosie and I don't like to make a fuss. Do we, Rosie?"

"That's right. We don't."

"And it's a good thing. Because if we were that kind of people, we could accuse you of harassing our daughter and obstructing her right to freedom of expression." Les leans back in his square-framed chair and rests his right ankle on his left knee. Suddenly all the power in the room has been sucked over to our side. Dr. Wohman looks shriveled. Even his desk seems to have shrunk.

I let out my breath, surprised to find that I was holding it. I still sort of hate my parents for bringing me to this place, but right now I want to kiss them.

The principal exhales slowly and digs his knuckles into the skin above his nose.

"I can help you with that," Rosie says.

"Excuse me?" Dr. Wohman glances up at her with a tired expression.

"Your headache." Rosie taps her own forehead to illustrate. "I know some pressure points that can release that tension for you."

"Uh . . . no. Thank you." His eyes fall on me. "Miss Dempsey? Will you please wait outside while I speak with your parents?" he asks at about one-third his previous speed.

"Yeah. Okay." As I rise to my feet, Les squeezes my hand and Rosie calls, "See you in a minute, doodlebug!"

Walking out the door, I catch sight of Dr. Wohman's expression. He looks kind of puny and wasted and totally drained of authority—like a plucked peacock. I almost feel sorry for the guy.

The school's office is in the exact middle of the main building, between the library and the cafeteria and right across from the student center. All the outer walls are made of glass midway up, so you can view office activity from any part of the student center. You can also easily see who's been called in to meet with the principal.

When I first took a seat in the chair outside Dr. Wohman's office, there were only a couple of students wandering about. They must have been trained scouts who quickly flew back to their hives with the news, because not long after, I had a group of six staring right at me.

Them I could deal with. But just two minutes ago, the bell for first lunch rang. So here I am, in a dress that fits like gauze bandages, perched awkwardly on a metal chair, trying to ignore the small mass of students pointing at me from the other side of the glass.

Now I know why monkeys throw their poo at people.

"Young lady," the secretary sternly says—meaning me. "I'm going to the teachers' lounge to warm up my lunch. Can I trust you alone for a few minutes?"

What does she think I'm going to do? Steal paper clips?

I nod mutely.

She holds my gaze for a moment longer, as if administering some telepathic polygraph test. Apparently I pass, because she gives me a satisfied nod, shoulders her Thomas Kinkade–print tote bag, and marches out into the corridor.

I stare at the door to the principal's office, wondering

what could be taking so long. I hope Rosie isn't making Dr. Wohman snort rosemary plant.

"Pssssst!"

I whip my head around, searching for the source of the noise, but I find nothing.

"Pssssst!" it goes again, this time more loudly.

Finally I notice Drip, the petite girl from the Helping Hands Club, standing inside the office. Her freckled, cereal-box elf face barely clears the front counter.

"What are you doing here?" she asks me.

"Dr. Wohman called me in."

"Are you in trouble?"

I shrug as much as my squeezy dress will let me. "Apparently he didn't like my outfit."

Drip makes one of those scoffing exhale sounds. "That's dumb! I don't like his spray-on hair, but you don't see me complaining!"

I laugh wheezily. Drip reminds me of those teeny tiny dogs that aren't afraid of anything. She might be a loser-dweeb, but at least she has spunk.

"Is he going to call your parents?" she asks.

"Already did." I wave my thumb in the direction of his closed door. "They're in there now."

"Good luck," she says, her forehead bunched in worry.

"Thanks."

Drip gives a little wave and heads back into the student center. Almost instantly people start crowding around her, obscuring her from view. After a while they bob up to stare at me. A few even shake their heads.

One guy I've never met pushes open the door and says, "Yo! Give him shit!"

"Yeah," someone shouts over his shoulder. "Screw baldie!"

Now even more students are wandering over to get the scoop. A few walk away, disappointed, but most stick around to give me supportive smiles.

What the hell is happening here? All this attention makes me feel sort of . . . dare I say it?

Popular?

Finally, just as I start losing all feeling in my posterior, my parents emerge from Dr. Wohman's office. Rosie is smiling and glancing around as if she were thinking about buying the place. Meanwhile Les and Dr. Wohman are laughing big hearty men laughs.

"And he said, 'What? I thought Yin and Yang were your lawyers!' " Les says, clapping the principal on the shoulder. The two amp up their guffaws even more.

Dr. Wohman holds a hand against his belly while he laughs, as if he's pulled a little-used muscle. Once his chuckles peter out, he straightens his suit jacket and turns to me. "Well now, young lady," he says breathlessly.

I stagger to my feet and meet his gaze. His eyes are glistening with tears from his and Les's laughfest, and a rosy tint has spread across his cheeks. He looks almost likeable.

"Here is a copy of our school dress code." He thrusts a piece of paper into my hands. "You are free to dress however you like, as long as you remain within these boundaries. Understood?"

"Yes, uh . . . yes, sir."

He gives a satisfied nod and turns back toward my parents. "Pleasure to meet you, Dr. Dempsey," he says, clasping Les's hand and giving it a vigorous pump.

"Call me Les."

"As long as you call me George."

For some reason they all laugh at this.

"You too, Miss Rosie," Dr. Wohman continues. "Thank you for the referral."

"My pleasure, George. Call us anytime. We just love your sunshine-filled school."

Luckily they're all so busy chattering in their little "Kumbaya" party they don't hear my disgusted moan. I have no idea what they talked about after I left the room, but it's obvious my parents worked their magic on him. I hope that doesn't mean he'll be coming around our place for astrology talks and dead head fruit snacks.

As Dr. Wohman goes into his office, Rosie claps her hands together and says, "Well, now. He was nice."

"There's an educator who supports a student's personal freedom," Les comments.

"Yeah, right," I mutter. "Only when he's afraid you'll sic the ACLU on his ass."

"So, sweetness," Rosie says, throwing her arm across my shoulders. "Do you have time to show us more of the school before you go back to class?"

At this my mind starts rolling a montage of embarrassing moments from my past: the time Les and Rosie decided to weed the flower beds at my school in Seattle . . . the way the junior high kids laughed whenever Les picked me up on our tandem bike, since every pair of pants he owned slid down to reveal his butt crack . . . the day both of them showed up during freshman English in full Elizabethan garb—codpiece and all . . .

I'm just about to tell them I can't when I suddenly spy those students gathered in front of the office. "Actually," I say brightly, "I'm about to go to lunch. You guys want to join me?"

"You betcha," exclaims Les.

"Sounds lovely," muses Rosie.

"Great," say I. And together we march off toward the cafeteria.

I figure if getting hauled in front of the Whoa Man somehow gained me cool points, the absolute best way to lose them is to be seen eating in the lunchroom with my mommy and daddy.

This is it. The perfect recipe for supreme dorkdom. I'm in the school cafeteria, dressed like a color-blind geisha, pulling food out of a *Star Trek* lunch box while sitting between my parents and across from Penny.

It's quieter than usual. Probably because everyone

around us is either blatantly staring or whispering behind cupped hands.

This is so great. After today I'll be considered reputation Kryptonite. No sane local teenager will want to get near me! For the first time ever, I'm thankful my parents are so different.

"You mean they don't offer a vegan tray?" Les is asking Penny.

She shakes her head. "And they run out of dairy-free options all the time. Last month the gravy gave me diarrhea."

I push aside my fried tofu and dig in to my cherries instead.

"Poor baby," Rosie croons to her. "Did you protest?"

"I told the nurse."

Les waves a carrot stick at her. "You should take action. You have a right to be served a meal that doesn't risk your health."

Penny seems to be enjoying all this attention. "I've told them lots of times," she says, pushing her lips out as she talks. "Last year when I got my third bladder infection, I told them they needed to offer cranberry juice. And then they did."

"Good for you!" Les cheers.

A few girls behind us start tittering like crazed birds. But no one except me seems aware of it.

"You know what else you should do for those infections?" Rosie leans forward and her beads tap rhythmically against the tabletop. "You should do vaginal exercises."

I hear a choking sound in back of me as one of the giggly girls starts hacking and coughing. Turning toward the noise, I find all six of them red faced. Five out of embarrassment, and one from lack of oxygen.

"Someone your age really should practice these movements," Rosie keeps on saying to Penny. "All of you girls should." She turns to include the group behind us. "It will aid urine flow and enhance pleasure during intercourse."

The girls exchange wide-eyed glances and start laughing incredulously.

"Here," Rosie says. "Let me demonstrate."

At this the girls' expressions change from amused to downright alarmed. It's all so horrible-wonderful I can barely handle it. As mortifying as it is to watch my mother launch into a sex-ed lesson in the middle of my school lunchroom, I almost feel a little proud.

Why didn't I invite my parents to lunch before now? Rosie and Les are managing to do in minutes what I haven't been able to do in over a week!

"All you have to do is think of . . . an elevator," Rosie says. "Your vaginal muscles are designed to squeeze upward"—her pitch rises and she slowly lifts her hands— "and relax downward." Her pitch lowers and her hands dip back into her lap.

Penny has abandoned her food and is listening

intently. I won't be surprised if she produces paper and pen and starts taking notes.

I look over my shoulder to catch Les's reaction, but all I see is his half-eaten carrot lying on the table.

"Where'd my dad go?" I ask Penny.

Keeping her gaze on Rosie's lesson, she absently points over her left shoulder. And there's Les, standing by the theater kids, juggling fruit. He keeps three oranges going in a quick circle and then pulls out the neck hole of his belted tunic top to catch them, one by one, in his shirt. The kids at the table clap and cheer.

"Do it again!" shouts one guy.

No, no, *no*! This is *not* part of the plan. He's supposed to be spooking the natives, not making friends with them.

I leap up and wend my way through a pack of lunch tray–carrying students. They're all trudging along, totally clueless to my emergency. Thanks to the kimono, the whole journey seems to take till retirement age. Finally I fight through the last of them and reach my father, who is now balancing an apple on his head.

"Um . . . Les? Come back and sit with us, 'kay?"

"Hi, sugar bear!" he says, greeting me, as if he weren't right beside me just five minutes ago. "Fellow players, this is my daughter." He carefully gestures toward me.

A couple of the kids say, "We know." Most of them go, "Hi."

"Hey, man. I heard you faced down Wohman today," one guy says to me. "Way to go!"

"Uh, thanks." I turn back to my father. "Come on, Les. I . . . need you to finish my salad for me."

"In a sec. I was just telling these guys about my Shakespeare days." He grabs the apple off his head and assumes an exaggerated stage posture. "Alas, poor Yorick!" he says in a deep and tragic-sounding voice.

"You played Hamlet?" someone asks.

"Not exactly. I was more of a comedic actor." He snatches a couple of the oranges off the nearby table and starts juggling them again. This time he orates as he tosses.

"I am the worse for my friends. They praise me and make an ass of me; now my foes tell me plainly I am an ass: so that by my foes, sir, I profit in the knowledge of myself; and by my friends I am abused." He ends the speech, catches the oranges, and takes a little bow.

Just as I feared, the students are all looking at him the way preschoolers regard a man who makes balloon animals.

"You should come talk to our class," says a guy in a *South Park* T-shirt.

"Yeah," chime in the others.

No! I scream silently. "Um . . . Les? The salad's getting soggy."

"Sure, Shug. Just let me leave my card." Les opens the leather pouch hanging from his belt and pulls out a business card. "I'd be honored to come speak to you," he says, handing the card to the *South Park* fan. "It reads Satya Nichols, but this is the number where you can reach me. I'm running Satya's store for a while."

"Hey, I know that place," says a redheaded girl, leaning sideways to inspect the card. "Our drama teacher sometimes gets costumes there."

"Oh, we have more than just costumes. We have all kinds of clothes. Speaking of which . . ." Les cranes his head and studies the nearby snack bar line.

For a nanosecond, I have no idea what he's looking at. And then I see her. Coming out of the frozen-yogurt station is Shanna, wearing the gently used jeans she just bought at our store.

Shanna spots Les, realizes he recognizes her, and freezes. Since she typically sports a deer-staring-down-a-diesel expression, no one else picks up that something is wrong. But I notice her hands tighten around the rim of her tray, making her drink wobble ever so slightly.

Les's grin broadens and I see his hand start to lift. But before he can wave to her, I grab his arm and tug it backward.

"Dad!" I shout.

That gets his attention. I never call him that. His head instantly snaps toward me, his mouth half-open in a Penny-like stare.

"Um . . . Rosie's looking for you," I mumble. Over his shoulder I see Shanna scurry to the safety of the popular crowd.

"Righty-ho." Les turns and bows to his newfound fans. "Always a pleasure to meet fellow thespians. And remember . . . 'some are born great, some achieve greatness, and some have greatness thrown upon them.' "

"Bye, Les!" they call after us as we walk back to our table.

"Why'd you stop me from saying hi to that girl?" he asks once we're out of earshot.

"Huh? What girl?"

He studies me for a second. "My mistake." I know he thinks I'm lying, but I also know he won't press it.

The truth is I really *don't* know why I wanted to stop Shanna's big secret from being exposed. It's not like I'm her friend or ever will be. Maybe it's because I gave her my word. Plus there was just something about the way she looked—all wild-eyed and shivery, like a scared bunny in designer wear—that kick-started my compassion.

When we arrive at our seats, all the girls at the table behind us are angled toward Rosie, listening intently.

"Tighten . . . release. Tighten . . . release," Rosie is saying, opening and closing her fists for effect. "One hundred reps a day is all you need. I'm doing them right now and no one can tell."

I look over her audience and catch the attention of the girl closest to me, a cute Halle Berry look-alike. I instinctively make so-sorry eyes at her.

She leans toward me. "Is that your mom?" she whispers.

I make myself nod.

"She's cool!" the girl goes on. "My mom never talks about stuff like this. You're so lucky."

I glance over at Rosie, who is now discussing the wonders of yogurt with active cultures. Les sits down beside her and slings an arm around her, pulling her close so that he can kiss her on the cheek.

"Yeah, I guess so," I whisper back. The girl smiles and leans forward again, tuning back in to the lecture.

She just doesn't understand. I don't feel lucky or grateful. Lately, instead of loving my parents, I love-hate them.

And right now, I sorta feel like kicking them.

"Tighten . . . release. Tighten . . . release. Rosie says it helps prevent your organs from falling into your vaginal canal."

Penny is relating our lunchtime follies to Helen, Mabel, Doris, and Barb as we get ready for water aerobics in the locker room. I can tell they're a little put off by all this sex-organ talk—especially Mabel. But they also seem to understand Penny's fascination with bodily functions and all things health related, so they don't complain.

"And it also helps prevent the loss of bladder control later in life," Penny goes on.

"Too late for me," Barb says gruffly.

Mabel gives her a horrified stare and Barb busts out laughing. "Gotcha!" she says.

"Is your mother a doctor?" Helen asks me.

"Not really," I reply as I try for the third time to tuck my hair into my swim cap. "But she's studied herbology and she's about to get a certification in therapeutic massage."

"Oh, I see," Helen says in a way that tells me she really doesn't.

"She just likes to give advice," I add, feeling the need to explain some more.

Helen must pick up on something in my voice, because she reaches over and gives me a reassuring pat on the shoulder.

"Come on, ladies," Barb bellows. "Time to hit the pool. That sadistic drill-sergeant teacher of ours will be out any second." She turns toward me and Penny. "You coming, young ones?"

"In a sec," I say. "I just need to get my hair up into the cap."

Penny watches them, rather longingly, as they line up by the exit. Then she looks back at me and chews her lower lip. Half of my hair has yet to be tucked into the swim cap and only one of my Aquashoes is on. The other is nowhere in sight.

"I'll wait for Maggie," she says morosely. I know how she hates not being on time.

Barb shrugs. "Suit yourselves."

As they head out the door, I hear Helen ask, "Should we worry about Barb getting into that warm water?" The rest of them crack up.

"You could have gone with them," I say. "I can get there on my own."

Penny plunks down on a bench. "That's okay."

"Sorry I'm so slow today."

I don't know what's wrong with me. All afternoon I've been draggy—and not just because my dress fit like a condom.

The Stabbies are back, worse than before. After lunch today, six different people came up to either congratulate me on standing up to Dr. Wohman or tell me how cool my parents are. One guy who high-fived me was even wearing galoshes. I told myself it was no big deal (after all, it's still muddy out from the storm), but it was scary anyway.

Each time someone was nice to me, I felt a sharp pain in the center of my midsection, as if I were getting a series of belly-button piercings. All this plotting to be unpopular is wearing me out. And it isn't even working.

"You look like you have a headache," Penny remarks. "Do you need one of those plants?"

I shake my head, causing another several strands to fall out from under the cap. "I'm just tired." I try to explain. "I just want to go away and do nothing. Like on an island somewhere. Me and no one else."

Except maybe Trevor. I zone out for a moment, imagining the two of us sneaking away and meeting up in some tropical paradise. We could live in a hut and eat coconuts and sleep snuggled up in a hammock together.

He would tell me how stupid he was to think he could ever let me go; then he would feed me bits of banana and pledge his everlasting devotion. . . .

"I used to want to live on a cloud," Penny says. "I'd be all alone up there, except for the birds, and I could float wherever I wanted."

I look over at her. She's staring off toward the showers, but her eyes seem to be focused on something beyond the painted brick walls. Her mouth is partway open, the way it always is when she's thinking hard.

I used to daydream about the same thing when I was little. Clouds always looked so soft and fluffy and safe from all the craziness on the ground. Just a poufy paradise where the only thing to worry about is the occasional jumbo jet.

Seems strange that Penny, of all people, would have this fantasy. She's always so darn literal.

In my distracted state, I loosen my grip, and my swim cap slips sideways, causing most of my hair to tumble back down.

"*Aaaauugh!*" I hate this stupid cap. I hate my stupid hair! I hate my parents for bringing me to this stupid place! "Crap!" I shout, grabbing the cap and whacking it against the bench. "Crap! Crap! Crap!"

Eventually the freaking stops.

Penny's jaw drops even more.

"Sorry," I mutter. I forget. She's probably allergic to high volume.

"You know, it's easier to do that in front of a mirror," she points out.

"Good idea." I smile to reassure her that I'm not crazy. Then I trot around the corner and start the whole process again before the mirrors above the sinks.

After a few seconds I hear the door squeak open. I figure Penny probably couldn't stand waiting anymore and decided to catch up with the ladies. Then I hear a familiar droning voice.

". . . need to get better subs. I mean, rully. No way am I getting a workout from that woman. Did you see her thighs?"

Caitlyn.

The door squeals shut, followed by a round of snickers. Penny must still be there, in the line of fire.

"Oh. My. God! Where did you get that swimsuit?" Caitlyn screeches.

"My mom ordered it off the Internet," Penny replies.

Like I said: literal. Her tone is wary, but she doesn't realize that the question is rhetorical.

"Looks like someone barfed up fruit salad," says somebody with a different, nasally voice.

Sharla.

Snorts and laughter echo through the humid air. I can't take it anymore. I let go of the cap, which snaps tightly around my skull, and march around the corner to the locker area.

What I see brings on a surge of anger so intense I'm

amazed I don't burst into flames. On one side of the dressing area stands Penny, with her knock-knees and protruding belly. She looks so pitiful I just want to pat her rubber-covered head. Meanwhile on the other side of the room stand Caitlyn, Sharla, and Shanna in their fancy workout wear, their hair neatly clipped or braided and their runway-model limbs cocked at huffy angles.

It's such a disgusting imbalance of power I want to retch.

"Don't listen to them, Penny," I say, surprising the three Bippies with my presence. "Orange is a much nicer color for swimwear than it is for *skin*." My voice echoes back to me, all high pitched and growly. I can't remember the last time I let myself feel so mad.

Both Caitlyn and Sharla look like they're trying to vaporize me with their stares. Shanna stands behind them, gazing into the distance. I used to think that look made her seem shallow and stupid, but now I see it for what it really is: fear. She's scared of them. And she's scared of me. She's afraid I'm going to rat her out.

I just might if this doesn't go well. I'm that mad.

"Well . . . ," Sharla says testily, breaking the silence before it becomes obvious I got them good. "What do you know, anyway? You two look like roll-on deodorants with those stupid caps on."

"Rully!" Caitlyn lets out a loud squawk of laughter, and Sharla grins smugly. Shanna concentrates on the nearby water fountain.

I take a shaky step toward Sharla. "Maybe. But did you know that whenever you make fun of people, your frowny rat face gets even uglier?"

It's a lame comeback—straight from third-grade recess. But it's the best I can do. When you're the child of peace activists, you're not very fluent in clever retorts.

I glance over at Penny, expecting a look of gratitude or an awkward high five, but her eyes remain neutral. Other than a few beads of sweat on her upper lip, there's no outward reaction to what's going on around her. It reminds me of those nature movies where an animal's only defense against a predator is to lie completely still and act dead. Makes me wonder if she'll roll into a ball if she gets any more confused.

"Stop it!" someone shouts.

I look back at Caitlyn and Sharla, but they seem just as surprised as I am. I watch them turn in unison to gape at . . . *Shanna?*

"Just stop it!" she repeats. Only we aren't doing anything—not anymore. We're too duhed by her outburst. Even Penny is staring at her. "Come on, guys," Shanna continues in an impatient whine. "Let's just *go!*" With that, she whirls about, pushes open the steel door, and stalks out into the corridor.

Caitlyn and Sharla exchange a look of astonishment. Guess they've never seen Shanna display so much emotion before either. After giving us one last follicle-frying scowl, they turn and follow her out.

"Go ahead!" I shout after them. "Keep glaring at people that way! You'll get even more wrinkles!"

I plunk down on the end of a bench and let out a long, moaning breath. Penny is still standing by the lockers, staring blankly at the door.

"You okay?" I ask.

She looks over at me and I can tell she's surprised by the question. "Yes," she replies. "Did the mirror help?"

It takes me a second to realize she's asking about my swim cap. "Oh yeah. Thanks."

"Sure. Can we go to class now? We're already late."

It's after two in the morning and I'm still wide awake. Thoughts and memories of Trevor keep coming at me, like an army of angry ghosts. After crying and moaning for a couple of hours, I give up on sleep, slide out of bed, and open my window.

So *this* is when it isn't hot.

I stand there, enjoying cool wafts of air as I listen to the whispery sounds of cars on a nearby highway. Austin doesn't have the in-your-face beauty of Portland, but it's nice, in a steamy scrubland sort of way. I could maybe even like it here, if I'd let myself. Which I won't.

I lean against the sill's scabby paint job and replay parts of my day—my run-in with Dr. Wohman, my parents' visit, my losing my temper with Caitlyn and her attendants. Things have never before gotten so crazy so fast. And yet nothing bothers me more than all the nameless students who smiled at me in the hallway today. That's not supposed to happen.

Maybe I should step up my plan a bit. Next week I'll wear *extra*-ugly clothes.

Of course, when the school paper comes out, that'll solve everything. As soon as everyone reads all the weirdo things I said (real and made-up), they'll run from the sight of me.

Thinking about that makes me feel better. I decide to leave the window open and climb back into bed, hoping the shushy waves of traffic will lull me to sleep. I've just gotten comfortable when somewhere in the distance a cat starts up a mournful yowl. Great.

The sound calls up a new memory. About a kitten I once had.

Actually she wasn't really mine; she just ran wild in the small commune we lived in outside Santa Fe. She had light green eyes and white fluffy fur with big peach-colored spots. I named the cat Gladys, because she always looked so glad to see me.

During the eight months I lived there, she and I developed a little routine. She would be waiting outside our door in the mornings for scraps of eggs. When I walked down the road to the parent-run community school, she would scamper along beside me. Then, after school, she'd follow me back home and play with the string toys I made for her. She'd hang around long enough for bits of dinner, wash herself, let me pet her awhile, and then disappear to wherever she spent her nights.

When we packed up to move (to an organic farm in Oklahoma), I begged Les and Rosie to let me bring Gladys with us. But they said no. They explained that Gladys didn't belong to me—that she didn't belong to anyone—and that she'd be happier and better off if I left her at the commune.

That was the beginning of my starting to question the way we lived. I cried and pleaded some more to take Gladys, but eventually I figured they must be right. After all, that was their whole philosophy about life. Les and Rosie don't believe in ownership. To them, people should share everything. I've seen Les give our last twenty-dollar bill to a drifter. And once, when a lady went on and on about how she loved Rosie's earrings, Rosie took them off and gave them to her. Sometimes I wonder if they would consider handing me over if someone made a big enough fuss. I'm sure they wouldn't, but when it's come down to it, they've always let me be free. They've never imposed their will on me or said I had to do things because they "said so."

After they announced that we were leaving Portland, I seriously considered refusing to go. Lorraine said I could stay with her, and I knew that Les and Rosie would agree to that if I really wanted it.

Staying behind would have meant I'd get to be with Trevor and keep building the life I'd started there. But I knew I'd miss Les and Rosie. And living with Lorraine would have had its problems. Her parents had gone through a warlike divorce and most of the time she stayed with her mom—who bought red wine by the case and flirted with all Lorraine's boyfriends.

After a lot of sleepless nights, I finally decided to go with my family. Trevor was really disappointed, but I truly felt that even though it would be tough, our relationship was strong enough to handle a year apart. So I left.

Now I completely understand what my parents were trying to tell me about Gladys. I don't belong here. And maybe, even though I would have been at the mercy of strangers, I could have been happier as a stray in Portland.

Chapter Seven: Cold Sweat

TIP: Be seen at all the wrong places with all the wrong people.

Or . . .

Threaten the crotch of the most popular boy in school with a sharp metal instrument.

This morning is Operation Green Clean, when the Helping Hands and other service organizations help clean up local parkland. Our club has been assigned a section of Zilker Park, a mongo green space next to the lake where lovers of the outdoors come to frolic. According to Mrs. Pratt, it's the largest park in the city, with a winding trail for joggers, walkers, and cyclists; a big open area for playing soccer or flying kites; and even a natural spring-fed pool for more amphibious types.

It's a glittery, sunshiny day. The kind when you almost have to be outside. The kind that, unfortunately, brings out hordes of loving couples.

I would have much preferred rain.

Each time I see a happy, hand-holding pair, something rips in my gut. Just a couple of months ago, that was me and Trevor. On a day like this, we'd be out paddling a canoe or hiking through Forest Park. We'd hold hands, tease each other, then find our tree and make out for a nice long while.

How can it be possible that I'll never do that again? I lived for those days. Now that they're gone, everything else seems so . . . beside the point. Life has become an endless parade of schoolwork, ugly clothes, and Penny ramblings, with nothing that really brings me joy.

But I guess that's okay for the time being, because I don't plan to leave any happy marks here in Austin.

I coast down a hill, following a map Penny drew for me, and start looking for our meeting place. Luckily I got a bike yesterday. Norm knows a guy who fixes them out of his garage, so Les and I went there and picked out a used Raleigh for only fifty bucks. The guy was cute too. Long blond ponytail. Bugs Bunny tattoo on his left shoulder. He reeked of pot and said "dude" a little too often, but that didn't bother me as much as his mom coming out and telling him to wash up for supper. I really hope I'm not still living with Les and Rosie when I'm twenty-five. When we got back home, I started filling out another university application—this one for UC Berkeley, Trevor's second choice.

Thanks to Penny's sketch, I find the bicycle rack exactly where she said it would be—right in front of the playground area. (She even included tiny stick figure kids so there would be no confusion.)

As I take off my helmet and slip it into my backpack, a lady walking her Labrador gives me the once-over. Following my new vow of never dressing normally in Austin, I managed to cobble together a practical yet wacky enough outfit from the shop: pink satin shorts with a matching satin jacket (which I've tied around my waist, because it's pit-of-hell hot), white tee with a unicorn design on it, white headband, and tube socks pulled up to the knee. My hair is in two long braids.

Penny's cartoon map is so detailed I have no problem finding the meeting place. She's already there, keeping a knock-kneed, mouth-breathing guard over a picnic table.

"I like your shirt," she says as I jog up.

"Thanks," I reply. "I like yours too." She has on a short-sleeved blouse with huge plastic buttons shaped like butterflies, big pleated khaki shorts held up by a white belt, and socks very similar to mine, also pulled up to the knee. On top of her head is a wide-brimmed gardening hat about the same width as the hood of a car. Between the two of us, it's a toss-up who looks more geeky. I find myself almost jealous of her effortless lack of style.

"Here," she says, handing me a tube of sunscreen. "Sunburn at our age increases the risk of skin cancer later on. Did you know that melanoma is the third most common cancer for people aged fifteen to thirty-nine?"

"No," I reply truthfully. I unscrew the cap and begin shellacking my arms with the greasy stuff. Penny has a way of reminding me of my mortality.

"Here come the others." Penny points to the top of the hill, where Jack, Drip, Carter, and the twins are loping toward us, each carrying various tools and supplies. Jack looks like a more athletic version of himself. His gray shorts reveal legs that are pale but surprisingly muscular, and his chest looks extra-broad in the RunTex T-shirt he has on. I wonder why he can't dress like this more often, instead of like an ad executive.

"Hey," he says, nodding at Penny and me. "Been waiting long?"

I shake my head.

"Eight minutes," Penny says, glancing at her watch. She scans the assembled crowd and frowns. "Where's Mrs. Pratt?"

"Not coming," Jack says. "Her back is acting up, so she's leaving the hard labor to us. But we're all invited to her house afterward for lunch. You all are coming, right?" he asks, looking right at me.

"Sounds great, but I came on my bike," I reply, trying to sound disappointed. I'll put in my hours of service for college requirements, but any extra socializing is totally against my rules. Especially if Jack is going to be there. I'm scared he might think I joined the club just to get near him.

"That's okay," Drip says, spraying bug repellent on her legs. "She only lives—what?" She looks over at the twins. "Two or three blocks from here?"

"Three and a half," answers Frank.

"More like four if you count the park trail," Hank counters.

"Or I can put your bike in the back of my truck," Jack offers. I'm sure to anyone else his smile is of the typical friendly-guy variety. But to me it seems like . . . wrapping paper. There are a whole lot of meanings hidden there; I just know it.

"Okay. Great." I haven't lifted a single tool yet and already I'm worn out. I have a feeling this sudden weariness is the prelude to something bigger—like that stretchy sensation that comes over you right before you get sick.

Suddenly I just know the day won't end well.

"What about this one?" Drip asks, holding up an empty Fritos bag in her gloved fingers.

"Uhhh . . . I know," Hank says. "Guy robs a gas station, but he's hungry too. So along with the cash register money, he grabs a large bag of chips. As part of his getaway, he detours through the park, sits on the grass, and eats them."

"Did he hide the money here too?" Frank asks.

"Nah. As he ate the chips and looked out over the empty playground, he had an epiphany and realized he was wasting his life. So he decided to become a law-abiding citizen and returned all the money."

"Didn't stop him from littering," Drip mutters, shoving the chip wrapper inside her garbage sack.

We've been here only an hour and already we've filled up six Hefty bags with trash. To make it more fun, the twins started up a game in which we try to guess how certain discarded items came to be here.

Fortunately, Jack is on the other side of the clearing, helping a park official remove a dead tree. With him gone, it's easier to relax and have fun.

"Your turn, Penny," Frank says, holding out a half-crushed Coca-Cola can. "Tell us about this guy."

"There are ants on it," she says. "Watch out. They bite."

Frank studies the can more closely. "Funny how they go in a line," he says. "Like they're having a parade or something."

"Maybe they're singing their national ant-them," Carter quips.

We all boo and hiss. Drip tosses a Styrofoam cup at him.

"Hey!" Carter shields his head with his arms. "Stop bio-degrading me!"

"It's still your turn, Penny," Frank says. He holds up

the Coke can as if it were the sword Excalibur. "Tell us, O Wise One. How did this get here?"

Penny hunches her shoulders and frowns down at the ground. "I don't know. Some person on a picnic dropped it," she mumbles.

"Yeah, but who?" Frank prods. "And who was he with?"

She gives an awkward shrug. "People who aren't very healthy, probably. Carbonated drinks are bad for you."

"Maybe they were carbon dating."

This time we all toss trash at Carter.

"Aw, come on!" he cries, protecting his head again. "We're supposed to be picking up here!"

"*Eeeeuuuw!*" Drip shouts suddenly. She steps into a clump of bushes and bends over something. "Maggie? Can you come get this with your stick-thingie?"

Even though we have tons of garbage bags, several pairs of work gloves, and a whole pack of bug repellent, we were only given two of those trash-picker-upper poles with the pointy ends. To make it fair, we're all taking turns using them. Penny and I have them right now.

"Stick-thingie coming through," I say, pushing past the twins toward Drip. "What did you find?"

"I think it's a dirty diaper," she replies, scrunching up her nose.

The guys make disgusted sounds and take a couple of steps back. Penny seems unconcerned.

"No, it isn't," I say in my best stage voice as I skewer the fly-infested plastic mound and dump it into Drip's sack. "It's an alien carcass."

The others laugh.

"The UFO landed about where Carter is standing and they sent this poor scout out to investigate the surroundings. Unfortunately he was hit in the head by a Coke can tossed by some careless, sugared-up picnicker and died instantly. Fearing for their lives, the others returned to their homeworld and immediately branded us a hostile race. They are currently debating whether to call a preemptive strike against us."

"Okay. Maggie wins," Carter says.

The twins are giving me looks that border on reverential.

"That was awesome," Frank breathes.

"Heavenly, I'd say," quips Carter. "Out of this world, even."

"Will someone *please* shut him up?" Drip shouts to the sky.

"Try putting one of those twisty-tie things on his mouth," suggests Frank.

"Uh . . . guys?"

We're having so much fun giving Carter grief that we don't hear Hank.

"Guys? Guys, listen," he repeats. This time there's a quality to his voice, all high and buzzy like an alarm, that makes us stop and look at him.

"We've got company," he says, staring over my shoulder.

I spin around and see a group of people standing on the hill behind us. Shielding my eyes, I'm able to make out Miles, Caitlyn, Shanna, Sharla, and a few other nameless Bippies, their silhouettes haloed by the shimmery sunshine, making them look like descended gods. All appear to be wearing swimsuits and carrying tote bags.

"What are you guys doing here?" Caitlyn asks as they stride down toward us. "Having some sort of dorkfest? Is it Geek Pride Week?"

The rest of them laugh a rather bloodthirsty laugh—all except Shanna, who again hangs back with her scared-rabbit stare.

I look around at my fellow Helping Hands. Almost everyone is in the same pose: back slumped, eyes averted, cheeks the color of pomegranate seeds. Only Drip and Penny dare to make eye contact with the tormentors. Penny just seems dumbfounded, but Drip's hands and jaw—hell, her whole body—are clenched and ready for battle. She looks like the fiercest, angriest, most ill-tempered sugarplum fairy you could ever meet.

"What are those?" Caitlyn continues, pointing to Frank's garbage sack. "Are they your sleeping bags?" More hellish laughter follows.

I watch as Caitlyn smiles and tosses her hair triumphantly. She's so enjoying this. I think about her stealing Penny's Ho Ho and making fun of her bad leg in middle school. And I remember the way she cackled at Penny in her swimsuit the other day. This girl totally abuses her power.

A tight, steamy sensation builds up inside me, igniting my organs. I have never hated anyone in my life. Not ever. There are people I've been disappointed in and annoyed with, and many I couldn't be good friends with, but there has never been an individual I've wanted to completely rub out of existence with a giant eraser.

Until this very moment.

"Actually we're picking up trash, Caitlyn," I say, waving my Hefty bag in my left hand. "So why don't you climb on in?"

A stereophonic gasp wells up from the crowd.

"What did you say?" Caitlyn hisses, her tangerine skin turning red and blotchy. "What did you say, you freaky-looking bitch?"

I don't reply. I halfway realize that I'm setting stuff in motion—stuff I really don't want to take on—but it's too late now.

Miles steps up beside Caitlyn. At first I think it's a show of solidarity with his Bippy princess, but then I realize he just wants a better view. Unlike the others, he doesn't seem the least bit shocked. Instead, his mouth has swiveled sideways, revealing his left dimple. He folds his bronzed arms across his chest and stands there gleaming like a life-sized Oscar statue.

For a moment there's nothing but the sound of gathering tension. Caitlyn's face is all tough on the outside, but something about her eyes is a little off. They look more sad—or is it scared?—than angry. Even so, there's no telling what she might do.

"Come on, guys. Why are we wasting time with these dorks?" Shanna whines. "Let's go swim."

The less murderous-looking Bippies nod in agreement and twist their upper bodies toward the pool, waiting for a signal from their leader.

"Yeah, come on, Cait," Sharla urges. "Who cares about these nobodies?" She looks right at me, screwing up her already severe features into a gargoyle-like expression.

"Fine," Caitlyn mutters, not taking her eyes off me. "Let's go."

Sharla and a couple of other bikini-clad Barbies lead a still seething Caitlyn off toward the pool. The rest of the group parade after them, each giving me a parting glance. Some look livid, others confused. Most just seem stunned. Shanna brings up the rear without regarding me at all.

Only Miles remains behind. He waits until his friends are out of range and then swaggers toward me.

"You know, you're really sexy when you're angry. Are you some sort of bad girl?" he asks, his voice low and husky.

I have no idea how to answer. A no would be asking for the usual torment. But a yes could trigger new and different abuse.

"What?" He opens his arms in a nothing-to-hide gesture. "Don't tell me you're afraid of me."

"No!" I snarl, then immediately regret it. I've fallen into a trap.

"Good. Then how about you and me go for a walk and . . . talk." He grins widely enough to expose his dimples, and again his eyes seem to gleam. Like metal hooks.

Mother Nature can be such a sarcastic bitch. How could she make a creature that looks so beautiful and acts so repulsive?

"Miles?" I say sweetly.

"Uh-huh?"

I raise my trash-grabber stick and point the sharp end toward the fly of his shorts.

"You should go catch up with your friends." I smile as if a halo frames my face. "Before you get hurt."

At first his perfect features go slack with surprise. Then his smug smile returns. "Yeah, right. Like you'd really do that."

"How do you know I won't?" I keep grinning like a supervillain. "You don't know anything about me. Maybe I *am* bad. Or maybe I'm just . . . mad."

He glances down at the spike hovering inches away from his crotch. Gradually his smirk falters.

"I'll say it was an accident. That I thought you were a big piece of filth, and accidentally shish-kebabbed you," I go on in a scary-sweet voice. "And besides, I have witnesses." I give a backward nod toward my fellow club members, hoping they're still there and not cowering in terror.

They must look convincing enough, because Miles appears even more uncertain. He meets my gaze and I finally see what I need to see. Fear blooms unmistakably in his ice blue eyes. He takes a step back. "Crazy bitch," he says sort of poutily. "What's your problem, anyway? Think you're too good for me?" Before I can reply, he does a quick about-face and starts marching toward the pool house.

Once he's a good distance away, I turn and face the Helping Hands. They're all just standing there, stupified, looking like they might dive for cover at any second. Penny's mouth is gaping wide enough for a whole burger, Carter is pearly pale, and the twins are waving in the wind, looking a little faint. Drip, on the other hand, is bouncing on the toes of her sneakers.

"That. Was. *Awesome!*" she says, uttering one word per bounce. "You rock!"

"I can't believe she did that," Hank says to Frank.

"I can't believe you did that," Frank says to me.

"Yeah," Carter adds. "Way to *stick* it to him."

Drip lets out an aggravated moan. "Maggie, can you chase him off next? *Please?*"

All of a sudden I hear a rhythmic footfall and the crunching of leaves. Jack is racing toward us, his T-shirt stained with sweat.

"Hey," he says breathlessly. "What happened? I saw those guys come over. Were they trying to start stuff?"

"Yeah, sort of," Drip replies. "But Maggie took care of them. Especially Miles." She and the others start laughing.

Jack turns to me. "Really? Are you okay?"

He seems worried. Maybe too much so. "I'm fine," I answer.

"But . . . what did he do?"

"Nothing. He just . . . talked trash."

"Yeah. And she almost bagged him," Drip cuts in.

Jack walks right up to me. "You need to stay away from that guy."

I stare back at him, thrown by his slightly pushy attitude. "I can handle Miles."

"She's right about that," cries one of the twins.

Jack rakes his fingers through his sweaty hair. "Look. Just trust me on this," he continues, his voice barely audible. "That guy is scum. You don't want to egg him on."

"Who says I was? And who are you to boss me around?" I can't believe this guy. My own parents don't lecture me the way he does. Does he think I'm some flaky kid who can't take care of herself?

"Okay. I'm sorry," he says. Only he doesn't sound sorry. He just sounds irritated by my reaction. "I just . . ." He pauses and lets out a sigh. "I just don't want to see anyone get hurt." He looks at me, and for a second it seems like he's going to say something else. Then he shakes his head and walks away, heading back to the dead tree.

A voice comes from below. *"Hmmm."* I glance down and see Drip staring after Jack.

"What?" I ask.

"Nothing," she replies. "Just . . . *hmmm*."

"You should have seen it. It was, like, ten to one."

"No it wasn't. More like twelve to one."

"What are you talking about? You were so scared you practically climbed the tree. You weren't even looking."

My standing up to the gang of Bippies has become a subject of debate for the twins. Once everyone started relaying the story to Mrs. Pratt, the facts seemed to go out with the Hefty bags. To hear it now, you'd think I was a weapon-wielding martial arts master and the Bippies had brass knuckles and chains. Frank keeps calling me Warrior Princess and Hank won't stop humming some superhero theme song.

After the incident with Miles and Caitlyn, the rest of the morning went fine, and before I realized it, it was time to pack up and head over to Mrs. Pratt's house. At first I wasn't sure about it. I really didn't want to see Jack again; that guy already had me wary before all this ordering me around. But I was hungry. And Norm was back at my place, getting ready for another astrology class. So I got Penny to draw me a new map and biked into the neighborhood behind the park.

"I'm so glad you joined our club!" Drip says for the seventh time, walloping me on the back.

The only ones not joining in the dramatic retelling are Jack and Penny and I. I keep shoving mini egg-salad sandwiches into my mouth so I won't have to talk. Jack is sitting in the leather recliner, listening to the others and shooting me disapproving looks every few seconds. And Penny, other than asking if the soup is dairy free, hasn't said much at all.

That's twice she and I have been in a confrontation with Caitlyn and the others, and Penny hasn't acknowledged either time. Is it because it bothers her so much she can't bear to talk about it? Or has she been beaten down so much by those types it isn't even newsworthy anymore?

"Well, now. Sounds like you guys had quite an exciting time out there," Mrs. Pratt remarks in a not entirely sincere voice. She's also been giving me strange glances, as if she were Jack's illegitimate mother or something. Probably afraid I might try to take over the club and turn them into a fighting force.

I'm really starting to regret losing my temper with the Bippies. Not because I fear retaliation—which is a possibility—but because I now realize it was the wrong thing to do. I don't mean ethically. I mean planwise. None of these Helping Hands members would have faced them down (except maybe Drip). I should have just hung my head and taken the abuse like a good loser.

"Okay, everyone. I hate to be a party pooper, but we do need to discuss some club business," Mrs. Pratt shouts from her seat on the couch. "The big dance is coming up soon and we still have a lot of work to do."

"Dance?" I look over at Penny, who is carefully lining up the plastic spoons. "What dance?"

"Every fall the Helping Hands Club has a dance fund-raiser for the charity of our choice," she says, as if reading from the official bylaws. "This year we decided to donate all the money from tickets and drinks to the Arts Outreach Program."

"What's that?"

"It's this organization that provides used instruments and supplies to kids who want to take music or art classes but don't have the money. I already gave them my old harp. And Carter gave them the tuba he stopped playing when he got braces."

She carefully nudges one spoon that's slanting away from the rest and then heads over to the couch, where the other kids are crowding around Mrs. Pratt. I hang back.

"Maggie? Are you going to join us?" Mrs. Pratt calls out, tapping a stack of papers against her knees to straighten them.

"I don't know. I think I should be getting back home," I reply. I really don't want to be here anymore. I'm all sweaty and mucky from our morning in the park, and the egg salad isn't sitting well in my stomach. Besides, something's wrong. It all feels a bit too chummy after my face-off with the Bippies, as if we're suddenly brothers-in-arms.

Mrs. Pratt gives me another probing stare. "This won't take long, but it is very important."

"Come on, Maggie. Don't go," Drip says, motioning me toward them. "The dance is our big thing. And this year we're getting a really cool DJ named Master-Man!"

"Yeah," Hank mumbles. "Maybe more than forty kids will show up this time."

"Please stay," Mrs. Pratt adds. "We have such a small club, one person's absence makes a big difference."

The others join in the urging.

They convince me. Feeling icky is too lame a reason to take off, and my overwhelmed brain can't come up with anything better. Anyway, if Mrs. Pratt gets all disappointed in me, she might not write a letter of recommendation like I need her to. She has major power over my future—and whether I ever get reunited with Trevor.

I yank my reluctant, weighed-down-with-egg-salad body over to their corner of the living room and sit down next to Penny. As Mrs. Pratt starts going on about the price of sodas and the cost of hiring a cleanup crew, my mind starts to wander. I'm in complete zonk-out mode when I suddenly hear my name.

"Huh?" I say stupidly.

"What do you think?" Drip asks me.

"Uhh . . ." I consider faking it, realize I can't, and

finally say, "I'm sorry. I was thinking about something else. Could you repeat that?"

"They want to know if we should serve just soda, or also a healthy alternative, like punch," Penny says.

"Whatever. Doesn't matter to me." I'm trying to be all easy-breezy but I can tell they're let down.

"Well, I guess that's all we need to cover today," Mrs. Pratt says, rising to her feet. "This meeting is officially over, but you all are free to hang around. I'm certainly not eating the rest of that food." She laughs heartily and then trots over to me. "Maggie, could I speak to you a second in the kitchen?" Her ultraquiet tone tells me this is serious. Again I ransack my mind for a way out of it but come up empty.

"Sure," I reply.

I follow her through a swinging door into her tile and stainless steel kitchen, where I somehow manage to stand and face her.

Mrs. Pratt gets right to it. "I'm worried about you," she says.

"What?" I practically choke on my own tongue. "Why?"

"It's obvious something is wrong. I've been watching you. Not just here today, but at school too. And I hear things in the teachers' lounge." She cocks her head, and her eyes narrow thoughtfully. "I have to ask, are you having a tough time fitting in?"

"No! Not at all!"

"Are you sure? It's just that you seem rather . . . aloof. I know it can be hard moving to a new place and finding friends."

"No. Everything's great. I have friends. Like . . . the Helping Hands. They're great." The Stabbies are on the assault, whacking away at my insides. How is it that she can sense all this about me? Have I been that obvious?

"Well, good. It's nice to know that. These are the sweetest kids. You've picked a good bunch to hang out with."

I nod vigorously. "Yeah."

"I'm sorry to pry into your business. I just wanted to be sure something serious isn't going on." She smiles at me—a warm, motherly smile—and it almost makes me want to cry. "You know, if there's anything you want to talk about, you can always come to me, or any teacher you trust."

"Nothing's going on," I say, making myself smile back even as a cloudy glaze covers my eyes.

But what *is* going on? First Norm, now Mrs. Pratt. Is Austin full of nosy psychics?

Suddenly the door swings open and Jack strides in. "Sorry," he says, looking from me to Mrs. Pratt. "Didn't mean to interrupt."

"No, no. Come in," Mrs. Pratt says. "I was just getting to know Maggie a little better. Did you need to speak with me?"

"Actually, I . . . uh . . . I wanted to talk to Maggie."

"Go right ahead." Mrs. Pratt turns and walks toward the sink. "I'm going to get these brownie pans soaking."

"Those were delicious," Jack says, never missing a chance for brownie points. In this case, literally.

"I know," Mrs. Pratt says, smiling wryly. "Why do you think I look like this?"

As soon as she turns the water on, Jack faces me. I figure he's going to start nagging me again, so I'm completely struck stupid when he says, "Uh . . . I was just wondering . . . would you like to go out to dinner with me tonight?"

A voice inside me starts screaming. This is the *last* thing I need right now—especially after Caitlyn and Miles and Mrs. Pratt. What exactly did my horoscope say for today? That if I don't hide under my bed, everything I don't want to happen will occur in the next twelve hours?

But what can I do? Just five seconds ago I assured Mrs. Pratt—no, I *pledged out loud*—that I wasn't being purposefully aloof, and that these people were at the top of my friends list. And even though she appears to be washing dishes, I can tell by the way her right ear is tilted toward us ever so slightly that she's listening in.

"Um, uh, sure," I say.

Jack's brows and mouth flip into perfect semicircles.

He looks as if he just captured a key voting precinct. "Great! That's . . . great!"

To my left, Mrs. Pratt starts humming as she scrubs her pans.

When did my life get so odd? Never did I imagine I'd someday be coerced into a date by a brownie-pushing history teacher. What's next? Frog rain? Abduction by Oompa-Loompas? Mrs. Minnow arranging my marriage?

Tomorrow I'm definitely staying under my bed. *If* I survive tonight.

After a long shower and some peppermint tea to settle my stomach, I head up to the roof with my Nokia. After this month, my Portland account will lapse. I could transfer it to an Austin area code, but there's no point, since we're leaving here soon. So I figure I'll use it while I can.

I settle into my shady spot by the door and power up the phone. I plan to check the news and maybe toy with sending a text to Trevor, but to my amazement there's a message flashing in the lower left-hand corner.

I've got e-mail.

Incredible. I haven't heard from anyone since I got here.

I wonder if it's from Trevor. My gut goes all twisty-tight and my hands are trembling, making it hard to click on the envelope icon. But of course it isn't from him. Because today is Everything-Goes-Wrong Day.

It's from Lorraine.

HEY MAGS!!!!!!

I can't help smiling. Lorraine is one of those all-caps people. Everything she does is big and loud and screaming for attention, and exclamation points are like her lovers.

GOD IT'S BEEN FOREVER!!! HOW IS
TEXAS? IS IT HOT? HOW ARE THE GUYS?
ARE THEY HOT? MEET ANY CUTE COWBOYS
YET???!!!!
    BENNETT MILLER ASKED ME OUT!!! SO
DID TERRYL BOOTH, BUT I SAID NO WAY
JOSE!!!! BENNETT TOOK ME TO THE
CARNIVAL AND GOT ME A PINK GIRAFFE.
THEN WE MADE OUT BEHIND THE HAUNTED
HOUSE. HE'S SO HOT!!!
    I'M SURE ALL THE GUYS ARE TOTALLY
SALIVATING FOR YOU!!!! YOU HAVE TO TELL
ME ALL ABOUT IT. AND IF THEY ASK YOU
OUT, YOU HAVE TO SAY YES!!! I HOPE YOU
AREN'T ALL MOPEY ABOUT TREVOR. HE'S A

JERKWAD AND A HALF. CANDACE THINKS
SHE'S GOT IT GOOD WITH HIM, BUT SHE
DOESN'T KNOW HIM LIKE WE KNOW HIM.

WELL THAT'S ALL FOR NOW. I GOTTA GET
SEXY FOR TONIGHT. BENNETT IS TAKING ME
TO A PARTY BY THE UNIVERSITY. IF I MEET
A HOT COLLEGE GUY, I MIGHT BLOW HIM
OFF!!!! HEE HEE!!!

BYE SWEETIE! MISS YOU!!!! BFF 4-
EVER!!!!!!!!!

LORRAINY

Candace thinks she's got it good with him?

Tears are dripping all over my lap. One slides down
my face and perches on the end of my nose. It itches and
yet I can't swipe at it. I can't move at all.

I stare at Lorraine's message until the letters go all
squiggly.

Trevor is with Candace Jacobi? Candace, who never
met a lacy camisole she didn't like? Candace, with her
too-tight jeans and stilettos and bloody lipstick shades?
He went from me to *her*?

Trevor and Candace? Candace and Trevor? Trevace?
Candor?

Maybe that was why he broke it off. Maybe it wasn't
the distance but me. Maybe I just wasn't *Candace*

enough for him. In fact, I'll bet that's why he was kind of weird on the phone the other day. He'd already hooked up with her!

My left hand shakes as it grips the phone, making Lorraine's message wiggle like a live, pulsating thing. I feel like screaming into the treetops. I want to break something, just really crush something into a chunky powder. The Nokia is the most logical victim, not to mention the only one in reach, but I still have enough sense to prevent that from happening. Or maybe I'm just too much of a wimp.

Finally I set the phone onto the gravelly surface of the roof and turn it so that her message is hollering at the building across the street. Then I pull my knees to my chest and fall forward, sobbing into my crossed arms.

I cry because my ex-boyfriend left me for someone cheap and obvious. I cry because I know I'll probably never see him or Lorraine or anyone from that chapter of my life ever again. And I cry because there's absolutely no one I can talk to about this. I can't write a mopey-dopey letter to Lorraine. All she would do is tell me to throw myself at the nearest rodeo star. I can't tell Penny because she's, well . . . *Penny*. I can't tell Drip or Mrs. Pratt or anyone from Lakewood High. And most of all, I can't tell Rosie or Les—because they're the main reason I'm in this sorry-ass state.

Clearly the peppermint tea didn't help that much, because it feels like a giant bear claw is squeezing my stomach. It's the Stabbies—only they seem to have morphed into something more monstrous.

One thing is made totally clear in this whole nuclear winter of a mess: I can't go through this again. No matter what, I can't let down my guard and get comfortable here in Austin. No friends, no fun, and *definitely* no love life. I'll still go out with Jack tonight (if I cancel, Mrs. Pratt might get all suspicious again), but I'll make damn sure I don't enjoy myself.

And Jack won't either.

Chapter Eight: Terribly Good

TIP: Boyfriends ARE strictly forbidden. If you find yourself accidentally out on a date, sabotage it with all your might. If all else fails, show pictures of your bare butt.

You'd think I'd somehow magically reunited the Beatles and asked them over for tea. Ever since I informed my parents that someone would be picking me up later—and that the someone was a guy—they've been all super-charged and extra weird.

Rosie is especially squealy. She keeps burning various incenses and draping the furniture with different-colored silk scarves.

"Do you think he'd like green tea? Or Red Zinger?" she asks, holding up a tin in each hand.

"Uhhh, neither? Because he's only picking me up," I reply, kind of irritably.

"What did you say this young man's name was?" Les asks me for the third time.

"Jack!" Great Gandhi. How can the name Jack be so hard to remember?

In keeping with my Strangest Day Ever on Record, my parents are doing more to get ready for my date than I am. Of course, that's not too difficult, since I'm doing nothing.

After letting my hair dry in the wind to obtain an electroshocked disco queen–type look, I went downstairs and grabbed the ugliest, most antidate outfit I could find: a hairy-looking wool skirt and matching jacket, both the color of lemon-lime Gatorade. I then added rhinestone-studded cat's-eye granny glasses and a pair of white nurse's shoes.

"I hope he likes Dylan," Les says, starting up *Blonde on Blonde* on the old-fashioned record player.

I hope he doesn't.

Rosie has apparently decided on green tea and has already started the kettle going. Now she's skipping about the apartment, spraying her rose oil–scented water.

"You guys! Why are you doing all this?" I whine. "He's only going to be here for a few seconds."

"Oh, honeybee! We're just so happy you've made a friend!" Rosie dances over and gives me a chest-compressing hug. When she lets go, she spritzes me a little with her water.

Just then, the downstairs buzzer sounds.

"I'll get it!" I shout, sprinting down the stairs in my thick-soled shoes. Rosie and Les come tromping after me.

It's Jack. I can see the stick-straight part in his hair through the transom window as I go down.

Okay. Let's just get this over with. I try on an expression I hope isn't too glum or too eager and yank open the door.

"Hi, there," I say.

"Hi," says Rosie.

"Hey," says Les.

Jack leans back a little, taking it all in. I can't tell if he's overwhelmed by the sheer ugliness of my outfit or the fact that my parents are grinning at him over my shoulders. I must look like a three-headed, windblown senior citizen.

"Hi," he says, reverting to his young bureaucrat self. "I'm Jack. Jack Krebs." He gives my parents a little wave.

"Rosie," my mother says, thrusting her arm out through the space beneath my right sleeve. Jack grabs her hand and shakes it.

"And I'm Les." His arm comes out the other side.

"Nice to meet you," Jack says, shaking his hand as well.

"Won't you come upstairs for some tea?" Rosie asks.

Say no! I command mentally. *No. No!*

"Sure. We have time," Jack replies with a quick glance at his watch.

He steps inside and gives me a smile. "You smell great," he says.

"Thanks." I can practically hear Rosie beaming behind me. At least he didn't say I *looked* great.

Unlike me, Jack has obviously taken extra care with his appearance this evening. His yellow shirt and khaki slacks seem freshly ironed and his cheeks have the faint gleam of a recent shave. He's even wearing a tie—dark blue with black slanted stripes. And as he heads up the stairs in front of me, I notice the glow given off by his loafers. Did he shine his shoes?

"Come on in!" Rosie sings, sweeping her arm toward the inside of the apartment.

"How do you like your tea?" Les asks Jack. "With sugar? Honey? Lemon?"

"Uh, just plain is fine. Thanks."

As Les disappears into the kitchen nook, Rosie practically pushes Jack into the fabric-draped armchair. "Please make yourself at home," she commands.

Rosie settles onto the overstuffed pillow at his feet and proceeds to grin at him. I perch on the ottoman directly across from Jack, enjoying his bewildered expression. It occurs to me that my parents' insisting on his having tea might not be a bad thing after all. What better way to show him how weird my home life is—how completely the opposite of his own?

"Look at that," Rosie mutters as she gazes at Jack. "You have the greenest aura I've seen in a while."

"I . . . I do?" Jack shifts his eyes toward me as if to ask "Is she for real?" I just smile back.

Rosie reaches toward him but doesn't touch him. "Do healing powers run in your family?"

"Well . . . I have an older brother who's studying to be an immunologist. . . ."

"See that? I just knew it." Rosie presses her hands together in front of her and nods at him—her ultimate sign of acceptance. "What about you? Are you going to heal people too?"

"Ah . . . no." He chuckles nervously. "I'm actually going into law."

Figures, I think.

Rosie keeps nodding. "I see. And why is that?"

"I don't know. I just find it interesting."

"Heeeeeeere's your tea!" Les steps into the living area as if he were bounding onto a stage and hands Jack a cup and saucer.

"Thanks." A confused look flits across Jack's face and I realize he'd been expecting *iced* tea.

"Isn't our baby beautiful, Jack? Isn't she a moonbeam?" Les walks over and grabs my nose, wriggling it until my granny glasses go all crooked.

"Yeah, she is," Jack replies, smiling at me.

Les has let go of my nose and is now gazing down at me all misty-eyed. "The midwife told us she'd never seen such a blessed-looking infant. Here. Let me show you." He hops over to a nearby shelf and pulls out a cloth-bound photo album.

"Oh no. Les, don't. Please?" I protest.

But as usual, my father doesn't choose to hear me. He plops down on the arm of Jack's chair and opens the book, holding it sideways for Jack. Rosie climbs onto the other chair arm and starts giggling and clapping her hands. "Oh, I just love these pictures!" she exclaims.

"See there? And there," Les says, pointing. "Doesn't she look wise?"

"So in tune with the Universe," Rosie muses. "And the most adorable dimpled butt!"

"I can see that," Jack says with an amused smile.

I let out a small groan and throw back my head, preferring the swirl patterns on the ceiling to the sight of the three people gawking at my naked newborn posterior.

"Wow. Where was that taken?" Jack asks.

"Mirror Lake, Alaska."

"And there?"

"That was in Little Falls, Minnesota."

"Wow," Jack says again. "Maggie said you guys have moved around. You've really seen a lot of the country."

"The world has so much to offer," Rosie says.

"See those shots?" Les goes on. "They were taken when we lived in Harpers Ferry. And these were from that Buddhist lodge outside Colorado Springs."

The campouts by the waterfall. The tepees in Sedona . . . Since it's one of our few material possessions, I have the entire scrapbook memorized.

All of a sudden I jump to my feet, remembering what's on the next page: our shots from the nudist colony in Palm Springs. Mind you, I was only ten years old at the time, but still. It's not the same as baby butt shots.

"Hey! Uh . . . don't you think we should be going?" I nod, gesture, and basically lean my whole body toward the stairwell. "Traffic can get kind of slow around now." I have no idea about the traffic. It just seems like an urgent thing to say.

"Right," Jack says. "The restaurant isn't far, but I don't know about their parking."

To my relief, Les closes the photo album and sets it back on the shelf while Rosie takes Jack's cup and saucer.

"Thanks so much for the drink," Jack says as he stands and smooths out his pants. "It was nice to meet you."

I see him start to offer his hand, but Rosie throws her arms around him and kisses him on the cheek. Then Les comes over and does his best Yogi bow. It's all I can do not to laugh at Jack's stunned expression.

"Come by whenever you like," Rosie says as she and Les walk him to the stairs.

"Thanks," Jack says.

They stop at the doorway and Jack joins me on the top step.

"You kids have a great time," Les says.

"We will. And don't worry"—Jack looks right at Les—"I won't keep her out late."

"Don't be silly. It's a beautiful night," Les remarks. "You two should do some stargazing."

Jack doesn't seem to know what to say to this, so I gently tug on his sleeve. "Let's go," I say.

"Right."

"Bye! Have fun!" Les and Rosie call after us as we head down the stairs and out the door.

Jack pauses on the back stoop and shakes his head, staring into the distance. "Your parents . . . ," he mumbles. "They're . . ."

Out of touch with reality? I finish mentally. *Full of nutty goodness?*

". . . nice," he says finally.

"Yeah," I mutter as I walk toward his truck. "That's one way of putting it."

Jack takes me to a semiswanky Japanese restaurant called Yin-Yang on the west side of town. The decor is all black-and-white funky and everywhere you look there's a giant aquarium. We're seated by a beautiful hostess in a kimono not too different from the one I wore to school. I wonder if that outfit made him think I'd like this place.

"I hear the fish is excellent," he says in an authoritative voice, pressing the end of his tie against him as he plops into his chair.

"I'm vegetarian," I declare loudly.

Just so you know, I am not one of those vegetarians who think anyone who eats meat should be made into burgers. I just figure my saying so will make Jack feel uncomfortable. Which it does.

"I'm sorry!" he exclaims, clapping his hand to his forehead. "Do you want to go somewhere else?"

I shake my head. "No. It's fine."

"Man, I'm sorry," he repeats. "I should have asked. That was stupid of me."

"Really. It's okay. They have nonmeat dishes here."

"Then I won't order meat either."

"Order whatever you want."

"But if it will upset you—"

"It's all right," I interrupt. I'd wanted to stress him out, but now it's just getting annoying. "Really. Don't have a cow." I start laughing. "Or *do* have a cow. Or a chicken. Or pig."

He smiles. "Mmmm. Sounds so appetizing when you put it that way."

"Hey, it's your colon," I say with a shrug.

"All right." He sighs. "Bean curd it is."

I manage not to laugh, but my mouth still boings up into a smile.

We sit and stare at our menus and listen to the gurgly noise of the aquarium beside us. Jack keeps yanking his shirt cuffs, and his Adam's apple bobbles with repeated swallows. Strange that he should be so nervous and extra careful when all I want is to have a horrible time and go home.

A waitress in a bright red kimono walks up to take our order. I envy how easily she moves in her outfit. I watch her to see if I can pick up any pointers, but all I can figure is that her body must have better contours for it.

I order the vegetables teriyaki and a cup of shiitake mushroom soup, and Jack orders the assorted vegetables in ponzu sauce and the miso soup.

"See? I can do the no-meat thing," he says after the waitress sashays off to another table.

"Actually, you didn't. Ponzu sauce has fish in it."

His face falls so quickly and completely that I crack up.

"Aw, man! I'm sorry," he says. "Maybe I can bring her back." He twists around and starts to raise his right hand.

"Stop!" I screech, reaching forward to grab his other arm. "It's okay! The sight of ponzu sauce won't make me faint. I promise!"

"All right, all right. Sorry," he says, facing forward again. Then he looks down at my hand on his wrist.

I quickly let go and pull my arms under the table. "No big deal," I mutter, rubbing my palms on my itchy skirt.

He grins another one of his top-hat-and-tuxedo smiles and I realize I've just given him some hope. I should have let him freak out about the fish.

"You know," he begins, leaning forward and resting his elbows on the table, "it was nice to meet your parents and see all those pictures."

"For real?"

"Yeah. I want to know more about you."

"Why?" The word just sort of pushes past my lips. It's been darting around inside me ever since he asked me out. *Why me?* I'm doing everything I can to be ugly and weird. He should see me as the world's most embarrassingly bad date, and yet here he is. Here *I* am.

His eyes blink wide. "Uh . . . because I just do. I think you're . . . fascinating."

"Why?" I repeat.

"I don't know. Because you're you." He shakes his head and lets out a meek little chuckle. "That was lame, huh? Some lawyer I am. What I mean is . . . I've never met anyone like you."

Oh. So *that's* it. I'm different. I'm a case he wants to crack open. A debate he wants to win. An Eagle Scout's wildest merit badge. As president of the Helping Hands and all-around brownnoser, he cannot resist the chance to adopt a poor, unenlightened savage like me.

"I've been wanting to ask you out for a while, but . . ." He trails off and shrugs.

"But what?" I ask, unable to help myself.

"I thought you'd say no." The grin returns, as if he suddenly remembers that I *didn't* say no, and that I really do want to be out with him.

Which I don't.

"Look"—I lean forward and meet his gaze—"thanks for thinking of me and stuff, but this isn't going to work out."

"Oh really?" Jack looks amused. He settles back in his chair, waiting for the punch line.

"Really," I echo, peeved that he's taking this so lightly. "Think about it. I'm one of the most radical people I've met—and I've met a lot of people—while you're like this Young Republican poster boy."

"I see. You're sure about that, huh?" He strokes his chin as he nods, humoring me—and pissing me off in the process.

"*Yes*. I can't hang out with Republicans."

"Why not?"

Oooh! This isn't fair. He's not playing this right at all! He should be all blustery and offended. Instead he looks positively thrilled.

"Because!" My voice has risen to that shrill

whiny-baby tone. "Because I can't stand Republicans. They're so narrow-minded and intolerant."

I'm totally shocked by what happens next. Jack tilts back his head and howls with laughter.

"What? What's so funny?" I demand.

"Sorry," he says between guffaws. "It's just hilarious. You hating all Republicans because they're so intolerant."

Hearing my words bounced back like that makes me realize how stupid I sounded.

"I never said I *hated* them," I mumble, all puny with shame. "I just don't agree with them on lots of stuff. Makes it hard to get along."

"I know." Jack goes all serious again. "Okay, fine. I'll be straight with you. I don't support any particular political party, but I am a conservative—at least fiscally."

"Right. You people believe in slashing any program for the hungry and poor in the name of financial responsibility. Blah, blah, blah."

"That's not what I said. What's wrong with thinking our nation should have a balanced budget and live within its means? A whole lot of debt isn't good for it."

"It's just funny how you guys never want to cut back on things like corporate subsidies or the military. It's always the things that are designed to help people that have to go."

"The military helps people."

I let out a snort. "Yeah? How?"

"Well, beyond the fact that it protects us, it also

funds education for those who might not be able to afford it."

"Sure, with the minor condition that you put your life on the line! Really sweet of them."

"It's how my dad got his college degree," he adds with a shrug. "Probably the only way he would have gotten out of the tiny town he grew up in."

"But it's not right that the least powerful people in this country are the ones we put on the front lines!"

"He knew what he was getting into when he joined the army. And at least his government assistance wasn't a handout. He worked for it."

I glower at him and pretend to be so put off by his argument that I can't even speak. But the truth is I can't come up with anything else to say. That's one way I'm not like my parents. They can debate an issue calmly, for days if they have to. Me? I always lose my temper and then can't think straight.

Jack, on the other hand, is almost James Dean cool. He talks in his bossy know-it-all voice, but he doesn't bully. And he doesn't get all superheated when I challenge him on stuff. He's wrong about being a bad lawyer. He's a good one—like TV-crime-show good. The jerk.

But what really pees me off is that he's still looking at me with that tickled expression, as if he's indulging a cute, babbling infant.

"Why are you so . . . condemning?" he asks.

"*I'm* condemning? You guys want to put poor people in trenches!"

He laughs lightly and I resist the urge to fling a Buddha-shaped saltshaker at him.

"You keep saying 'you people' and 'you guys.' But what makes you think you and I are so opposite?"

I make a face. *"Please!"*

"No, really. Tell me."

Just then, the waitress shows up with our soup orders.

"I like your glasses," she says to me.

"You do?" I absently pat the almond-shaped studded rims.

"Yes," she says, giggling. "They are so cool."

"Thanks."

"You're welcome. Enjoy the soup!" Once again she easily glides away.

I welcome the chance to take a break from Jack's lawyer-savant questions and start digging in to my soup.

"Uh . . . Maggie? You were saying?" he prompts. "You think we're so different . . . ?"

I swallow and nod. "It's true. We're night and day."

"Uh-huh. You sound so sure about this."

It occurs to me to try a little interrogating of my own. "Let me ask you something. What's the first thing you do when you wake up in the morning?"

His eyes swivel up and to the right. "Um . . . I make my bed."

Now it's my turn to laugh. "See? I don't understand why people do that. I mean, it's just going to get messed up again in another—what?—sixteen hours?"

He shrugs. "I just like doing it, I guess. I'm in the habit. What about you? What's the first thing you do?"

"Look out the window."

"Really? Why?"

"I don't know." I suddenly realize I don't have an answer for this. I take a moment to consider. "It's just a way to connect with the day, you know? Like I'm taking a little peek to see what I'm in for."

Jack smiles at me. Only this is one I haven't seen before. It's more subtle, and his face has this toasty-warm glow about it.

What the hell is happening? I'm doing my best worst-date stuff and trying hard to convince him we're opposites, and yet he seems to like it.

I break my eyes away from his adoring gaze and instead focus on the last little tablespoon of soup in my bowl. One lonely mushroom is floating in the broth. Seems a shame to leave it, but it's too shallow for those big flat spoons they gave us.

Suddenly I get a boost of brainpower and I realize what I have to do. Gripping the china bowl with both hands, I lift it to my lips and loudly slurp the rest of the contents into my mouth. After working it as long as possible, I set the bowl back down and end with a cartoonish "*ah!*"

Just as I hoped, Jack is staring at me in utter horror.

"In other cultures, it's bad manners to leave part of your meal behind. And the louder you eat, the more of a compliment it is to the chef," I say, making it up entirely.

Jack glances fearfully to the left and the right and then picks up his own bowl. "Yeah, well. Guess we shouldn't waste food," he says. Then he puts it to his mouth and sucks down the remainder of his soup with an even louder squelch.

Damn! I shout inwardly as he deposits the bowl on the table with his own happy *"ah."*

Something better go my way soon, because I'm seriously considering picking my nose.

Dinner did not go as horribly as I wanted. I brought up all sorts of crazy tidbits about my family—like the way Rosie talks to her plants, and Les's philosophy of doing Tarzan yells to let out stress. I even mentioned that my father had once been interrogated by the CIA because he studied hammock making from a guy who wrote crazy letters to the president, but nothing seemed to freak Jack out. When I mentioned that Rosie hoped to study acupuncture someday, he said his brother saw lots of benefits in it too and felt it had a place in the white-jacket medical world.

Jack also felt comfortable enough to talk about himself. I found out tons of stuff I didn't know before. Like that he wanted to start a film club at Lakewood, but Dr. Wohman nixed it, saying there was no educational benefit. And that he only goes to school for four straight periods, not including lunch, and leaves at one-thirty for his internship at a law office. This is why he dresses like a right-wing boy wonder. It's also why he's always late for the Helping Hands meetings—because he isn't even on campus.

When the check comes, I open up my fake-alligator handbag and pull out three ten-dollar bills.

"No way," Jack says, putting the money back in front of me.

"Why not? This isn't the fifties. I can pay my own way." I plunk the tens back onto the bill tray.

"But *I* asked *you* out." He lifts my hand, places the money on the table, and sets my hand on top of it. "I'm a modern guy. You totally have the right to ask me out. *Then* I'll let you pay."

Once again, I find myself with nothing to say.

I feel panicked. I really wanted to embarrass and disgust Jack so much that he lost this stupid fascination with me. But I have the uneasy hunch that so far he's enjoying himself. And the really scary thing is I haven't had such an awful time either.

We thank our bubbly waitress (who I noticed got a nice fat tip from Jack) and step outside. The sky is now a dark shade of charcoal-violet and the air is cooler but no less sticky.

I want to go back home, and yet I don't. I feel like I still need to do something to make him lose all interest in me. Something crazy weird.

"So, there's a special screening of *The Return of Martin Guerre* at the Alamo Village," he starts.

"No. Don't wanna."

"Uhhh. Okay. What do you want to do?"

I glance around, trying to decide on my next move. On the other side of the parking lot is a section of the Austin greenbelt, with a jogging path, a playground, and a small duck pond. "Let's go there," I say, pointing.

"But . . ."

"Come on!" Without waiting for an answer, I take off through the grass and head right for the swing set. By the time Jack catches up with me, I've already got one going higher than his head.

"You really want to do this?" he calls out.

"Why not? Try it. There are other things to do in a park besides clean it up."

I lie back in my swing, enjoying the breeze I'm creating. It feels good to do nothing but pump my legs and soar over the ground. When I was little I used to spend whole hours on swings. Rosie and Les loved them too, and we made up special moves—like the elevator, the wrecking ball, and the seven chakras.

Jack gets on a swing and awkwardly starts it going. He seems so out of place in his office wear and shiny shoes. I'm sure I look stupid too, but at least I'm into it.

He's moving like some cement statue a fairy princess just breathed life into.

"Hey, listen," he says, his voice Dopplering as we pass each other. "About what happened at the park today with Miles and the others . . ."

I let out a groan. "Oh no. Don't start."

"What?"

"I know what you think. I saw the way you looked at me. Listen, I'm a pacifist. My parents are, like, professional peace activists. But I also think sometimes you have to stand up to people like that. No one got hurt, so . . . stop with the you-ought-to-know-better lecture, okay?"

"But that's not what . . ." Jack stops swinging. "Look, it wasn't like that. If I seemed sort of down on you, I wasn't. I was mad at me. Mad that I wasn't there to help you with Miles."

I stop pumping my legs and slowly come to a stop. I think back to the look on Jack's face at the park and the way Drip went, "Hmmm."

"He's such a creep. You don't understand." Jack's right hand closes into a fist. "He lives on my street and I've known him for years. He's done a lot of really mean things to people."

"To you?"

"Yeah, to me!" he snaps. "Sorry," he says, catching himself. "It's just . . . I really wish I could have taken care of that jerk for you."

Jack twists his swing toward me and I meet his gaze. His face seems all stretched and serious. His mouth isn't exactly turned down, just drooping at the edges. And his eyes and eyebrows are arched toward a wavy point in the top middle of his forehead. He looks so worried about me. It would be sweet if it weren't so scary-awful.

"Please!" I say, getting to my feet. I walk over to the merry-go-round and sit down. "You really are right out of the fifties." I lie back against the metal, which is still warm from the ninety-nine-degree day, and stare up at the purple sky.

"Wait." I hear him walk over. "What are you talking about?"

"You! You think I can't take care of myself!"

"No way! I wanted a chance to deal with him because I can't stand him. And I don't like him messing with my . . . club. I have no problem with a girl taking charge."

"Oh yeah?"

"Yeah."

"Push me."

"Huh?"

"I'm taking charge. Push the merry-go-round. I want a ride."

There's a brief pause and then the platform I'm lying on starts to turn to the right. I hear him running and thumping against the support bars and soon it's whirling at a really good speed. After a while, Jack bounds on with a loud, gonglike sound and stretches out on another wedge of the platform.

I close my eyes and enjoy the rush of velocity. "Whooo," I say. "God, I love this."

Jack lets out a small moan. "I think my ponzu sauce fish are trying to swim upstream."

This cracks me up. "You did a good job," I call out. "Taking orders from me, I mean."

"See? I'm not such a Nazi."

"Sure you are."

"Prove it."

This again. I really don't want to ruin the fun with another argument, but then, I'm not supposed to be having fun. I'm supposed to be sabotaging our evening. Discussing taboo topics on a date always makes things squirmy. It didn't exactly work before, when we argued politics, but there are other cringeworthy subjects. It might be tough to bring them up in the natural course of conversation, but maybe in a quiz format?

"All right," I say, feeling recharged. "I'll name a topic and you tell me how you feel about it. Okay?"

"I guess."

"Where do you stand on abortion?"

"Oh, so you're starting with the easy ones?"

"Just answer."

"Fine. . . . Well, I don't ever plan on having one

myself. I don't think it's wonderful, but I think making it illegal isn't the best way to stop them." Spoken like a true debate captain.

"What about religion?"

"Okay. Uh . . . I go to church, if that's what you're asking. I don't know if I accept everything they preach, not literally anyway, but I like the whole do-unto-others part. That makes sense."

"Drugs?"

"I'm a squarehead. I don't even know where to find them."

"Sex?"

He goes silent. Fortunately, he can't see my face, which, judging by the stinging sensation that seeped up from my neck, is now the color of watermelon flesh. I'd been so caught up in rattling off a laundry list of controversial topics that I didn't stop to think about what I was saying.

"Sex is . . . nice . . . I mean, probably. I mean . . . What do you mean?"

Jack's tone is all over the place, as if he's going through a sudden second puberty. It was a total accident, but at least I finally got him flustered.

"Sex is a wonderful, natural thing," I reply, repeating what Rosie likes to say about it.

"Oh."

It hits me that he probably takes my answer as an indication that I've already had sex, maybe lots of it. For some reason, that bothers me. I don't want him to think that.

"I mean . . . I'm sure it must be," I add.

For a moment, we just lie there quietly. The merry-go-round has slowed, but my body still feels all whirly. I try to concentrate on the little patch of stars above me, but my vision keeps sliding sideways, as if the whole world is tilting to the right.

"So, did I pass?" he asks.

I don't answer. I'm still trying to focus my eyes and thoughts.

"I passed, didn't I? Admit it. I'm not such a bad guy. I'm not your polar opposite after all."

He's stretched out his leg and keeps nudging me with his foot. That movement, plus the fact that he didn't do too badly on my test, really gets on my nerves. "Trevor!" I snap.

There's a pause. "Who's Trevor?"

Oops. Where'd *that* come from? "He's . . . uh . . ." At first I'm not sure what to say. I'm still loopy from spinning and mad at myself for letting my mind jump to Trevor. And then it hits me: what's the number one taboo subject when out on a date? *Exes!* "He's a guy I used to date in Portland."

"Huh." Jack sounds weird. Is he worried? Threatened? I can't tell. "So . . . I remind you of him?"

"No way!" I cry. "You guys aren't alike at all. Trevor was really outdoorsy and liberal. He was also vegetarian."

"Why'd you guys break up?"

I guess it's a fair question, especially since I quizzed him about abortion and stuff, but I'm totally unprepared for it.

"Because I moved," I reply. It's the truth. I'm positive it's the only reason we aren't together anymore—the only reason he ended up with Candace. But it still comes out sounding kind of lame.

"You guys didn't want to try keeping it going?"

I don't answer. My torso is shuddering. I want this conversation to stop now, thank you very much.

"It's just . . ." Jack sits up and starts pushing his foot into the dirt, making the merry-go-round swivel back and forth. "If it was me, I'd be running up the phone bill and trying to buy frequent-flyer miles on Craigslist."

I lift my head and gape at him, bolstered by the fact that his back is to me. I can't believe Jack said that. That's exactly what I'd been hoping Trevor would do. "Yeah, well . . . we didn't want to go to all that trouble," I say, blinking fast so that the wetness in my eyes doesn't glob into tears.

"You seem worth the trouble."

I let out a little sarcastic hoot.

"No, I mean it." Jack turns and stares right at me. "I think you're . . . special."

His comment is so real and naked that I have to look away. No need to spin the merry-go-round. I'm wobbly just lying here. I can't even put a tag on what I'm feeling.

I'm mad-sad. Up-down. Hot with anger that my date isn't a fiasco (at least for him) and cold with terror that I kind of liked hearing him say those things.

I miss feeling special. Trevor used to make me feel that way. But I don't want to feel special here.

Jack is waiting for a reaction. But how can I respond with the same amount of honesty? What I truly want to do is run away. Just turn and start racing into the night. I've already got the practical shoe wear.

I slide off the metal platform and start straightening my outfit. For some reason, I feel extra itchy and swampy. Why didn't I choose something ugly yet practical, like those muumuu dresses Mrs. Pratt likes to wear?

In a daze, I start unbuttoning my suit jacket.

"Uhhh . . . are you okay?" Jack asks. It's understandable he's a little thrown, since he can't tell I have on a shirt underneath to protect me from the itchy stuff— and also since I have a history of losing clothes in front of him.

"It's all ooky out here," I explain. "I just want to cool off."

"I know what you mean," he agrees, noticeably more at ease now that he can see my brown racer-back tank. "I've been thinking about wading in that pond."

Zing! New flash of brilliance.

"Hey, yeah!" I sit down on the steps of the slide and start taking off my shoes.

"Actually, I was just kidding," he adds.

Of course I knew he wasn't serious. That's why it's so perfect. I can change the subject, get refreshed, and shake him up all at the same time.

"You know . . . we *do* have poisonous water snakes in Texas," he calls out as I skip toward the water's edge.

I ignore him. I don't care if they have anacondas; I just want to get away from all talk of Trevor and "special" me.

"It might not be all that great." He keeps yammering. "Probably warm from being in the heat all day, and we haven't had rain in a while. Could be kind of stagnant."

I hike up my skirt to midthigh and slowly step into the pond.

"Watch out. It might be slipper—"

Splash!

My feet just hit some moss-covered rocks, and they went sliding forward at highway speeds, making me fall backward into the murky and, yes, stagnant water. He's right about the temperature too. It's as warm as a bath. "Uck!" I shout, blinking froth out of my eyes.

"Hang on! I'll get you!" I can make out Jack's silhouette yanking off his loafers.

I thrash about in a sitting position, with stinky, sudsy water up to my ears. "I'm fine!" I cry, insulted that he thinks I need rescuing from a two-foot-deep pond. "I can take care of myself!" I try to get up, hit yet another slippery spot, and go tumbling back again.

Okay. So maybe I could use a little help.

Jack steps into the water, just to the edges of his rolled-up khakis. "Give me your hand," he instructs.

I reach forward, but I'm too far out to grab it.

Jack wades in deeper, drenching the ends of his pants. "Just a little more," he says, egging me on as I crawl along the slimy bottom toward him.

Finally I'm able to grab hold. "Ready?" he asks. "One . . . two . . . three!"

Instead of lifting me toward the pebbly shore, Jack loses his grip on my hand. For a couple of seconds, his arms wave wildly around, pushing against thin air, and then his whole body goes whooshing backward into the water.

Splash!

He comes up sputtering beside me.

"Gee, thanks," I mutter. I'm beyond frustrated. I'm chilly and gross-smelling and I've lost my granny glasses.

"Hey! It was your idea to do this!" he retorts.

"I wanted to get cooled off!"

"Well, are you?"

"Yes!"

We glare at each other for about four seconds and then bust out laughing.

"My hero!" I tease, splashing him in the face.

He splashes me right back and we spend the next several minutes attacking each other with mucky water. By the time we finish, there isn't a dry spot on us.

We manage a slippy-slidey crawl onto the rocky bank and stand there, panting and dripping.

"Now what?" he asks.

This time I can give him a completely honest reply. "I have no idea."

Since we're completely soaked and pond scummy, I ask Jack to go ahead and drive me home.

"Sorry about the smell," I say as we bump along in his Ford pickup.

"No big deal," he says. "It'll go away eventually. I'm just glad I have leather seats instead of cloth."

"Not me. I'm vegetarian."

"Yeah, yeah. At least I didn't eat whatever they made my seats out of."

I smile in the semidarkness, then immediately stop. This is bad. And I don't mean the fact that I probably have a whole population of mosquito larvae in my hair. The way Jack and I talk and tease each other, it's so . . . comfortable. And being comfortable makes me nervous.

At least the night is over.

Jack pulls his F-150 into the alley behind our shop and parks beside the Dumpster.

"You don't have to get out," I tell him when I see him unbuckle his seat belt.

"It's okay. I should probably help explain to your parents."

"They're already asleep," I lie.

"Yeah, but I could still help you if you slip and fall." He flashes me a mocking grin and hops out of the car.

My skirt makes squishy noises as I cross the pavement to the back stoop. I'll probably have to throw it away, since I'm pretty sure it's dry-clean only. I sure ruin a lot of clothes when I hang out with this guy.

We reach the back steps and Jack turns toward me. "So . . . ," he begins. "I had an *interesting* time."

"It was terrible," I remark as I squeeze another cupful of water out of my hair.

Jack laughs. "It wasn't so bad."

"Oh yeah? I just found a dead tadpole in my *mmmmph*." The last sound is the result of Jack's lips suddenly being clamped onto mine. I didn't even see him coming. One second I'm picking gross stuff out of my crevices, and the next thing I know, his face is mashed up against mine.

At first it's awkward and, truth be told, a little yucky. His nose is squashing my nostrils, and his mouth is covering mine so completely I can't breathe. Plus I'm so startled I go all lock-jointed. If he didn't have such a good hold on me, I would reel backward.

And then everything just . . . softens. His head finds that perfect tilt and his lips push gently against mine. Even my swirly brain seems tranquilized. All I can think is how good it feels to be held again. My hands, which were stiff at my sides, soar up and under his arms, seeking out fingerholds along his wet back. It's so warm and cushiony I feel like I'm dissolving.

And then . . . everything deepens. Our mouths open. Hands slide everywhere, frictionless on our drenched clothes. I can't stop myself. I don't want it to stop.

And then . . . *he* stops it.

Jack suddenly lets go and takes a giant step back, shaking his head and making a sound like *eeyah*. I stagger about, disoriented. If it weren't for my shock-absorbing shoes, I probably would drop to the ground.

"I . . . should go home," Jack says, smiling crookedly.

"Yep" is all I can say. I cover my mouth, partly from shock, partly to prevent any more stupid replies from flying out, and partly because my lips are still throbbing from so much intense activity.

Jack strolls backward toward his truck, so slowly it looks like he's drifting. Eventually he hits the bumper and stops. I study him in the shadowy light. His clothes are soaked and rumpled, and the breeze has half dried his hair into a crinkly Beatles-esque do. I've never seen him look so disheveled—or so cute.

I feel a sudden chill and wrap my arms about me, the way he was just doing, and the movement seems to jolt us both awake. He shuffles his feet on the pockmarked asphalt and rubs his hands along the front of his pants. A little weirdness has returned.

"So . . . bye," he says with an awkward wave.

"Yep," I say again.

As Jack climbs into the cab and starts the motor, I head through the shop's back door. I stand shivering in the foyer, listening as his pickup rumbles away.

Crap! Double crap! Crap covered in crap sauce!

I've gone and done the exact thing I promised myself I wouldn't do: I've found something to like about Austin.

Chapter Nine: Old News

TIP: REVEL IN GROSSNESS. LEAVE FOOD IN YOUR TEETH. PROUDLY DISPLAY FEMININE HYGIENE PRODUCTS.

I HAVEN'T BEEN to school in three days. I told Les and Rosie I didn't feel well, and they took my word for it. But really, I didn't want to see Jack.

If you didn't already think my parents were unusual, get this: the other night when I walked up the stairs half-delirious, completely wet, and smelling like dead fish, the only thing they did was ask if I had a good time. Of course, to be fair, midnight swims are a standard date for those two—only they like to skinny-dip.

I mumbled that it was okay, then went off to take an hour-long shower. While I was washing green gunk out of my hair, I thought about the evening's events. By any-one's standards, that date should go down as one of the worst in history. And yet . . . it really wasn't that bad. I kept reliving little moments in my head and smiling. Then I'd realize what I was doing and have a mini nerv-ous breakdown. That was when I got the idea of playing sick. So for seventy-two hours I stayed home, wore paja-mas, drank the different tea concoctions Rosie made for me . . . and mentally replayed my kiss with Jack every minute on the minute.

That kiss . . . that wonderful-horrible kiss. Weird how something can be simultaneously wowee-nice and scary-bad. Even my body has gone split personality. Whenever I rerun the moment, my heart dances about joyfully, but I also get a crumpling sensation in my mid-section, as if my stomach is being wrung out.

I haven't felt this way since Trevor and I first got together—which freaks me out in such a major way. I can't like Jack! And if I do . . . does that mean I'm get-ting over Trevor? And if I am . . . does that mean I'm freeing myself up emotionally for Jack? And if so . . . does that mean it's going to kill me all over again when we move in three months?

Oh god! I hate my parents!

After three straight days of losing my mind, I finally came up with a theory: the kiss was great—but only because it was nice to be kissed again, not because it was with Jack. Right? Because Jack is so wrong for me. . . . Right?

No, I'm still hung up on Trevor. My mind is just playing tricks on me. I was so lonely and wigged out over Lorraine's e-mail I was looking for a stand-in. And Jack simply happened to be there at the right time. Or maybe the *wrong* time.

Even if I do like Jack a little, I can easily make myself *not* like him. How? I have no idea. I was hoping that by the end of my sick leave I'd have a plan of action, but my brain was too busy TiVo-ing the kiss to do me any good. So today I'll go to school and hope for the best. I'd stay home again, but on the fourth day of illness, Rosie gets out the home-enema kits.

I woke up early so I could find myself an outfit in the shop. After digging through some new inventory, I decide on a white padded silk jacket and matching pants, plus another pair of galoshes, this time with a ladybug design. When I get back upstairs, Les and Rosie are up. Les is making breakfast and Rosie is running around the kitchen with a handheld fan, shouting, "This way! Over here, you!"

Lately our apartment has been overrun by flying, bitey things. Austin is buggier than most places, but I wonder if I might have carried home insect spawn after my dip in the pond.

Usually Rosie and Les don't mind sharing their living space with critters. But they believe in using humane, catch-and-release methods if they can't. So Rosie's latest idea is to blow the bugs out the window and then shut it, thereby safely relocating them.

"Shoo! Shoo!" she's saying, jabbing her fan at a small swarm near the fruit bowl.

"You know, I think more bugs are coming through the window than going out of it," I observe.

As I enter the kitchen, one of the red gnat-thingies flies toward me. Since I don't follow a no-kill philosophy on anything that multiplies by the thousands, I try to clap it between my hands. No luck squashing it, though. So I try again and again. Each time, I perfectly line up the target, but when I study my palms, there's nothing there.

"What the heck?" I grumble. "Do they teleport?"

"They escape on the air currents your hands make while clapping," Les points out as he slices melon. "You're actually pushing them away instead of trapping them."

"Great," I mutter. Yet another way my actions end up having an equal and opposite reaction.

I'm beginning to think Austin has its own laws of physics.

I notice that something is different the minute Lakewood's brown brick exterior looms into view. Usually mornings follow a lazy, dreary pace as students reluctantly prepare for another day at school. But today there's an energetic hum.

At first I figure they're psyched after a big football win; around here, lots of people's moods depend on the final score of some game. It's only when I'm halfway across the lawn that I realize everyone is looking at me.

That limited omniscience returns, as if it's the first day of school all over again. My range of vision seems to widen several degrees and my hearing adjusts to include whisper frequency. The students stop whatever they're doing to watch me pass by. Many of them are smiling. Some giggle to each other. A couple of them even nod hello.

What's going on? Did they forget how weird I am in just three days?

Suddenly, with my second-first-day bionic vision, I spy something across the yard. It's Goth girl again. She's wearing gray galoshes with her black dress, and hanging from her wrist is a colorful cartoon-themed lunch box with "Yu-Gi-Oh!" written across the side.

Now that I'm closer, I notice that one of the drama kids has on industrial coveralls. And I see two more lunch boxes—one with Strawberry Shortcake and one with someone called Lizzie McGuire.

Holy crapoly. Was Dr. Wohman right? Am I really being *copied*?

The stares follow me as I head up the walkway toward the Kingdom of Miles. I haven't seen him since our showdown at Zilker Park. I didn't want to come to school, and I'm really freaked out by everything I see, so when Miles steps out from behind a brick pillar and says, "Hey!" I completely lose it.

"What?" I growl, whirling about with an angry stomp.

For a second, gravity takes over his face. His features go slack with surprise and his mouth hangs open a half inch. "You know," he starts, slowly going back to his rooster pose, "you were a real bitch the other day."

"Deal with it!" I shout.

"Yeah!" A cry comes from somewhere to my left.

I turn and scan the vicinity. Several students have crept closer to tune in to our conversation. A whole variety pack of them—from thugs to theater kids to extrabold band nerds. I can see the top of Drip's head in the center. I'm pretty sure she was the one who hollered.

I feel like I'm on display. All this attention goes beyond simply checking out my latest crazy outfit. It's as if they're all . . . waiting for something. But what? What do these people want from me?

Suddenly I really do feel sick. Without another word, without even a final glare at Miles, I wheel around and stomp through the front doors.

Once inside I race to the nearest girls' bathroom and shut myself in a stall. My breath is all weak and gaspy and I have the heart rate of a scared squirrel. I don't understand. What happened? I'm the one wearing Michael Jackson's reject clothes, but everyone else has gone crazy.

I'm not sure I can go through with this day.

Noise suddenly fills the room. Through the small

crack in the door frame, I see that a whole group of girls has come in. One of them is sobbing while the others coo and shush at her.

"It's not fair!" says the crying one. "It's just so . . . wrong! She probably doesn't even care about it!"

"It should have been you, Sharla."

Sharla? What's she blubbering about? I recognize Caitlyn as one of the cooers.

"Whatever! I don't care!" Judging by Sharla's big sniffles and quivery voice, I think she *does* care. "At least you and Shanna got in."

"When are they announcing it?"

"After the bell rings."

Sharla lets out a wail and cries for the next full minute while the others make hushing sounds

"Let's not go to class, okay?" Sharla says once she's regained control of her breath. "I swear I'll totally lose it when they call her name. That bitch!"

"Don't worry. Coach Eden will get us out of it."

"She wants us to finish painting the run-through, anyway."

They push open the door and head into the hallway, leaving behind the smell of hair spray and a high-pitched ringing in the tiles.

At least I'm not the only one having a bad day. Sounds like all is not well in the Barbieverse either. I start wondering which class they're going to skip out of. Then I realize I don't care. Tears or no tears, they're the ones who have it easy—which is why I usually try to join their ranks.

And of course, I didn't this time, which might be why things are extra screwed-up for me now.

When I walk into Mrs. Minnow's class, Jack is already there. He leaps to his feet as soon as he spots me, as if my passing through the doorway triggered an eject button on his seat.

"You're here," he says, striding up to me.

"I'm here" is my stupid reply. I'm upset that I'm glad to see him. My cheeks go all flushed and I feel a ghost pain where his arms clutched me the other night. Is it possible he has gotten cuter in the past few days?

"Where have you been?"

"Sick."

"Sorry." His face twists into that ultraconcerned look. "Think it was the gross water?"

"Maybe."

"You've got to give me your phone number. I've been trying to call you since Sunday. Here." He hands me a piece of paper and pencil. "Write it down for me."

I hesitate. Phone number equals time with Jack—which is the way-wrong answer to my problem.

"I don't have a phone at home." This is not a lie. Even though we are completely set up for phone and Internet service, my parents still haven't bought a phone. I could give him the number to the shop, but I don't want to.

Jack looks confused. "Do you have a cell?"

I shake my head. This is also not entirely a lie. In a couple of weeks, my cell account will be null and void.

Just then the late bell rings and it seems to me a beautiful, celestial noise. As Jack cups his hands and hollers at the others to be quiet, I quickly scurry off to my seat. In another small gesture of pity, the Universe arranged for Caitlyn, Sharla, and Shanna not to come to class this morning. No doubt off on their urgent cheerleader mission.

"*Psst!*" A girl a couple of rows over is waving her arms and trying to get my attention while another girl giggles and whispers in her ear.

I raise my eyebrows in a what's-up stare.

"We're having a party this weekend," she says. "You want to come?"

I'm too stunned to reply. I don't even know these girls' names.

"Is that one of your disco outfits?" asks the giggly one.

"Huh?"

"Hey, man! Hey! Hey, you!"

I turn around in my chair. A guy diagonally behind me is gesturing with a tabloid-sized newspaper. "You're that girl!" he says.

"What girl?"

"The one in the article!"

Suddenly I remember. The school paper. Has my interview been printed already? And if so, where's all the ridicule? I'd expected new, improved taunting and maybe a nickname or two. Instead everything seems . . . better. Better than better.

"Can I see that, please?" I ask the guy.

He folds the paper in half and wings it toward me.

"Yeah, you're cool, man!" he continues. "Way to stick it to the Bippies."

I quickly skim the article, which carries the headline NEW STUDENT BRINGS WEST COAST WAYS TO LAKEWOOD. It's a much bigger feature than I thought it would be. The thing takes up half the page. Did that reporter girl print every single word I said to her? They even have a picture of me trudging down the hall in my coveralls and galoshes.

"When did this come out?" I ask the guy.

"Monday. People can't stop talking about it."

"Really?" Is that why everyone rubbernecked during my arrival this morning?

"Yeah," says the girl who invited me to her party. She and her friend are leaning across their aisle, listening in. "They love how real you are. It's true what you said about the Bippies. How they tell people how to act and how they're so fake all the time. Everyone agrees."

"Everyone who's *not* a Bippy," adds her friend. "That's probably why Caitlyn didn't come to homeroom today. She knows we're all tired of her crap."

"But . . ." I can only sit there, gulping air. This makes no sense. How could people have taken that article the wrong way? Sure, I went off on the popular kids, but I also gave crazy-person answers! I raved about cheesy seventies dance music and said stewed beets were my favorite snack, which they *are*—I'm weird that way—but *still*!

"Oh, you saw it." Jack nods at the paper as he sits down in Shanna's usual seat. "It's good, huh?"

No. "How did they even take this picture?" I mumble.

He shrugs. "A couple of our school photographers can be like paparazzi. Some guy was probably waiting behind lockers for you to walk by."

I finish glancing over the article. Obviously that writer girl didn't get me at all. The way she wrote it, I don't really come off as some creepy nutjob. Instead she made me sound like an artsy trendsetter. She even has the nerve to call me fun and authentic and totally natural. I wanted her to make me look like a lunatic!

Tired of staring at my five-inch-high self, I refold the paper and chuck it back to the guy behind me.

"You should go by the journalism room and get a couple of copies," Jack says, so helpful.

Yeah, and authentically punch a sophomore reporter in her totally natural face. It would be fun.

"By the way," he adds, "Mrs. Minnow needs the note from your parents excusing your absences."

I dig through my Star Fleet backpack, looking for the note Les scrawled out for me, but I can't remember where I put it. In my hurry, I almost toss out a couple of maxi pads I had stashed in there in case of an emergency. I start to safely tuck them out of the way when it suddenly hits me: *why not let everyone see them?* Yes! That's it! I can humiliate myself back to loser status!

"Whoops!" I exclaim as I purposefully knock the two pads out of the bag. "Look at that! My *maxi pads* just fell onto the floor!"

The students down front take one look at them and break into nervous laughter. Then more kids bob up for a peek. I pretend to fumble with them so that as many people as possible can catch sight of what I'm doing. I try not to smile as the laughter grows. My mind spins up a lovely daydream in which groups of onlookers smirk and call me Maxi Maggie. . . .

"Man, don't you hate it when that happens?" says the girl who invited me to the party.

"Yeah," goes her friend.

"Don't feel bad," says another girl to me. "One time I was reaching in my purse for a pen and I pulled out a tampon. Right in the middle of class."

Everyone laughs at that.

"Man, guys have it easy," says the party girl, pouting.

Others nod and mutter in agreement.

Suddenly I'm the center of a female-bonding session. I glance around at the guys. Jack at least has the sense to look embarrassed for me, but no one else seems all that bothered.

I finally find my note and hand it over to Mrs. Minnow. She exchanges it for a bright blue excused-absence pass and whispers something about a homework grace period. By the time I make my way back to my seat, the whole feminine-hygiene incident has passed. And from what I can tell, it didn't leave the slightest pencil mark on my reputation.

As soon as I retake my seat, there's a crackling sound above my head and Dr. Wohman's voice comes over the intercom. "Good morning, ladies and gentlemen," he says. "May I have your attention for some announcements?"

Funny how they always *ask* for our attention, as if we really have a choice in the matter.

"The nominees for homecoming queen have been selected. Congratulations to the following young ladies: Hannah Hirsh . . . Caitlyn Ward . . ."

"Please!" someone snorts.

Someone else groans.

"Shanna Applewhite, Tenisha Lewis, and Sugar Magnolia Dempsey."

What?

Several people in the room clap. Jack smiles and says something I can't hear. My heartbeat is twanging loudly, and everything around me looks a little off, as if I'm staring out from a fishbowl.

So *this* is why Sharla was sobbing. She didn't make the cut and I did! I, Maggie Dempsey, loser extraordinaire, am now a nominee for *homecoming queen*?

If only Sharla knew that, right now, I feel like crying too.

• • •

"How did this happen?"

"They passed out the ballots yesterday while you were gone. The top five vote-getters become the nominees."

"I know how it works but . . . why me?"

"I don't know. I wrote down Hannah Hirsh. She once tried out for *American Idol*."

I'm sitting in the cafeteria with Penny, hoping to return to some normal strangeness after a morning full of *strange* strangeness. But I can't even eat. The Stabbies are back—this time set to puree.

"Are you coming to water aerobics today?" Penny asks, carefully spearing her green beans so that no tine goes empty.

"I don't know," I mumble. "I'm not feeling all that great."

"Helen probably won't be there. She just had surgery."

"She did?" I'm sorry to hear that. I really like Helen.

"She hurt her knee. Apparently it was all swollen up with fluid and they had to stick a tube in and drain it. . . ."

I push aside my thermos of cauliflower soup and rest my head on my hand. The day's only halfway over and already I'm wiped out. All morning I've been greeted and congratulated and quoted to from the article. I've seen Pokémon, Kim Possible, and Teenage Mutant Ninja

Turtle backpacks. I've seen Winnie-the-Pooh and Trans-former binders. One girl had a Scooby-Doo purse I really envied. And even now there's a drama kid at the next table eating from an Elmo lunch pail.

"Way to go!" A pretty Hispanic girl pauses at our table on her way from the lunch line. "I voted for you, you know."

I suppress the urge to grab her by her shoulders and shout, *Why in hell would you do a thing like that?* Instead I mumble, "Thanks," and shove a big glob of cauliflower into my mouth, making further conversation impossible.

The girl grins at me as if we're sharing a secret and continues on to her seat.

"So after that they slice off part of the cartilage . . . ," Penny is saying.

I force myself to chew the cauliflower, trying not to choke. I see the girl sit down with her friends at the end of the table. Their heads dip together and they start up a chat storm, pausing occasionally to look over at me and smile.

Why do all these wonderful things have to happen to me? It's not fair! First Jack. Then this stupid home-coming nomination. It's like the Universe is determined to see me succeed. In the past, I would have been groggy with joy. But not now. Not when I have three months before I take leave of this place.

Take leave. What a weird saying. Seems to me you either take something or leave something. But if you *take leave*, what happens to the something? Does it get canceled out?

Maybe that's why I'm so tired. I'm literally being used up.

My gaze wanders over to the popular table. Lots of people over there are watching me, including Miles. He's nodding to something a guy in a baseball cap is saying, but his eyes keep drifting in my direction. Caitlyn and Sharla are glaring at me like two mustache-twirling cartoon baddies. Sharla's face is all puffy and splotchy, and I find myself feeling sorry for her. She was right. I don't belong in that list of top-tier females. And strangely enough, I don't *want* to be there. Not here. How could people have voted for me when I've been acting like a supreme loser for weeks?

It feels like my stomach is folding itself up. Halfs. Quarters. Eighths. Sixteenths. Maybe it's possible to implode from stress. Maybe the force of the Stabbies will pull everything inward until there's nothing left of me but a wavy distortion.

What happened to what's-her-name?

She collapsed under too much strain and became a black hole.

"Hi!" Another total stranger—this time a girl with thick red hair and glasses—has come up and tapped me on the shoulder. "I just wanted to let you know that my friends and I are going to vote for you. Good luck!" She gives me a wide smile and walks away, her Hello Kitty backpack bouncing along behind her.

"Wow." Penny's sparse brows push together as she scrutinizes me with all her mouth-breathing might. "You're really . . ."

No! Don't say it!

". . . popular."

After school I hide in the bathroom, waiting for most people to clear out before I leave. Forty minutes and twenty-two pages of *Gulliver's Travels* later, I finally decide it's safe to venture outside.

The halls are empty except for the custodial staff, and the bus pickup point is deserted. I head down the sidewalk, wondering if I should do the bathroom-hiding thing every day until we move. Maybe I can arrive early in the morning and stake out a stall then too. Maybe I can even convince Penny to eat lunch in there.

I turn onto a street parallel to the one I usually take. Once again I'm following one of Penny's elaborate maps. I told her I'd pick up the flyers for the Helping Hands Halloween Dance. The print shop isn't far off my route home, so it's no big deal. Besides, our next meeting is tomorrow after school, and if I show up with the flyers, it might earn points with Mrs. Pratt. I just hope Jack doesn't decide to ask me out in front of her again.

My brain starts rolling footage of the kiss, and once again that squashy feeling comes over me. I don't know what to do. I'm really trying not to like him, but my mind is still confused. Just seeing his wide smile this morning and breathing in his clean, papery scent made me want to fall into his arms all over again. At least I managed not to give him my phone number. I just have to keep putting him off until he gives up.

I repeat these thoughts as I head into the print shop, pick up the stack of papers, pay for the order with the tax-free account number Penny gave me, and wander back outside. The smell of coffee wafts over me from a nearby café, and I suddenly get the urge for an iced chai latte.

As I meander down the sidewalk, I pull one of the orange flyers out of the stack and study it. The design is hokey but cute. There's a sketch of some ghosts, witches, mummies, and vampires dancing under a full-moon disco ball, and across the top it says "Join the Helping Hands for their Spook-tacular Halloween Dance. We'll be dancing to DJ Master-Man and 'goblin' up treats!" Something tells me Carter helped with the wording.

Finally I reach the café. As I cross the red and black checkerboard floor, I suddenly sense the speed and temperature in the room change. Glancing up from the flyer, I see several beautiful and familiar faces looking right at me. I've wandered right into a hive of Bippies. The gleaming tans, as well as the smell of salon products, should have been a tip-off.

"Nice of you to join us," says someone in a drawling voice. It's Miles, hanging over the back of a chrome bistro chair.

Beautiful.

He gets to his feet and stalks toward me, all smirky and snakelike.

"Watch out, dude," says one of his chucklehead friends. "Or she might jab you with her big trash stick."

"Yeah, I got a big stick for her," Miles quips.

Lovely.

Forget the chai. Forget the notion of ever having a moment's peace in this town. I spin around in my rubber boots and head toward the door.

"Hey!" Miles steps in front of me, causing me to veer left. Only he keeps matching me pace for pace until I end up wedged in the corner between him and the window. "Hey, chill! Don't be so pure. I was just joking."

"Please move out of my way," I whine.

"Wait. Just listen, okay?"

He has me trapped. I really can't leave. So I fold my arms across my chest and raise my eyebrows impatiently.

After a quick glance back at his pals, he hunches his shoulders and says, "I know you act like you don't like me, but that's crap. You and I could be great together as soon as you stop." His tone is sulky yet demanding. "So how about tonight? The Golly Bums are at the Hole in the Wall and I can probably get us in." He dips his head and levels his eyes at me in a sultry sort of look. "Come on. I'm not so bad. You'll see."

What is *with* this guy? I think I made myself pretty clear at the park. Why does everyone in this whole crappy city seem determined to like me no matter what I do?

"*No,*" I say as firmly as I can.

Miles looks surprised, then insulted. "No you *can't?* Or no you don't want to?"

"Just *no!* No to everything. Always. Forever and ever."

He blows out his breath and rakes his hand through his choppy haircut. "What is your deal? I just . . . don't get you." All the swagger has left his voice and posture. For the very first time, Miles is being straight with me. "You act like you're too good for everyone, but then you go and hang out with those weirdo kids."

"Maybe I'm a weirdo."

"No, you *aren't.* And you know it."

He says this with such total conviction all I can do is stare back at him. I'm seriously freaked now. It's as if Miles just barged into my mind, kicked up his feet, and started reading my innermost thoughts. Does he know? Can he really tell I'm faking it?

Miles shakes his head. "I don't know why, but you're trying to pull something here. Whatever it is, it's just . . . sad."

He gives me a long, dissecting stare. It's like Norm looking at me—if Norm were gorgeous and had better breath.

I feel my neck starting to flush. In a moment my face will be like one of those flashing lights on top of emergency vehicles, all red and glowing and obvious. I have to end this. Fast.

"You don't know what you're talking about. Just leave me alone." I push past him, but not before I see a triumphant grin wriggle across his face. *Wonderful.* Of all the people I've met in Austin, it has to be Miles who figures out I'm up to something.

In my hurry to skirt him, a few of the flyers fall from my grasp and zigzag lazily to the floor. I don't bother picking them up. 'Cause that's me. Maggie Dempsey. Liar and litterer extraordinaire.

But the Universe isn't done with me yet. As I cross the checkered tiles, heading for the exit, who should sashay in but Caitlyn. She glances from me to Miles, quickly charts the direction I'm coming from, and gives me her sneeriest look.

Somehow, though, that makes me feel better. At least Caitlyn still hates me. She knows a weirdo when she sees one.

"Do they make these in extra-large?" I ask Penny as I try for the third time to shove all my hair under the swim cap she loaned me. I still can't seem to get the hang of it.

"Maybe," Penny says. "For people who have really big heads." The other ladies giggle at this.

I wasn't going to go to water aerobics, but then I decided that thrashing about in liquid that isn't slimy might do me some good.

Even Helen is here, hobbling about on crutches. It's still too early for her to restart her exercise program, but she said she was going nuts sitting at home all day and decided to come in for a visit.

"And I wanted to thank you in person," Helen says to Penny. "That was very sweet of you to mow my lawn."

"I thought you said you didn't know who'd done it," Barb calls from across the locker room.

"I didn't. But my neighbor described her and I figured it out. Why didn't you just tell me, Penelope?"

"I don't know. I forgot."

"Wait a minute." I give up on my swim cap and face Penny. "You mowed Helen's lawn?"

Penny nods. "My dad and I did. I remembered her saying how hard it was with her knee hurting, and that her son was going out of town for a while."

"Wow," I exclaim. "That was really nice of you, Penny."

"Such a good girl." Doris trots over and pats her on both shoulders.

"A real sweetie." Mabel pinches Penny's left cheek.

"Hell, I'm not surprised," bellows Barb. "She brought me so much food when I had the flu, even I couldn't eat it all."

Penny's ears have turned bright red, and she's staring down at the floor, panting hard. Suddenly she straightens up and blurts, "Maggie was nominated for homecoming queen!"

Now all eyes are on me.

"She was?"

"My, my!"

"Congratulations!"

"And she was in the school paper, too." Penny pulls a neatly folded copy of the paper out of her backpack. "Here, look."

The ladies swarm around our bench and stoop forward for a better view.

"Well, now. How about that?" Doris exclaims, standing on her tiptoes to look over Penny's shoulders.

"My, my!"

Barb lets out a whistle. "Just look at that picture."

"Horrible, isn't it?" I say with a chuckle, unable to hide the pride in my voice.

"Actually, I think you look nice," Helen says.

"But . . . but I'm in that hideous jumpsuit," I point out—rather needlessly, I think. Is Helen having problems with her vision too?

"You know," Mabel says, "it *is* rather becoming on you."

"Hugs your curves," Barb remarks.

I frown down at the photo, wondering if some sort of group hysteria could be taking place. That outfit was my greatest accomplishment in the art of dressing like a loser. Not only was it weird, it was gross-ugly. How can they possibly think it's flattering?

"Okay, girlfriends," Barb shouts. "Time to get our

heinies down to the pool." She opens the locker-room door and gestures toward the hallway. "Move it! You too, hop-along."

Once again, I'm running behind. "You go ahead," I say to Penny.

"That's okay. I'll stay. We'll see you guys down there," she calls to the ladies.

They nod and scurry out the door, Helen tottering after them on her crutches.

"Go on," I say to Penny. "I know you hate being late."

"Yeah, but we're a team. We should go together."

I notice she didn't use the word "friend," which makes me feel better. Still, I have to wonder. Maybe all the positive attention I've been getting at school makes her worried that she'll lose my company.

"Penny?"

"Yeah?"

"Why am I suddenly popular?"

She mouth-breathes for a moment, considering. "Because you're real."

"I'm what?"

"Real. You know. You don't act like you're better than everyone."

Strange. Just two hours ago Miles accused me of doing exactly that.

"And you have nice hair," she adds.

I start laughing, then realize she's totally serious. "Thanks," I reply.

"You're welcome."

I stop stuffing my hair into the cap and stare at her. "You know, you have pretty skin," I observe. She really does. Her complexion is creamy white with pale pink shadings, like the inside of a seashell, with not a single blemish in sight.

Penny's cheeks and ears turn a deeper shade of coral. "Thanks," she mumbles.

"You're welcome."

I hear the door creak open behind me, followed by some swishing sounds. An expensive citrusy smell wafts over us—the same scent I picked up this morning in the restroom.

"Hi, y'all!" Caitlyn greets in a slushy, fake-sweet voice.

"Hi," Penny says.

"It's *rully* good to see y'all." Caitlyn continues gushing. "Isn't it, guys?" She glances back at her cohorts.

"Oh yeah," adds Sharla, incapable of disguising her sneer. "Real good."

Shanna, of course, just lurks behind them like a sulky little mannequin. For some reason, she hacks me off the most today.

"We want to invite you guys to a party!" Caitlyn squeals.

Penny's eyebrows fly up to the edge of her swim cap. "A party?"

"Yeah! The Belles are having their annual Fall Ball

on the Saturday before Halloween! You just *have* to go! *Everyone* will be there!"

"Saturday before Halloween?" repeats Penny, her face going saggy. "But . . . that's when we're having our dance."

Caitlyn lets out a loud gasp. "*Rully*? I didn't know that. Did you, Sharla?"

"No," Sharla replies, little snorts of laughter escaping through her nose.

A staticky sensation sweeps over me. I suddenly remember dropping the flyers in the café . . . the look on Caitlyn's face when she saw me with Miles . . .

"You did this on purpose!" I shout, leaping to my feet.

Caitlyn places her hand on her chest, which is bulging out of her trampy athletic top. "I don't know what you're talking about. I'm just inviting you to our party."

"Yeah. We're being nice," Sharla adds.

"But the dance is a fund-raiser!" I continue. "It's for a good cause!"

Caitlyn drops her act. She throws her hands on her hips and takes a couple of sashaying steps toward me. "So? What do you guys pull in? Twenty bucks in Coke money? Please!" She tosses her ponytail and lets out a tweedling laugh.

"You're so full of crap!" I shout, making everyone go quiet. I've really lost it now. I've never wanted to smack someone so much in my life. If Rosie and Les could see me, they'd be heartbroken. "The Helping Hands are actually trying to do something good! All you guys want to do is hang around with your snob friends!"

"Rully?" Caitlyn rapidly taps her right tennis shoe, making her smug-looking head bobble around. "Well . . . you've got your thing coming up, and the Belles have theirs. We'll see who has the better turnout." She turns to leave and then pauses. "Oh, and also," she adds, glancing back with an evil grin, "we just got a rully cool DJ. His name is Master-Man. Maybe you've heard of him? He thought he was booked, but some dweeby club still hadn't paid down a deposit. So we did."

At that, she heads out of the locker room with a flouncy twirl, closely followed by her sidekicks.

I glance over at Penny and find her practically hyperventilating on the bench.

"Don't worry," I say. "It'll be fine."

"You think so?"

No. Not rully.

Chapter Ten: Fine Mess

TIP: Align yourself with the lowly and meek.
Piss off the powerful.

"It's going to be a disaster," whines Hank, holding the top of his head as if he's afraid it'll pop off.

"We'll be totally humiliated," says Frank, clutching his skull too.

"Maybe we should just call it off." Carter also looks sad and deflated. And he hasn't made a single bad pun since we started the emergency meeting fifteen minutes ago.

Pretty much all anyone has done so far is sit around and heave noisy sighs. Not even Mrs. Pratt is her typical cheerful self. The whole classroom has a dank atmosphere about it—like one of those rainy graveside funeral scenes in an epic drama. But there is one bright spot, at least for me. Because the meeting was last-minute, Jack couldn't get off work from his internship. This means I don't have to feel his moony eyes on me every few seconds or make up some reason to sprint down the hall when he asks to talk to me.

"I'm sorry I didn't pay Master-Man his deposit yet," Drip says morosely. "I was going to this weekend."

"It's not your fault," I say, patting her on the arm.

We lapse into another sigh-filled silence with no one knowing what to say.

Eventually Drip lets out an exasperated grunt. "I don't understand," she says. "Their ball is always in November. Why'd they move it up?"

"To mess with us," I grumble.

"But why?" Drip continues. "And how'd they know when our dance is? Or find out about Master-Man? We haven't even put up the flyers."

I chomp down on my bottom lip to prevent my guilt from spouting out.

"If we haven't put the flyers up, and they're all wrong about the DJ now anyway, maybe we should just . . . you know . . . move it? Or even cancel it?" Frank suggests.

"That's not possible," Mrs. Pratt says. "We've had this hall rented for months now. We probably won't be able to reschedule."

"And the Arts Outreach people are counting on us," Penny adds.

We hang our heads and process this.

"Okay, but . . . if no one comes to the dance, we won't make any money anyway," Hank points out.

"What makes you so certain no one will come?" Mrs. Pratt asks.

"Hmmm . . ." Drip taps her chin in a phony deep-thought gesture. "Our dance is in a bingo parlor, probably with homemade mix CDs and a boom box. Their thing is in a renovated mansion with a really cool DJ, fog machine, light display, catering . . ."

"And lots of rich beautiful people," Carter adds.

Again we sit silently, listening to the *chug-a-chug-a* of the building's old air-conditioning.

Mrs. Pratt studies each of our faces. "Well, if you really think it's not worth it . . . I suppose we could cancel it this year."

We all exchange pained expressions, but no one speaks. I feel like a grub. Lower, even. Like I've devolved into the same primordial swill I fell into at the pond. If it weren't for me, they wouldn't be in this mess.

"No!" I shout, finding myself on my feet. "We have to do it!"

Drip rolls her eyes. "Come on, get real."

"I mean it. We can't just fall on the ground and let those snots walk all over us. This is a good thing we're trying to do here! It's *our* thing. We should fight for it."

They all look as if they're trying to figure out how to medicate me. Then suddenly Penny stands up too.

"She's right. We can do this. We have to!"

Penny's pink-tinged expression is both ferocious and frantic. I've never seen her so worked up. And judging by the others' bulging eyes, I don't think they have either.

"You know . . . I bet I could get some people to come," Drip says.

"Me too."

"The other tuba guys won't go to their thing. They hate Miles."

"So do the oboes."

Gradually they all pull out of their funk and start chatting and planning. Mrs. Pratt nudges me and smiles.

"All right, let's give this some thought over the weekend and reconvene next Tuesday," she shouts over the din.

We all start walking toward the exit, strategizing as we go. But as soon as we reach the doorway, someone blocks our path.

It's Jack.

"I got here as soon as I could," he says, panting. "What did I miss?"

Major emergency here. I'm in an empty classroom with Jack. Mrs. Pratt apparently puts so much stock in his honor-roll-kid reputation that she's letting him lock up after we're done. I really hated the knowing grins on everyone's faces as they filed out the door, leaving us in privacy. Even Jack seemed a little smug.

Now I'm staring at the wavy pattern on his forehead so I don't have to meet his gaze. I'm breathing through my mouth so I don't catch a whiff of his pencil-eraser-and-fresh-laundry scent. And I'm gripping the insides of my checkered apron dress's pockets so my hands won't impulsively reach out for him.

It would be scary easy to fall in major like with this guy. But I can't. I don't want him to be just another one of those rolling stops in my life. A faded entry in an address book, or an e-mail folder that eventually becomes a string of unanswered *Sent*s.

I can handle this. All I have to do is avoid his gaze and be cool. . . .

"So, what's been going on?" he asks.

Augh! I just met his eye! Look away! Look away now!

"Not a lot," I mumble.

"Listen, uh . . ." He pushes a renegade strand of hair back off his forehead and shuffles his feet. "You want to try the dinner thing again tomorrow night? I found a vegetarian restaurant called Mother's that's—"

"No."

"No? Uh. Okay." He pauses and I realize he's waiting for an explanation.

"I've got a lot of stuff to do. Gotta help my dad with the shop. Busy time right now. You know. Halloween and all."

"Right." He nods quickly. "Maybe some other night?"

"Maybe." *No! What am I doing?*

"Okay. So . . ." He hesitates. His eyes lock on to mine and his body tilts ever so slightly forward. Suddenly I get it: *he's coming for a kiss!*

Of course he is. Wasn't like I fought him off the last time.

"See ya," I say, quickly backing toward the exit.

Jack catches himself. I have just enough time to see his surprise switch to disappointment before I head out the door.

Okay. Good save. But not totally. I still have that swoopy feeling I get around him. In fact, it's stronger. And Jack still doesn't seem all that discouraged yet.

I've got to do something major. Something that will make him give up on me for good.

But what?

In a way, I wasn't lying to Jack. The store *is* wacky busy lately. Part of it is due to upcoming Halloween celebrations, but it's also because Les has made some pretty cool changes.

The shop feels more open since he rearranged it. Crystal sun catchers hang in the front window, plants are everywhere, and old forty-fives hang in groups like mobiles. He even set up a small table in the middle, between two zigzag-patterned easy chairs, where customers can help themselves to hot tea. For background music he keeps the old stereo system set to a seventies-era album-rock station. The whole place has a funky-cool vibe—like a fun but eccentric relative you always love to visit.

After the meeting I came home and found Les trying to assist five different people by himself, since Rosie was off at class. I jumped in and helped a couple of university students find some Western-style shirts to wear to their gigs. Seems like every third person in Austin is in a band.

"You've got to hire some people to help you," I say to Les when the last two guys walk out the door.

"Yeah, I know. But everyone I talk to needs evenings and weekends off." He arches his back and starts rubbing the back of his neck. "Thanks for pitching in like that."

"No problem. I need to find something to wear for tomorrow, anyway." I head to my favorite rack and start flipping through my size. "What happened to all the work jumpsuits?"

"Been selling them."

"Really? For Halloween?"

He shrugs. "I don't ask."

Damn. I really liked them—even if what Barb says is true and they do emphasize my minor curves. They were weird yet comfy. I just figured I'd get baggier ones.

I hear the back door open and Rosie breezes in, her crystal and magnet jewelry rattling with each step. "Hello, loved ones!" she sings. She walks over to Les and the two start up some major aerobic kissing. "How was your day?" she asks when she finally comes up for breath.

"Excellent!" Les exclaims. "Finally figured out something to do when the customers don't know what costume they want. I just ask them their birthday and go by their sun sign. Aquarians really like the superhero stuff."

"How clever of you!" She smooches him on the cheek and then turns toward me. "Oh, doodle! Why so stressed?"

I didn't even realize my tension was that obvious. But here comes Rosie, swooping in with a bear hug and a scalp massage. I have to admit it does help.

"What's wrong, bee-bee?" she asks. "Is it school?"

"Sorta," I say, my head bobbing under her expert fingertips. "Just club stuff."

"Like what?" Les asks.

I hesitate, not sure I want to tell them. I've been keeping so many secrets from my parents over the past few weeks, I'm scared I might say something that will reveal too much.

On the other hand, I really could use some advice. After my little locker-room pep talk with the Helping Hands, I left school wondering, *what now?* At the time all I cared about was not letting Caitlyn win. Now I'm not sure how to keep us from failing abysmally.

"Well, see . . . I'm in this club . . . and we're having this dance . . ."

As Rosie strokes out my tension with her fingers, I

manage to tell the whole story one phrase at a time—careful that I don't launch into how the whole mess got started.

"I don't understand," Les says, stroking his goatee in that wise-old-man way of his. "Why are you so sure the students will go to this other party instead of your dance?"

He sounds just like Mrs. Pratt. I swear, sometimes adults can be so naive.

"Because they're popular," I explain.

"Popular?" Rosie stops massaging. She and Les stare back at me, totally confused. You'd think I'd said "uffnerblatt."

"Yes!" I take a yogic breath, trying to hold on to the effects of Rosie's rubdown as long as possible. "Those kids are going to have a DJ and all kinds of cool things. We just have . . . us. And whatever music the twins download. And a few cases of Coke."

"But that doesn't mean the *people* at the other party will be more fun than you," Rosie says.

Obviously she has never hung out with the Helping Hands.

"Whatever." I shake my head, letting go of the idea of gaining insight from them. "It'll work out. No big deal."

"Well, I'm going to have a drink on the roof and watch the sun go down," Rosie croons, doing a backward dance toward the stairs. "Who wants to join me?"

"You go ahead," I say to Les. "I'll close up. I still need to find something to wear."

"Okay, sugar pie. Thanks for the help." He charges up the stairs, and I hear Rosie let out a girly shriek.

I rummage through the inventory for twenty minutes, searching for the right wrong clothes. It looks like there's nothing left except for way-too-big or way-too-small things. I'm finally at a point where I have to repeat outfits. The kimono is still there, but I don't think my organs have recovered from being squished up the last time. Too bad Jack was the only person to see the wool suit before I trashed it. That thing was perfectly ugly.

I hear a customer come in. I quickly toss the prairie-girl dress and some puff-ball pants behind the counter—on the off chance this person will want to buy them—and head to the front.

It's Shanna. And man, if anyone's in need of an emergency Rosie session, it's this girl. Her face is all bent up and creased—almost Sharla-like. And her posture is so stiff her shoulders practically reach her ears.

"Hi," I say.

"Please, please, please don't tell anyone I was here," she says in a strained voice.

"You know I won't."

Shanna nods. She steps forward, nervously weaving a lock of hair through her fingers. The strawberry pink polish on her nails is all chipped and tacky-looking, and her honey highlights have grown out about an inch. Her big round eyes, which used to appear empty to me, now just seem full of fear. Has she changed? Or am I just really seeing her for the first time?

"Um . . . listen. I'm sorry about all that stuff Caitlyn's doing," she says. "She's just . . . really threatened by you."

"Threatened by *me*?" I let out a snort. "Why?"

"Because you're real and people love that."

Real. There was that word again. If only people knew I've been a total phony since day one.

"Even Miles really likes you," she adds.

"Miles doesn't like me. He just wants to conquer me the way he has everything else in that school."

"Maybe." She shrugs. "I'm just sorry Caitlyn and Sharla are being such bitches. I want to say something, but I can't. I've got to stick by my friends, you know?" She gives me a pleading look.

"Yeah," I mumble, suddenly jealous that she gets to make friends and stick by them for more than three months.

"Besides"—she pauses, biting her chapped-looking bottom lip—"I'm not brave like you are."

I think about my hiding in the bathrooms and let out another snort. Yep, I'm brave all right.

"Is that why you came by? To tell me all that?" I ask.

"Yeah. And also . . ." She smiles sheepishly. "I need to buy a dress for the dance. You know, the one that . . . that . . ."

"The cool one?" I finish.

"Yeah." Shanna's smile fades and she looks down at her slightly less chipped pedicure. "Can you help me?"

I suddenly feel like Rosie—wanting to personally push and shove all the stress out of Shanna. Guess even princesses can have it bad.

"I think so," I say, smiling. "So, when's your birthday?"

Chapter Eleven: Live Recording

TIP: Look like a dweeb on local TV.

For two whole weeks now, this has been the daily routine of Maggie-the-So-Called-Brave: Wake up. Dress as freakishly as possible. Eat. Walk to school. Ignore Miles by playing loud mental rock music (note to self: buy MP3 player as soon as possible). Hide in bathroom until bell rings. Go to homeroom and pretend to stress over homework. Avoid all eye contact with Jack. If Caitlyn and Co. are there for a change, ignore with more loud mental music. Try to be out the door before Jack. Go to classes. Eat lunch with Penny. Listen to fascinating details about skin diseases or digestive-tract problems while consuming as much food as the Stabbies will allow. Go to more classes. Hide in restroom for twenty minutes. Go home. Act like everything is peaceful-cool.

Same show the next day. And the next. And the next . . .

Strangely enough, my only high points have been at the pool with Penny. I've finally got the swim-cap thing down, and it's been really great getting to know the other ladies. Barb told us stories about her days as a roller girl; Doris made us her famous sticky-chocolate cookies (which, Barb pointed out, totally negated the effects of our workout); and Mabel has been babbling about her new grandbaby. Helen, meanwhile, has been cheering us on from the sidelines. She also seems to have picked up on Penny's discomfort with praise. Now she quietly takes her aside to thank her for her casseroles and grocery runs.

But through all of these days, the most nerve-racking thing has been the looming Helping Hands dance. Every time I spot one of those pumpkin-colored flyers with "DJ Master-Man" x-ed out in black marker, it's like my belly turns into one of those claw machines.

In spite of my little pep rally, and no matter how much the Hands talk it up to their friends, it's obvious this is going to be a complete fiasco. The kind you see on the news, with its own title and some nifty graphics. "Halloween Dance Horror" or "World's Worst Charity."

And tonight is the night.

At seven this morning I awoke with my chest all tight and thumpy. I had dreamed I was caught in this fierce windstorm and was getting blown all over the place, bouncing off cars and getting caught in branches before wheeling through the air some more. There was no way I could relax and get back to sleep again, so I slid out of bed and looked out the window at the dim, quiet street. After a few meditative moments, I felt sort of hungry and padded out into the kitchen.

This is the only time I feel like the old, typical me: early in the morning when I'm still in the cotton short sets I wear to bed and the world hasn't started making demands of me yet. And since today is a Saturday, my near normalness can last a bit longer than on school days. I can have at least a few hours of peace before the dance insanity starts up.

I put on the teakettle and dig through the fridge for some soy milk.

"Morning, butterfly!" Rosie is coming down the stairs in her robe.

"Were you on the roof?" I ask.

"Yes indeedy," she replies. "I was doing my sun salutations directly to the rising sun."

I want to ask if she was doing them naked, but I don't. I'm a little scared she might say "good idea!" even if the answer is no.

"I have some good news for you," she sings. She

takes off her robe to reveal sensible stretch pants and her favorite yellow T-shirt with the Mayan calendar on it— my last birthday gift to her.

"Oh?"

"Actually, I heard about it last night at my class. I wanted to tell you when I got home but you'd already gone to bed. I even thought about waking you up, but you looked like you were in REM state and they say that—"

"What is it?" I interrupt, still too dozy for Rosie's chipper voice.

"I think I know how I can help you guys out with your dance!" She grins and wiggles excitedly.

Ho boy. No telling what sort of idea Rosie would come up with. Group meditation? Harmonic convergence? For some reason she believes all you need for a positive outcome is a channeling of positive energy. As if you can just *make* good things happen.

I used to believe that myself. But it's been a long time since a really good thing has happened to me. Especially lately, with all the bad-is-good and good-is-bad craziness.

"How?" I ask.

"There's this rock band called the Gum Daddies or Golly Dads or . . ."

I suddenly remember the day Miles had me cornered. "The Golly Bums?"

"Yes! That's it!" She claps her hands together and

starts bouncing up and down. "Apparently they had a gig fall through for tonight and they said they'd be happy to play your dance!"

"You . . . ? How . . . ? *Huh?*"

Somehow Rosie understands me. "One of the boys in the band, Chip Walker, has a girlfriend who is studying massage with me. We were talking and I mentioned your dance for the Arts Outreach Program, and how worried you were that it might be a bust. Well, she told Chip. Apparently when he was studying music in high school, Arts Outreach loaned him the instruments for free since his family couldn't afford them. So he offered to play and help out!"

Her voice has steadily lifted into the range of a flipped-out squirrel, so it takes me a few seconds to process her last two sentences. Once I do, I start hopping on my toes too.

"Really?" *Bounce, bounce, bounce.*

"Yes!" *Bounce, bounce, bounce.*

"Thank you!" I throw my arms around her and we sway back and forth in a tight circle. I can't remember the last time I experienced joy like this. I feel all airy and sparkly and ready for takeoff.

Rosie pulls out of my embrace and trots over to her bag. "Here," she says, pulling out a business card and handing it to me. "You're supposed to call him on his cell."

"Okay." I start running for the stairs to use the shop's telephone.

"Wait!" Rosie calls out. "It's too early. He's a musician."

"Right." I spin around and head back into the kitchen for tea, my mind already laying out plans for the day.

"And, sweet pea?"

"Yes?"

I glance up at Rosie. She's stopped her hopping and is just standing there, smiling at me. Her eyes are all shimmery and the morning sunlight has put a shine on the tip-tops of her cheeks. It's what Les calls the Rosie Glow.

"It's so good to see you happy."

I bike down Shoal Creek Avenue to a medley of honks, shouts, and hysterical laughter. This is easily the most ego-shrinking thing I've ever done in my life—or any past lives, for that matter. But this will all be worth it soon. At least, it'd better be.

Luckily I found the perfect outfit for tonight. For half an hour, I poked around the shop, looking for something loser-dweeby. You'd think that since every day is Halloween for me, this would be easy, right? Well, it was kind of not. Eventually Les brought out this big red thing I had thought was drapes, but was in fact a costume for someone called Queen Amidala. At first I refused, since it was one of the more expensive items. Then Les said that he didn't think it was going to sell anyway, and that every time he pulled it out for some girl, she would laugh and say "no way." That was when I knew I had the winning losing look.

So here I am, wearing a heavy scarlet robe with black trim and a thick scrolly section down the front. On my head is a giant PVC piece that resembles the lid of an ornate teapot, with a knob, two antenna-like spires, and a big fake red jewel hanging down my forehead. And as if my poor noggin weren't weighed down enough, attached to the headpiece is a stretchy brown wig-thing that bags up my hair and makes it seem like an enormous dark caterpillar has wrapped itself, leechlike, around the back of my skull.

Les even insisted on doing my makeup to match the photo on the tag. Now my face is ghostly white, except for dark lines along my eyebrows and tiny splotches of red on my cheeks and lips. Having never seen the *Star Wars* movie that the tag tells me she comes from, I don't know who this Amidala is. I assume she's some sort of space geisha who shoots lasers and transmits intergalactic messages with her helmet. One thing's for sure: I bet she didn't have to ride a bicycle in this getup.

I've pushed the front dangly thing over my shoulder, and the robe is all twisted about my middle so as not to get caught in the spokes. Of course, it's hotter than a convection oven outside, and the combined weight of clothes, hair, and *Star Trek* backpack has kicked my sweat glands into high gear. My sneakers definitely don't go with the outfit, but they're the only comfortable things I have on; and besides, no one can see my feet when I stand up.

"What's the matter? Forget your spaceship?" calls out some guy in a convertible.

Fortunately, I soon hit a nice downhill slant and manage to coast awhile, letting the resulting breeze cool my overworked pores. A moment later I turn a corner and the Happy Trails Bingo Hall appears on the right.

Jack's truck is in the parking lot. Instantly, I feel a tightness across my middle—which stays even after I've parked the Raleigh and unwound my regal robes. Avoiding him at school is one thing, but I'm not sure I can do it all night.

I approach the glass doors and catch sight of my reflection. There's some dampness on my forehead, but otherwise Les's makeup job seems to have held up. Guess those years of summer stock taught him something other than twitty monologues. I head into the main hall and find the Helping Hands scattered about the room. Penny, dressed as a cat, and Drip, in a pirate outfit, are setting up the drinks table. Hank and Frank are balanced on stepladders to hang orange and black streamers. For some reason, they are both wearing black fake-leather trench coats and sunglasses. In a back corner, Jack, who isn't in costume, is helping set up the sound system with Carter, who's dressed up as Spider-Man.

The twins are the first to spot me.

"Whoa," says Frank, dropping his end of the twisted crepe paper. It flutters to the ground by my feet.

Hank lets out an annoyed grunt, then sees me and does the same thing. "Maggie?"

"Yeah?"

"You look so . . . awesome."

I try not to laugh. Their slack-jawed stares totally don't work with their pseudocool outfits.

"Maggie!" Jack is crossing the room toward me. There is so much speed and purpose to his stride that I'm taken aback. Plus he looks extra-good with his sleeves rolled up and two buttons undone on his shirt. "I need to talk to you." He places his hand on my shoulder and nods in the direction of the foyer.

Uh-oh. I quickly try to spin up some way to prevent this alone time, but I'm too tired from my bicycle ride.

"Everyone wants to quit," he says once we're out of earshot. "We've hardly sold any tickets and all we've been hearing about is how fun the other thing will be. It's going to be sad."

"Do you want to quit too?"

He pauses for a second, before nodding. "We all do. Well . . . not Penny, but everyone else does. The only thing keeping them going is you."

"*Me?*" That's dumb. How can I possibly have that much power when I'm the newest member? "Actually . . ." I break into a grin. "I think we should definitely *not* call the dance off. In fact, I can make you guys feel completely better about this."

Jack gives me his most skeptical are-you-on-meds expression. "How?"

I smile secretively and walk to the middle of the hall. I've been eager to do this all day. It was what kept me pumping that bicycle up and down hills in my dork wear.

"Hey, guys," I call out. "Come here for a sec. I've got the best news ever."

The others exchange looks of doubt as they trudge over.

"What?"

"What's up?"

"Are you and Jack getting married?"

I completely ignore the last comment. "This is how we're going to get people here tonight," I say. Unzipping my backpack, I turn it upside down and dramatically dump out a new stack of flyers. Luckily the print shop still had our original, so I talked the guy into lopping off the reference to Master-Man and adding "Music by the Golly Bums!" in capital letters across the top.

"What the . . . ?" Drip picks up one of the new flyers. "We can't lie. That won't work."

"It's not a lie," I say, restarting a calmer, headpiece-friendly version of Rosie's bouncy dance.

I explain about Rosie's connection to Chip Walker, and Chip's connection to Arts Outreach, and how the band's previous gig fell through. As I go on, the Helping Hands seem to rise slowly off the floor. By the time I wrap up with Chip's offer to play our dance, they are pumped up past their full heights. Even Drip looks tall.

"Ohmigosh!" Drip exclaims. "The Bums are the coolest band in town right now!"

"You are the awesomest girl ever," Hank says.

"Yeah," adds Carter. "She's saving us from the Dark Side."

"Wow. Thanks," Jack says, stepping up beside me. He's gazing at me intensely, as if trying to map every single freckle. My gut cramps up tighter.

"So what do we do now?" Penny asks.

"We get the word out. Forget streamers. Forget the tablecloths. We need to pass out flyers and tell as many people as we can before the dance starts."

"I'll send out an e-mail alert," Frank says.

"I'll put it on the band discussion board," adds Hank.

"And I, of course, will post it on the *Web*," Carter says, doing a bumbling Spider-Man crawl.

"Dude!" Drip gets right in his face and jabs him in the chest with her plastic sword. "Stop making us look uncool!"

"Fine," Carter mumbles. "I'll hang up flyers in the coffee shops and stuff."

"Great, guys. I'll see you in a little while." I gather up a few flyers and start putting on my backpack.

"Where are you going?" Jack asks.

"I've got to bike over to some TV station. The Golly Bums are going on at five to plug their new CD and Chip said he'd mention our dance on the air."

"TV?" Drip echoes. "That's so cool!"

"You are the awesomest girl ever," Hank says again.

Jack takes out his car keys. "Then let me give you a ride."

"That's okay. I've got my bike."

"Leave it. You're cutting it close and I can get you there faster." He's using that presidential voice of his—the one that implies that I should let him take over since I'm way too flaky to handle things myself.

Only . . . he's right about there not being much time, and I'm really not looking forward to riding around in this outfit again. As much as I don't want to, I should just give in.

"Okay," I say. "Thanks."

At the TV station we're made to stay in the lobby while a couple of people run back and forth to Chip Walker and the station manager, confirming that it's okay to let us in. The Miss America reject at the front desk keeps giving me up-and-down looks. I have a feeling she was a Caitlyn in high school.

Finally a woman with short red hair and blue square-rimmed glasses comes out and shakes both of our hands.

"I'm Elsa," she says. "Please come this way."

Jack keeps clearing his throat and dusting invisible specks off his slacks. "This is a great station," he says in his best kiss-up voice.

"Thanks." Elsa just keeps marching through the corridor at a brisk pace.

"So . . . ," he continues, falling slightly behind us as he gawks at framed promotional posters of the anchors. "Are you the director?"

"I'm the head camera op," she replies without glancing back. "The director is busy with the show right now."

She leads us into a smallish office with a nice view of downtown. Sprawled in a chair is a cute twenty-something guy in black jeans and a black vintage shirt. He stands up when we walk in and holds out his hand.

"Hi, I'm Chip," he says. "Are you Maggie?"

"That's me." I push up my floppy red sleeve and shake his hand.

"Great outfit."

"Thanks. This is Jack." I gesture behind me, and my sleeve accidentally whacks Jack in the face. "He's . . . also in the club."

"Hey." Chip extends his hand.

"Nice to meet you."

"Mr. Walker, you only have seven and a half minutes until your segment airs," Elsa says. "I'll be coming to get you soon."

"That's cool. I'm ready whenever."

Elsa shuts the door and the three of us smile and nod at each other.

"Where's the rest of your band?" Jack asks.

"Not here. It's a lot easier to set up when it's just me and my guitar. Especially since we only get to play one song. But don't worry. You'll get the whole gang tonight."

"We really appreciate you doing this," I say. "You're saving us."

"Really," Jack adds. "You have no idea."

Chip laughs. "Yeah, I might have some idea. It wasn't *that* long ago that I was in high school. Although I try not to remember it if I can help it."

"Why?" I ask.

"I had kind of a rough time—being a real geek and all."

"You were?" Jack looks stunned.

"Uh-uh!" I exclaim.

"Oh yeah. Ask anyone who was there. I was a royal nerd. Even other weirdos picked on me."

"How'd you survive it?" I ask.

"I don't know. I had my friends. I really liked band. And I guess I just knew it wasn't going to last forever. I kept my focus on what would happen *after* graduation."

Jack nods briskly. "Yeah. Yeah."

"I can't wait for high school to be over either," I mumble, thinking about the freedom of college. "It's so much crap."

"Aw, don't be that way," Chip says. "I'm probably being too harsh. In a way, I should be grateful for all the bullshit I went through back then."

I wrinkle up my nose. "Seriously?"

"Yeah. Sometimes people who have it easy in high

school think they're going to automatically have it easy out in the world. And when they don't, they freak. But those of us who go through stuff . . . we have experience handling crap. We can deal with it."

"Yeah. I guess so." I never really thought of it that way.

"Did it help you work hard at your music?" Jack asks. "Did it help you achieve all this?"

"It helped me with everything, man." He gives each of us a smile.

There's something very Jack-like about Chip. On the surface, he seems like the anti-Jack: sloppy, stubbly, slouchy, and with a lazy drawl of a voice. But they both have the same friendly-faced cuteness. And they both hold their gazes a little longer and deeper than most people.

I try to picture Chip as a ganglier, less fashionable teenager. Somehow I can.

Elsa pokes her head through the door. "We're ready for you, Mr. Walker."

"Cool. Can I bring my new friends?"

She hesitates for a second, giving us a good glance-over. "I think we can make that work."

We follow her down the corridor into the main studio. On one end is your stereotypical bean-shaped anchor desk, where a fluffy brunette sits reading notes. At the opposite end they've set up a makeshift stage with a microphone and two amps. An electric guitar sits on a nearby stand.

While Chip goes over to do a quick sound check on the equipment, Elsa positions me and Jack along the wall behind the cameras.

"Stand right here and don't make any noise at all," she says. "Absolutely none. Okay?"

"Yes, ma'am," I reply.

A moment later the director does a countdown and the lady behind the anchor desk goes all perky. "We have a special highlight for you in our studios today," she says through her smile. "Chip Walker of the band the Golly Bums is here to sing us a song off their new CD, *Freezer Burn*. Hi, Chip. What are you going to play for us today?"

Elsa gives Chip a little hand wave and he breaks out in a grin.

"Hey, Tanya," he says to the camera. "This is a song called 'Stomped.' "

Chip starts up a melody on his guitar and begins singing in a surprisingly soulful voice. It's an upbeat, frisky song, and yet I wonder if it has something to do with his high school years. I don't catch all the words, but it talks about getting kicked and stampeded. He also mentions army boots a lot.

Jack and I bob our heads along with the rhythm. Even a couple of camera operators are tapping their feet slightly. Meanwhile the anchor lady just keeps reading her notes. I notice she's now been joined by a mannequin-looking guy anchor.

When Chip finishes, everyone in the studio claps.

"Thanks," says Chip. "That's the first cut off our CD. Y'all should go out to Waterloo Records and buy it."

He fiddles with his guitar and even plucks a couple of strings. I wonder if he's nervous.

"Tonight the Golly Bums have a special gig," he continues. "I want to introduce you to a friend of mine who can tell you all about it. Maggie, will you come up here?" He holds his hand out toward me.

What? No way.

"Go on," Jack whispers. Elsa looks at me, and her stare is the equivalent of a shouted command.

All righty then. My limbs feel strange, as if someone else is controlling them, but I manage to make the required number of steps over to his side.

"Tonight Maggie and her friends are holding a dance to benefit a great group of people called the Arts Outreach," he says to the camera. "Tell them where and when, Your Highness." He takes the mic off the stand and holds it in front of my mouth.

"At the Happy Trails Bingo Hall at Congress and Winona," I hear myself say. "Doors open at seven. Admission is five bucks a person."

"And you're going to be there?" he asks.

"I'm going to be there."

"And you're going to dance?"

"Yup. Gonna dance."

"So, how *do* they dance on the planet Naboo?"

Naboo? I have no idea what he's talking about. "They . . . naboogie?"

Chip cracks up. Even Elsa's shoulders are jiggling in silent laughter.

"Ha, ha, ha, ha. Very good," cuts in the anchorman, with his sugarcoated voice.

"Yes. Ha, ha, ha," the female anchor chimes in.

"Chip Walker of the Golly Bums, thank you for being here and telling us about your new CD," says the guy anchor. "And thanks to your friend Maggie, too."

Elsa gives a little signal and the red light on top of our camera goes out.

"Sounds like a fun dance, doesn't it?" says lady anchor in a fake chatty voice.

"It sure does," replies dude anchor. "I just might naboogie on down there myself."

"Ah, ha, ha, ha!" Lady anchor just about pops a facial muscle on that one. "We thank you for joining us this evening. We hope you'll tune back in later tonight."

"And . . . we're out," shouts the director.

I blow out my breath.

"You did awesome," Chip says, playfully shoving my padded shoulder.

"Really? I thought I sounded stupid."

"Naw, you seemed fun."

I smile gratefully.

Jack strides up to us. "You were really great. Both of you."

"Thanks," we say in unison.

"Uh . . . Mr. Walker?" Jack says, still nervously dusting his pants. "Is there anything we can do to help you for the gig tonight?"

"Yeah. You can stop calling me Mr. Walker."

"He can't help it," I say. "He's time-traveled here from the fifties."

"Hey, *you're* the one in the alien costume," Jack retorts.

Chip laughs and shakes his head. "You guys are classic. Really. Y'all make a great couple."

"I hope a lot of people see it. Except . . . I hope they aren't too turned off by my lame 'naboogie' joke. Don't know what happened there. It's like I channeled Carter or something. If I'd known he was going to put me on camera, I would have prepared something to say."

I can't stop babbling as Jack and I cross the parking lot toward his truck. I'm still hyped-up from the broadcast, plus I'm hoping that constant noise might prevent any analysis of Chip's "great couple" remark.

When I finally pause for a breath, I sneak a glance at Jack. He's staring straight ahead, seemingly lost in thought, his right hand nervously tugging his left sleeve cuff.

A question pops out, something I've been wondering for a while. "Aren't you going to wear a costume?"

"No. I don't do costumes," he replies. He's still using

that high-polished voice he used in the TV station. I wonder if he'll ever loosen up to Chip Walker levels.

Suddenly he stops walking and turns to face me. "Hey, um . . . can I talk to you for a sec? I need to tell you something."

Damn! I should never have quit jabbering. "Now?" I ask, glancing around.

Jack nods and swallows. Then he swallows again. "Look, I keep thinking about when we went out that night," he says, staring down at the pavement. "And I want to apologize for . . . coming on so strong."

I don't know what to say. So I say nothing.

His expression wavers and I realize he takes my silence as a request for more information.

"I think I was trying to be more like you."

Huh? Now I really do want an explanation. "What are you talking about?"

Jack bunches up his face, as if trying to squeeze out the right words. "You're so free. You're not afraid to be just you. But I'm more . . . uptight, I guess. More worried about rules and things. That's why it's so great being with you."

Maybe my plastic headdress is cutting off circulation to my brain, but nothing he's saying makes sense to me. "I still don't get it," I say.

He blows out his breath and looks past me at the highway. "See . . . I always try to do the right thing. I know it's boring, but it's me. I spend a lot of time worrying before I actually do anything. But you don't. You just dive right in and do what you feel. Like turning cartwheels or wading in duck ponds. It's . . . different. It's . . . great." His eyes slowly find mine. "So I guess that night, when I kissed you, I was just doing what I felt like doing . . . without worrying about it."

Oh, this is bad. That swoopy, swirly feeling is back. I try to break my eyes off his, but I can't. They're the only things holding me upright.

All I want him to do is grab me and kiss me again.

Only . . . I *don't* want that.

But I do.

But I don't. Because of . . . some really good reason I can't think of right now.

"Anyway . . . I'm sorry. I can tell I sort of freaked you out. I just want you to know that I'll give you all the space you need." He looks away and it's as if two megawatt heat lamps have stopped blazing down on me.

I blink and glance about, remembering where I am and what I'm doing. It occurs to me that I should be thrilled. He's doing exactly what I wanted, sort of. He's laying off me.

Yay?

"Thanks," I mumble, only because I feel like I should say something.

"No problem." He grins stiffly. I can tell it's a cover—a Band-Aid on his wounded pride. "Can I ask just one favor, though?"

"Sure. What?"

"Will you save me at least one dance tonight?"

Just one dance? I stop to consider, feeling relieved-confused, grateful-disappointed. But it all brings me to the same answer.

"Sure."

Chapter Twelve: Found Missing

TIP: Be a horrible, treacherous, conniving person.

I wish I could see Caitlyn's face right now. I would laugh for the rest of my life.

Our media blitz worked. Seems all we had to do was mention the Golly Bums and suddenly we were the ones with the coolest party. And the most amazing thing is it really *is* a cool party. There are hundreds of people here. Most are from Lakewood, but some are just regular folks who heard about our fund-raiser. Hardly anyone is in costume, but who cares? The dance floor is so packed I'm a little scared it might buckle.

The Golly Bums have already played one set, taken

a breather, and gotten back onstage for a second. Strangely enough, even when the twins played their mix CDs during the break, people kept on dancing. And when Mrs. Pratt got up to talk about Arts Outreach, everyone clapped and cheered.

The Helping Hands are all wearing the same astonished look on their faces. I wonder if they've ever been a part of anything so wildly popular. I'm not sure I have—even at schools where I've been inside the superelite cliques.

We've all been so busy we haven't had much of a chance to dance or socialize. But that's okay. It's been fun just watching the crowd swell and listening to them have a great time. As we scurried back and forth fetching Cokes for the band or worked our respective shifts at the door and the drink tables, we'd pass along exciting bits of news.

"Mrs. Pratt has to go buy more sodas again!"

"The whole drama club is here!"

"We've already made over three thousand bucks!"

Finally Mrs. Pratt offered to let a few Lakewood kids in free as long as they worked a shift, and she told us we needed to enjoy the fruits of our labor.

So here we are, staring out at the crowded dance floor, toasting each other with Dixie cups full of soda.

"To Maggie! The awesomest girl ever!" Hank shouts.

"Who-ooo!" cry the others.

I'm so blissed-out happy my whole body feels fizzy.

It's kind of like my windstorm dream. Only this time I can fly.

Jack raises his cup and gives me another semisad smile. He's been slightly out of it tonight.

But who cares? Not me. I'm Queen Abi-something. Ruler of high school dances. Able to conquer conniving cheerleaders and rival parties. Not only is our fundraiser a major success, but Jack has agreed to give me space. I can leave here in a couple of months without any regrets.

I down my Coke in three big gulps and slam the cup against the table, squashing it a bit. "Come on, guys! Let's dance," I say as the Golly Bums start up a new, funky number. I twirl onto the dance floor and the Helping Hands follow.

"Go, Maggie. Go, Maggie. Go, Maggie. Go, Maggie," they chant, forming a circle around me.

I hike up my robe, sashay into the middle of the ring, and do an interpretive dance number that would have made Rosie proud.

"Go, Carter. Go, Carter. . . ."

Carter takes the middle and stalks about in the classic Spider-Man crouch, except with an added buttwiggle. We all start laughing.

"Go, Dri-ip. Go, Dri-ip . . ."

Drip swaggers out to the center of the circle and starts expertly popping up her shoulders and stomping her feet into a blur. I'm so stunned by how good she is I almost forget to sway and clap along. She looks like some sort of hip-hop, swashbuckling windup toy. Other people have stopped dancing to watch.

"Go, Hank . . . and Frank. Go, Hank . . . and Frank. . . ."

"Do your *Matrix* moves!" Carter shouts through his cupped hands.

The twins do their best supercool strut into the middle and face each other. In time to the beat, Hank slides his feet and bends himself backward until I'm scared he's going to fall on his butt. At the same time, Frank sweeps his right hand toward his brother, missing his nose by mere millimeters. Then they reverse the move, with Frank arcing backward and Hank's arm serving as the limbo pole. It's really kind of awesome, and I notice even more people are watching us now.

"Go, Penny. Go, Penny. . . ."

At first Penny resists, but we keep chanting her name over and over, never letting up. Finally she steps cautiously into the circle and glances around, huffing through her mouth. Just when I think she's not going to do anything but breathe, she raises her arms over her head and starts curving them from side to side. Then she lifts her left leg and swings it back and forth to the rhythm. Suddenly I recognize the movements: it's our water-aerobics routine. And the strange thing is it totally works as a dance. By the time she does the figure eights with her arms, all the Helping Hands are joining in. All except Jack, who just stands there and claps to the beat.

Now just about everyone around us is watching. I notice a couple of half sneers, but mostly they appear to be enjoying our little dance-off.

"Go, Jack. . . . Go, Jack. . . ." The guys start chanting as Penny moves back into her spot.

He holds up his hands and shakes his head.

"Go, Jack. . . . Go, Jack . . . ," we urge.

Just then, the song ends and the whole place goes seismic with applause. Jack looks totally relieved.

"Thanks. Thanks a lot." Chip's voice echoes throughout the hall. "Now we're going to slow it down for you a bit. This song is called 'Definite Maybe.'" The bass player plucks out a few mournful notes and Chip's guitar lets out a weepy-sounding wail. All over the dance floor, couples clutch each other and start swaying.

"This is more my speed," Jack says, walking up to me. "How about that dance now?"

I pretend to catch my breath as I think it over. It's just one dance. Now that he's agreed to back off, I probably don't have to worry so much. Besides, I did promise.

"Okay," I say, stepping into his arms.

We nestle together perfectly. The spot beneath his right collarbone is the ideal place for my head. If it weren't for my headdress bumping against his face, everything would fit just right. I clutch Jack tightly, still whirly from our group routine, and inhale his clean, starchy scent.

"This is the best dance I've ever been to," I say. It's the truth. I've never experienced such all-out, fluttery fun. I'll bet there are sparkles in my aura.

"Me too," he whispers back.

"We did it," I say. "We actually pulled it off."

"*You* did it," he murmurs into my ear. "You're amazing. The awesomest ever."

I look at him, and suddenly the temperature in the air between us spikes. There might even be steam. I don't know. Everything else seems clouded from view. I can see only Jack's trancelike eyes and those tidy grooves combed into his slightly slick hair. I want so badly to muss up that hair and unbutton those top two buttons of his shirt again. I want to run my finger over the smooth hollow below his cheekbone and trace the slope of his large nose.

My brain is no help. I've downshifted out of all rational thought. Right now I'm just a series of impulses.

Me . . . Want . . . Touch . . . Warm . . . Kiss . . .

The next thing I know, I'm falling forward, closing the small gap between us. My right hand reaches up and my mouth finds the perfect flight path toward his.

No. Wait. Stop! A little dart of reason shoots through me, but it's enough. I freeze in place, lips slightly parted, hand hovering near his cheek. I quickly go into a full reverse, but not before he notices.

Jack stops swaying and I can almost see the question marks in his eyes.

"I—I'm sorry," I stammer. "I don't know why . . . I was only . . . I guess I'm just having too much fun."

"It's okay. I understand," he says with yet another glum smile. "I know you need to get over that guy Trevor."

Trevor. Right. He's the one I really want. . . . Isn't he? *Wait a sec . . .*

Now that I think about it . . . it's been days since I've had one of my regularly scheduled mopefests over Trevor. I quickly scan my feelings, desperately searching for that heartache, the oh-so-familiar agony of having to leave him behind. But it's just not there anymore. I can *remember* it, but the pain itself is gone. All that's left is a cold spot, a deadened scab of a memory.

Oh my god . . . I'm over Trevor? How can that even be possible? He meant so much to me! For months he was in almost every single one of my thoughts. I planned everything around him. The hurt of our breakup was the whole reason I started Operation Avoid Friends!

But it's true. I'm through missing Trevor. Instead, for some weird reason, I miss the misery. That constant ache meant that Trevor and I had had something real and special. It was like this little string that kept me connected to him.

Now our relationship is no big deal—just something that happened during one of our many stops.

How can something that felt so important turn out to mean nothing?

I close my eyes and picture Trevor's face, but his

features twist into Jack's. Then I open my eyes and look at the real Jack and again feel that strong pulling sensation, that urge to snuggle in close.

An awful thought occurs to me, bringing on a severe case of the Stabbies: *I failed*. I had this wonderful plan to hate this place and to be hated too. Only now look at me. I'm dancing with Mr. Wrong, who feels like Mr. Right, partying with a group of kids I shouldn't like but do. I'm having the best time ever. And the worst part is it doesn't mean anything! Apparently love and friendship can be cleansed from your system the way toxins are flushed out of your liver by Rosie's herbs.

Nothing matters.

I break away from Jack and take a few irregular, almost seizure-like steps backward.

"Maggie?" Jack looks truly worried. He cares. That really sucks.

I whirl around and go crashing through the crowd, whipping people with my robe and knocking heads with my big teapot crown-thing. Everywhere I look are smiling, dancing partygoers. The whole place reeks of happiness, but I want no part of it. It's all a bunch of crap, anyway.

I've got to get away from all this meaningless fun before I go crazy.

Maybe it's too late.

• • •

I'm hiding in a corner of the bingo hall, next to a big blue drapery panel. It's dark and deserted and it offers me a great view of the crowd. I've watched Jack make a couple of loops around the dance floor, searching for me, but fortunately he couldn't see my white face peeking around the curtain folds.

I still feel all jerky, but at least some normal brain activity has returned. Between reminders that I am so monumentally screwed, my mind did manage to come up with a plan of action: I have to get out of here. Fast.

All I have to do is make sure Jack isn't watching. Then I can sneak out the door and bike home before any key people notice.

I peer around the drapes, trying to make out Jack's tall, well-groomed shape among the bodies on the dance floor. I don't see him. At least, not nearby. I could leave now . . . but what if he comes this way before I make it to the door?

I'm staring straight ahead so intently that I don't see a small group approaching from the left. Eventually I hear them talking.

"Is that her?"

"Yeah. I remember that costume from TV."

"Maggie?"

They step toward me, further into the light, and I make out Shanna in the pretty peach-colored dress she picked out at Dudz. With her are two girls I recognize from school and the run-in at Zilker Park. They're second-string Bippies—more of Caitlyn's followers. But I don't see Caitlyn anywhere. Or Sharla, for that matter.

"This is such a cool party!" Shanna exclaims.

"I saw you on the news," says a blond girl. "It's so cool you know the Golly Bums!"

"Yeah," says the other girl, a really tall brunette.

I frown at Shanna. "What are you doing here? Why aren't you at the other party?"

"Oh, that was lame," she replies.

The other girls nod and roll their eyes.

"Everyone is so tired of Caitlyn and all her crap."

"She told everybody not to come here, so we did."

"She's probably the only one left," Shanna says with a smirk. "Except maybe Sharla."

"And that sorry DJ who kept trying to get us to line dance."

I slowly inch sideways, hiding behind them in case anyone looks this way from the dance floor.

"This is Simone," Shanna says, gesturing at the blond girl. "And this is Bree." She points to the tall one.

"Hi," I mumble, all stupefied. Why are these Bippies talking to me? I'm glad for the extra cover, but I wish they'd just go away.

"Chip Walker is sooooo cute!" exclaims Simone.

"Let's go to one of his club gigs sometime," Shanna suggests. "You could get us in, right?"

"Uhhh . . . I don't know," I say, ducking behind Bree a bit. I just thought I saw Jack, but it was some other guy.

"Hey, what are you doing after the dance?" Shanna asks, grabbing my arm. "You should totally hang out with us afterward. We're going to Simone's lake house."

I have no idea why these Bippies have rebelled against Queen Caitlyn, but it's amazing how different Shanna is. She seems so much more relaxed and happy.

"Could you invite Chip to come?" Bree asks. "Tell him there's a hot tub."

"And lots of booze," adds Simone.

I can't believe how friendly these girls are to me. All because of a dance? Just hours ago they would never have let me or the other Helping Hands into their precious soiree, and now here they are crashing ours. What two-faced snobs.

My god. That's *it*. That's where I went wrong!

When I started this school, I avoided these girls and their scene because I didn't want to make any friends. So I joined the Helping Hands—the "loser" club. But *these* people are the real losers! *These* are the ones I won't be sad to leave behind. If only I'd chosen them!

Maybe it's not too late. . . . A new plan starts to formulate itself in my mind. A new game of switcheroo . . .

"Oh my god. Look at that." Simone points toward the dance floor, where Carter is doing more Spidey moves for the crowd. "You should go dance with him, Bree."

"Not me. I'm allergic to dorks."

I open my mouth to tell them to shut the hell up,

and then stop myself. I have to quit caring. No sense fighting over something I'm giving up anyway.

"Oh god. Oh, look!" Simone breaks into a fresh fit of giggles. "Look at those two!" She gestures toward the twins, who are trying to do hip-hop moves in their trench coats.

"Oooh. Twice the fun," Bree says sarcastically. "What do you think, Maggie?"

"I think . . . leather has never looked so uncool," I reply. It feels awful to say it, but the girls give a good roar.

Shanna peers at me quizzically. "Wait a minute. Aren't they your friends?" she asks. "The ones from that club?"

"Hey, I'm only in it because my parents are making me," I lie. "They think it'll look good on my college application."

"Parents can be such a pain," Bree says sympathetically. "Mine want me to get all active in church. Nine o'clock Sunday morning? Hello-o? I'm not even awake yet."

"Or back at home," adds Simone. The three of them hoot hysterically.

Suddenly Bree doubles over, her squeals of laughter getting higher and stronger.

"What?" we demand.

At first she can't even talk; she just keeps waving toward the Helping Hands on the dance floor. "Look," she gasps. "Check out that girl!"

Penny has now become visible. Her eyes are closed

and she's doing the water-aerobics moves again. Sure, she looks a little funny. But she also looks sort of . . . happy.

"Oh, that is so wrong," snarls Simone.

"I think I have to go to church now," Bree adds.

I realize it's my cue. "She looks like . . . she's trying to tread water. Like she's drowning or something."

The girls genuinely laugh at that. My stomach feels like it's turning inside out.

"Hey, Maggie!"

I glance up. Carter has just spotted me. He gestures in my direction and then he, the twins, Penny, and Drip (who I couldn't see in back of the others) come rushing over, all smiley and dancey.

"Come 'naboogie' with us," Carter urges.

"Yeah," says Drip. "We want to do another dance-off."

"Mrs. Pratt might even join in," Penny adds. "And Jack's been looking for you."

My heart is pounding more loudly than the band's rhythm section. Being mean to these guys behind their backs is one thing, but to their faces?

But I've got to do it.

"No," I say slowly. "I don't think so."

"Aw, come on!"

"Why not?"

I stare into their shiny, joyful faces. They think I'm the awesomest girl ever. They've made me feel welcome and happy and included. But I can't let them do that to me anymore.

I try to think back to when we first met and the way I automatically looked down on them.

"Please!" I exclaim, switching to my popular-girl voice—the one I thought I'd never use here in Austin. "Do I really have to be seen with you all the time? I mean, I know this is a charity event, but I've got to draw the line somewhere."

Wham, wham, wham, wham, wham. Five expressions fall automatically. And just like that my awesome status is gone.

"What the hell are you talking about?" Drip asks.

"Look, I did my part," I reply. "I got the band and helped the dance and earned my brownie points. Now I'm done. Now I can be with my own kind."

They keep standing there, pummeling me with those pathetic, hurt-shocked faces. Penny's confused look is especially painful. *Why won't they just leave?*

"So . . . that's it. Goodbye," I say impatiently. "Seriously, guys, get a clue. Don't you have somewhere to go?"

"Yeah, run along and play," says Simone.

Gradually they start to amble backward, still staring at me, all bewildered.

"Come on, guys," Drip says, narrowing her eyes at me. "Let's get away from these snobs."

One by one they turn and follow Drip back toward the crowd. Penny is the last to go. She lingers behind for a few seconds, practically wheezing in confusion. By the time she walks off, I feel rotten inside. The Stabbies are painfully bad, like I'm getting shot in the gut with a nail gun.

"God, I thought they'd never leave," snarls Bree.

"Me either," I mumble.

"They are so weird! How can you stand to be in a club with them?" Shanna asks.

"I can't," I reply, watching my former friends disappear into the shadows. "Not anymore."

Amazing how fast things can change. Just twenty-five minutes ago, I was so happy I was literally dancing. Now suddenly the music seems too loud and harsh, the air seems claustrophobic, and the crowd seems way too lively.

"And she says in this whiny voice, 'That's not very nice,' " Shanna describes, mimicking Penny's overenunciated way of talking. The other girls laugh. I force a chuckle out of me. "Caitlyn ate it right in front of her face."

I'm standing with my new "pals," listening to the story about the stolen Ho Ho. According to Shanna, someone dared Caitlyn to take it and she did. Shanna seems determined to make Caitlyn look as awful as possible and has been telling us all kinds of tales about her. Apparently Caitlyn rose to fame by doing just about any wild thing that would earn attention.

"Caitlyn can be so mean," Bree remarks.

Just then, a familiar guy shape comes toward us through the shadows. It's Miles. His gorgeous face is raised at a high angle, as if in victory—or to make sure as much light as possible hits it.

I'm pissed to see him here. He doesn't belong; none of them do. But I really can't do anything about it. I'm one of them now.

"You made it," Shanna calls out.

"Hey, y'all," he says, stepping into our foursome. "Hey," he says just to me.

"So, what's happening over there?" Shanna asks. "Is Caitlyn crying because we all left?"

"Like I care," Miles replies. "She's the stupid hag who wanted to move the date up, even though it meant we couldn't get the lights. And that DJ she wanted so bad turned out to be lame."

"Tell me about it," Simone agrees.

"You know . . ." Miles sidles up beside me. "You look kind of hot in that costume."

"Thanks," I mutter. I'd forgotten that making this my new crowd would mean I'd have to hang out with him.

Miles's grin curls sideways. "Hey, Shanna," he says, keeping his eyes fixed on me, "I'll pay you back if you buy me a Coke."

Shanna snaps to attention. "Uh . . . okay. Come on, girls."

Crap tart! What just happened? I watch helplessly as my new so-called friends head off toward the drink table, leaving me alone with His Hotness.

I press myself against the curtained wall, hoping to melt through it by sheer force of will.

"So, where are your nerd friends?" he asks.

"I don't know," I reply truthfully.

"You here alone?"

"Yeah, sort of."

"So you finally decided to drop the act, huh?" he goes on in his real voice—the one I heard the other day in the coffee shop. "I knew you wouldn't be able to stand it forever."

I don't say anything. Being so close to him makes me feel evil.

"I'm right, aren't I?" He looms forward, contouring himself around me as if shielding me from gunfire.

I lean sideways, trying to find light and air and to see if those stupid girls are coming back yet. Shanna, Bree, and Simone are nowhere in sight. But I do see something else. Something that makes my throat jam up with trapped screams.

Jack is charging out of the crowd, right toward me. His jaw is set and his face is all fired up. I've never seen him look so pissed.

"I need to talk to you," he says to me.

"Whoa." Miles turns around and glares at Jack. "I don't like the way you're speaking to her."

"Butt out," Jack snaps. "This has nothing to do with you."

Miles takes a step toward him. "I think it does."

"I need to talk to Maggie," Jack says through his teeth. "Move out of the way. Now."

"I don't think so." Miles grins menacingly. " 'Cause you see, I don't think she wants to talk to you. So get your dork ass out of here before I rip you a new one."

"*Stop!*" I shout. I can't stand to see fighting. And this night is bad enough as it is. "You!" I point to Miles. "Stay! And you!" I point to Jack. "I'll give you two minutes. That's all!"

I stomp away from the wall to a somewhat empty area of the room and cross my arms, waiting. After a brief stare-down with Miles, Jack follows.

"What?" I say shakily. It's hard to look at him. I feel like I'm going to burst apart, spewing flesh and bone and tatters of red cloth all over the bingo parlor. I'm way beyond Rosie's help.

"What's going on with you?" he demands.

"What do you mean?"

He huffs impatiently. "Drip told me what you did."

I stare past him. Over his right shoulder I see that Shanna and the others have rejoined Miles and are watching us intently. Over his left I see the Helping Hands standing with Mrs. Pratt. They're also peering at us curiously.

"So?" I say, sounding like a six-year-old.

"So *why*? Why are you being such a bitch to your friends?"

I meet his angry gaze and it literally hurts me inside.

Don't back down, I tell myself. *If you do, it'll hurt even worse when you leave.*

"Whatever," I say, reverting to my popular-girl voice. "I have new friends now."

"Who? *Them?*" He nods at Miles and company. "They aren't your friends and you know it."

"They are if I say so." Once again I feel like I'm a first grader having a shouting match with the teacher's pet.

All of a sudden the anger leaves his face. "This is about your boyfriend, isn't it?"

"Leave me alone!" Now I'm the angry one. I keep wanting to get away but people just won't stop talking to me and telling me all about myself.

"Is it something *I* did?" he asks.

"Just go away!" I try to walk past him but he grabs my arm.

"No," he says. "I'm not buying it."

Oh yeah? thinks my suddenly six-year-old self. *I'll prove it!*

I break away from Jack and go stomping over to Miles. He has a split second to look shocked before I wrap my arms around him and kiss him right on the mouth. Just when I'm about to pull back, he seems to snap out of his surprised state. He yanks me closer, clamping his lips even harder against mine and shoving his tongue all around. I feel my helmet fall off, and my hair goes tumbling down my back. My lungs are squashed and his expensive-smelling cologne is making me dizzy. I feel like I'm suffocating.

Finally I heave myself backward and terminate the kiss. Miles's cheeks and mouth are smeared with white makeup and he seems a little dazed too.

I glance around for reactions. Shanna and the girls are frozen in shock. The Helping Hands look thoroughly disgusted. Mrs. Pratt is shaking her head.

And Jack is gone.

Chapter Thirteen: Open Secret

TIP: Screw up all your chances at friendship.
Be a sorry-assed bitch.

My ears are still ringing at about a B-flat from the Golly Bums show. There's a leftover band of pressure around my scalp where the Queen Amidala helmet gripped my head. And the whole right side of my body is throbbing. After pretending I needed to go to the bathroom, I snuck out of the dance last night and started pedaling home as fast as I could. I was crying by then and wasn't paying very close attention. That was when my robe got caught in the spokes, and I flew onto the pavement. I went home with a bent bike, a ripped costume, two bleeding scrapes, and a case of the Stabbies so intense it hurt to breathe.

I'm never getting out of bed again. The only thing I want to do right now is hibernate until moving day.

I thought it would be so simple: I'd just act horrible to the people I cared about and be nice to the ones I disliked. I figured it would put things in reverse and undo all the mistakes I've made. Jack would forget about me, the Helping Hands would go back to their normal uncool status, I wouldn't have any friends, and order would be restored to the Universe.

Only . . . it didn't exactly work that way. Sure, I managed to make my friends hate me, and Jack wants nothing to do with me, but I overlooked one major detail: my feelings. They aren't exactly cooperating. I keep telling myself that it's all bullcrap—that I can get over this the way I got over Trevor. But my emotions just aren't buying it. The real truth is I've started to like it here. And no matter what happens, it's still going to hurt when we leave. Bad.

I first realized this about midnight and I haven't stopped crying since. I'm not even sure if I slept. The whole night passed as a parade of horrible memories of people waving goodbye to me—Trevor and various old friends, some of their faces faded and half filled-in. Or maybe it was just a series of bad dreams. Sad that I can't tell the difference between my life and a nightmare.

I might be over Trevor, but I'm not over having to live life as one big sightseeing expedition.

I'm so tired of change. I want everything just to be still—at least long enough for me to figure some things out. But since the planet won't stop that stupid rotation business, I'm doing all I can to put myself in suspended animation. I'm lying in the fetal position, cocooned inside my waffle-weave blanket, staring at the orange-peel texture of the wall.

"Butterfly? You up?" Rosie knocks on the door. The joyful bell sound of her voice makes my stomach squirm even more.

I close my eyes and try to close my ears as well. Maybe if I don't respond, she'll go away.

"Wake up, ladybug. Les made berry parfaits."

La, la, la! Since I can't shut myself down, I try my mental iPod trick. But she just keeps on pounding. Eventually I hear the door open and her soft footsteps on the creaky floorboards.

"Doodle?" She sits on my bed and starts stroking my back. "It's after nine, sweetie. Time to face the sunshine."

Again her peppiness makes me nauseous. Normally I love that about my mother. Her zing and sparkle are what make her, well, *Rosie*. But not today. Today she's about as charming as an ax murderer.

"Leave me alone," I croak.

"Is she up?" I hear Les's voice and footsteps.

"Nope. She's being lazy."

"Did you tell her about the parfaits?"

"Yes, but then she got all grumpy."

"She probably ate lots of junk food last night with her friends."

"Oh, she wouldn't do that."

"I'm right here!" I shout, sitting up like a shrouded, reanimated corpse. "You're standing in my room talking about me and I'm right here!"

"Good. You're up!" Rosie exclaims. "We have a big morning today."

"No!" I groan, clutching my skull. "I don't want to do roof yoga or eat berries. I just want to sleep. Alone. In the *quiet*."

Suddenly they're both helicoptering over me, their faces scrunched in worry.

"What's wrong, Sugar?" Les asks.

"Your aura is all muddy," Rosie remarks. "Maybe you should have a colonic."

"No!" I can't stop myself. I'm just too weak from stress and lack of sleep. A loud sob breaks out of me and I lurch forward, crying hard.

"Honey bee? What is it?" Rosie coos, smoothing my hair and wiping tears off my cheeks.

For some reason, all her attention just makes me mad. Something weird is happening. My limbs are shaking and an intense pain is shooting through my middle. It's the Stabbies. It feels like they're mulching my organs. I hug my knees to my chest and rock back and forth, trying to make them go away, but nothing helps.

"Les?" Rosie is freaking. "Les, do something!"

Les puts his hands on my shoulders and tries to steady me. "What is it, Shug?" he asks, sounding equally worried. "Are you sick?"

I take a breath and open my mouth, and suddenly all my pent-up poison comes steaming out. *"Yes!"* I shout. "I'm sick of everything! I'm sick of my life!" Somehow this makes me feel a little better. So I keep on, picking up volume and speed. "I'm sick of moving all over the stupid planet and never staying put! I'm sick of missing people! I'm sick of feeling homesick . . . and I've never even had a real home!"

Rosie and Les exchange one of their mind reading glances.

"I don't understand," Rosie says. "What brought this on all of a sudden?"

"It's *not* all of a sudden!" I wail, my voice all choked and shuddery. "I've felt like this for a long time."

"Why didn't you say anything?" Les cuts in.

"I tried! But you guys wouldn't listen!"

They stare back at me, looking utterly lost.

"I used to think I didn't have a choice, that I *had* to live this way," I go on, unable to stop. "But lately I can't stop thinking about how unfair it is. I mean, you guys have each other, but who do I have?"

"You have us!" Rosie exclaims.

"That's not the same. I love you guys, but I never chose you like you chose each other. I never chose this life!"

"But . . . we thought you loved your life," Les mumbles, sounding really hurt. "You always seemed so happy."

"Until recently," Rosie adds.

"I did! I was! You guys showed me the world. But now . . . now I want to figure out *me*. Only I can't do that if I'm always getting used to some new place."

They sit silently for a moment, both of them staring down at my square-patterned blanket. The agony in my gut has dwindled and I feel a little lightheaded. Now the guilt is starting to set in.

"I'm sorry you've been unhappy, Sugar," Les says. "But you know, in a way, you've made us feel better about something that's happened. We weren't going to tell you just yet, because we thought it would be hard for you, but . . ." He stops and looks at Rosie.

"We've decided to stay in Austin," Rosie finishes. "For good. Or at least for a few years."

"You . . . *what?*"

Rosie interprets my shock as rapturous joy and her face breaks into a huge smile. "It's true!" she says excitedly. "Les has done such a good job with the shop that Satya wants him to take it over."

"And Rosie has been offered a position at that day spa," Les adds. "They love her and want her to start as soon as she's done with her certification."

They beam at each other and Rosie bounces happily on my mattress.

"Wait a minute!" Shock waves of panic shoot through me. "*Now* you guys want to settle down? *Here?* In the one city where I've made such a mess of things I can't even leave my bed?"

Rosie and Les glance quizzically at each other, totally thrown by my sudden burst of anger. Les is probably thinking I need berries and yogurt and Rosie probably wants to irrigate my large intestine. They just don't get me. They haven't in a long time.

I can't take this. They're the two things that never change around me and I can't stand looking at them. So I do what we Dempseys are good at doing: I leave.

I bounce out of bed and head through the door, running barefoot for the stairs. Forget hibernating in this cave. I need to be alone.

Because that's how I feel.

It's hard to do an angry, stompy walk when you're wearing flip-flops.

After leaving my parents staring at each other, I didn't want to go back and change out of my sleepwear. So I raced down to the shop and grabbed a trench coat and the first shoes I could find—a pair of sparkly red flip-flops.

So here I am, wandering down Rio Grande, looking like a flasher with bed-head and trying to figure out a destination. Preferably someplace where I can think and cry and not be carted off to the state hospital.

I suddenly smell bergamot, and it's like when wisps of smoke form beckoning hands in those cartoons. I follow the scent to that coffee shop where the beautiful people hang out—the one where Miles cornered me.

There's hardly anyone inside. Too early for partying high schoolers. I tramp up to the counter with visions of hot tea and red currant scones dancing in my head.

"Can I help you?" asks a hipster dude as he dries a large soda-style glass with a white cup towel.

"Yeah, I . . . oh." All of a sudden I realize I don't have any money. I know it's only tea, but I'm so disappointed I feel like crying again. "I'm sorry," I mumble. "I forgot my purse."

"Hey, aren't you the girl who works at Dudz?" He leans across the counter, peering at me closely.

"Yeah," I reply tentatively. "How'd you know?"

"I was in there the other day. You helped me."

I cock my head and study him. He does look familiar. Then I remember. "You and your friend bought those shirts for your gigs."

"Right. Hey, whatever you want, it's on me. You guys gave me a deal, so it's the least I can do."

"Thanks." I start to tear up a little—this time out of gratitude. I'm really frazzled. "Earl Grey tea and one of your red currant scones, please."

"You got it." He flips the cup towel over his shoulder and picks up a pair of plastic tongs. I'm trying to tele-pathically guide him toward the big oblong one with the most currants when another aproned worker appears be-side him. A tattooed girl with dyed black dreads.

"Isn't that her?" she asks the hipster guy.

"That's her," he replies, grinning at me.

She turns and drapes herself across the counter toward me. "Weren't you on TV yesterday with Chip Walker?"

"Yeah," I say. "How'd you even recognize me?"

"Ian knew it was you," she answers, nodding toward my hipster savior dude. "And you still have some white on your neck."

I reflexively put my hand to my throat, wishing for a mirror.

"You're, like, famous around here," the girl continues.

"I'm *what*?" I make a face.

"Maggie from Lakewood, right?"

"Uh . . . yeah." I stare at her in a daze, half mesmerized by the metal studs glistening in her nose. I've never met this person but she knows my name.

"We hear all about you," she continues. "We went to your shop the other day and bought a couple of jumpsuits. My friend's going to paint hers." As she stares at me, I notice a sort of manic glimmer in her eyes—the kind people have when they meet famous idols.

And yet she's looking at me. *Me!* Some whacked-out teenager with too much hair, too little sense, and zero friends.

"Here you go." The guy leans in front of the girl to plunk down my tea and a plate with two scones.

"Thanks," I mumble. Still half-stunned, I grab the plate and the saucer and shuffle over to a table—in the same corner where Miles basically told me I was full of it.

I eat and sip my drink, but it's all mechanical. I can't taste anything. The Stabbies are back. I thought I'd purged them during my shouting session with Les and Rosie, but apparently that was just a temporary lull. Here they are again, needling me from all directions, as if I swallowed a baby porcupine. It doesn't help that the girl and the guy behind the counter keep watching me, grinning as if they really know me. Which they don't. Which no one does.

Including me.

I find it grotesquely ironic that what I really need right now, more than tea or scones or the fantasy of brand-new, boring parents, is a friend. Someone who'll let me confess everything and then convince me it will all be okay. But since the reason I'm hurting is that I purposefully drove off everyone who genuinely liked me, I can't have that.

After forcing down some breakfast, I continue walking around the city, sobbing off and on and wondering if there's anyone I can talk to. Not Lorraine, who hasn't sent one of her updates since she got a new boyfriend. Not my parents, who are basically the candy center of the whole mess. Not the coffee shop workers, who think I'm some sort of seventeen-year-old trailblazer. And definitely not my new Bippy "friends" or any of my

Lakewood admirers. They don't care about me. They just want me to dress weirdly and make appearances at their parties. It's almost funny, in a way. They say I'm real, and yet they don't see me as a real person.

I could barely stomach everything when I thought my time here was almost up. But now that we aren't moving . . . I just don't see how I can survive.

As I shamble along the sidewalk, crying and sniffling and lost in thought, it occurs to me that I'm heading toward the bingo parlor. Is it coincidence? Is it my guilt directing me back to the scene of the crime?

Maybe it's the Rosie in me, but I see it as a sign. The Helping Hands are supposed to be there cleaning up right now. I should probably go and clean up my mess too.

I turn onto wider, busier streets and cross a few major intersections. Several people gawk and a couple of drivers honk. I'm hoping that they're just wondering about the wild-haired girl dressed as an old-timey private eye and that they don't recognize me.

Eventually I reach the parlor. I see Jack's truck and feel a butcher knife–sized Stabby. This is going to be hard.

I pause, trembling, outside the front door. It's like first-day jitters times one thousand. Then I push into the foyer and head into the main hall.

They're all there—everyone except Mrs. Pratt. I expected them to be playing music and living up their success some more, but they aren't. Instead they're sweeping and packing and pulling down those lame cardboard Halloween cutouts with the draggy pace of a funeral march. Jack is at the far end of the room doing something with the electrical outlet.

At first no one sees me. Then Drip, who's closest, looks up from her tablecloth-folding and lets out a yelp of surprise, followed by an angry "Oh no!"

Everyone stops and gapes at me—including Jack. No one says anything. I feel a strong, tingly rush, as if every atom in my body is getting stirred up and set on fire. I move my mouth a little, but no sound comes out. All I can do is stand there and get scorched by their stares.

Suddenly Penny walks over and frowns at me. "You look bad," she remarks.

"Yeah," I reply, my voice all crackly. A shudder comes over me and the sobs restart. For a moment I just cry while everyone watches.

Eventually I take a breath and meet Penny's concerned gaze. "I'm sorry," I rasp. "I didn't mean it. Everything that happened last night, it was all an act."

Drip seems completely unmoved, and the others just look blank. Only Penny appears to be truly listening.

"You see . . . I had this plan. I wasn't supposed to make friends. . . ."

They all appear a little more interested now. I tromp over to a nearby folding chair and sit down to relieve my shaking knees. Penny follows. Then I take a deep breath and tell them everything—about my strategy and how it totally went wrong. I don't mention Jack by name, but I describe how I started to have real feelings for people and it scared me; and how all my past relationships ended up being a whole lot of nothing and I didn't want that to happen again; and how I thought becoming a Bippy would cancel it all out and help push them away.

The Helping Hands listen intently, their semi-shocked, semifascinated expressions never wavering. It feels good to confess finally, and by the time I describe how I went home and started regretting everything, I've completely stopped crying.

I wipe my eyes on my sleeve, waiting for them to say something. I don't expect them to forgive me, at least not right away, but maybe now that they know the whole story, they'll at least stop hating me.

Penny looks up at the ceiling. She seems to be mulling it over pretty hard. "So . . . ," she begins, "you wanted to hang out with me . . . because you knew you'd never think of me as a friend?"

"Um . . ." I don't know what to say. That's it, essentially. I just managed not to make it sound so awful. "Well, yeah. I mean, that's what I thought at first. Only because you were so . . . different. From me," I say rambling. "But that's not how I feel anymore! You *are* my friend. I mean, I hope you are. I really do like you!"

One by one the others turn away. First Drip, then Carter, then the twins. Jack is still staring, but Penny won't even look at me. She gazes down at the flecked vinyl tiles while a ruddy tinge spreads over her face and neck. Suddenly she whirls around and starts trotting toward the girls' restroom.

"Penny?" I stand up to follow her.

"Stop!" It's Jack. He's striding across the room in that superboy-on-a-mission way of his. "Just stop!" He halts right in front of me. His eyes look too soft for him to be mad, and for a second, I think he's going to stick up for me. "What you did," he begins, his lips quivering, "was disgusting. I can't believe I liked you. I thought you were different, that you didn't care about stupid things like popularity. But you do."

"No, I don't!" I protest. "I was trying to be *un*popular!"

"So what!" he shouts. "Obviously it matters to you or you wouldn't have gone to all that trouble. If you really liked us, you would have stuck by us, even if it meant getting hurt down the line. But you just wanted to protect yourself. You never cared how it made us feel."

I reach back to grab hold of the metal chair, reeling from his words. He's wrong, but he's right. I hurt them, because I liked them and didn't want to lose them. I was only thinking of myself, because I assumed they'd be fine. I never thought I could make that much of a difference in anyone's life.

"You might as well stay with Miles," Jack goes on, his eyes hardening. "You're just as shallow and selfish as those guys."

I start crying again, but this time it's different. It's

worse. I'm not crying because I hurt. I'm crying because I hurt them. "Please . . . I'm so sorry," I mumble, gasping and blubbering. I don't care that my face is a snotty mess. I just want to make things better.

Jack's face goes cold. "You need to leave. *Now*," he says loudly and firmly. "You don't belong here, and you know it." Then he too turns away from me.

That's it. There's nothing I can do. Everyone hates me and I deserve it. I literally asked for it.

I leave my chair and walk shakily back outside. Even though it's sunny and warm, it seems like I've just gone through a terrible storm. I feel all battered and blasted apart. I don't know what to do. I don't even know what to think.

I've made so many mistakes. Mistakes upon mistakes. Mistakes inside mistakes. My whole stay in Austin has been nothing but one big mistakefest. And I can never make it right.

And the worst part is now we aren't leaving. I'm going to have to live with it.

Chapter Fourteen: Stop-Motion

TIP: Cry in front of two thousand people.
Tell the scary, embarrassing truth.

I've just had the worst day ever. I'm talking Greek-tragedy bad. The kind that, if I went on a talk show and told the whole world about it, would make millions of people gasp and say, "Man! I'd really hate to be you."

So after I trudge all the way back to our apartment, who's the first person I see? Norm, of course.

I mount the last step and turn into the apartment and see him standing in the corridor outside the kitchen.

"Hello, moon child," he says, revealing multicolored teeth as he grins. "I brought something for you." He hands me a small package wrapped in a piece of brown grocery bag and tied up with a dingy string.

I'm too wrecked to protest, so I snatch it and say, "Thanks."

Just then, Les and Rosie step out from the kitchen and tentatively walk up beside him.

"You okay, Sugar?" Les asks.

I can only shake my head.

"I should leave," Norm says. "Thanks for the parfait."

I stay rooted to my spot as my parents walk Norm to the stairwell, mumbling about star charts and sustainable foods. After a while I hear the downstairs door shut, and Rosie and Les come at me from both sides.

"Sit down," Rosie says, pulling me toward the kitchen table.

"Drink this," Les commands, setting a lime-colored frothy liquid in front of me. Probably a green tea frappé.

For a long time they just sit close and watch me sip my liquid. They don't ask where I've been or what I've been doing. It's not their style anyway, but considering I ran out of here hours ago, screaming and babbling in my pajamas, I was sort of expecting a mini cross-examination.

After I left the bingo hall, I roamed the streets, thinking about everything I'd lost. The Helping Hands, Jack, Penny, probably the water-aerobics bunch too. No doubt I also lost Mrs. Pratt's faith in me, which means no letter of recommendation and little chance of getting accepted to a top university. So I lost my future plans as well.

But the thing is I wasn't feeling sorry for *me*. Not really. I realize that I brought this on myself. All these weeks I've been completely self-obsessed. I've used other people as part of some grand scheme, without thinking about how it would affect them. I'm just as bad as Caitlyn—worse, even. I don't deserve any friends. Not even the Bippies.

After two hours of wandering, my feet were blistered and bleeding where the straps of the flip-flops had rubbed against the skin. So I decided to go back home.

I slurp my frappé and toy with the string of Norm's gift, trying to figure out what to say to my parents, but I'm too drained. At least the drink seems to be helping. I can feel it seeping through me, refilling my energy stores and quenching the hunger pangs in my gut.

Oh yeah. That's something else I lost. The Stabbies. They're gone—only I'm not sure why or how. Maybe they've disappeared for good. Or maybe they've just grown so much they've completely taken me over and I'm now one giant walking Stabby.

"Doodlebug . . . we need to talk to you about something," Rosie says.

She seems tired. The corners of her smile have drooped several millimeters and that flicker of light in her eyes has switched to a lower wattage. She looks older somehow. Les too. There are lines around his eyes that I haven't noticed before, and his hair and beard have new streaks of gray. Did that just happen today?

"We want to apologize to you," Rosie continues. "We're sorry we took you away from so many places when you didn't want to go."

"We just didn't see it your way," Les chimes in. "You saw it as leaving somewhere, but we always saw it as going somewhere."

Rosie reaches for my hand and squeezes it. "We never minded saying goodbye to a place. We felt that all we needed was each other, and you." There's a tremor in her voice, and a sheen of water covers her blue eyes. "We just assumed it was enough for you, too. But now we realize we were . . . we were . . ." She trails off.

"Selfish," Les finishes. He strokes his goatee wearily and sighs down at the tabletop.

"It's true," Rosie says in a hushed voice. Like me, she seems totally wiped out. At first I thought she grabbed my hand to give me strength. Now I wonder if she did it to gather some. "We were still finding ourselves, still living like free spirits. We told each other it was good for you to see the country and meet so many wonderful people. We didn't stop to think how . . . *unstable* it was for you."

"To tell the truth, Shug," Les says, jumping in, "it hasn't been all that good for us either. At least not lately. I know we look it, but we're not that young anymore." He gives me a wink and a weak smile.

"We're so sorry," Rosie says, squeezing my hand superhard. "We should have asked you what you thought about moving. Just like we should have asked you about staying here. So . . . if you really want to leave Austin . . . we will."

They look at each other, exchanging information in that secret way of theirs. This time, though, I feel like I can pick up some of it. I can tell that this is hard for them. I can tell that the thought of moving again makes them tired. They've found jobs here that they like and that they're good at. They're ready to start a new adventure: settling down. But they'll give it all up for me.

Rosie and Les. My parents. At least *they* still love me.

I stare down at Norm's shabby little package and curiosity gets the better of me. I let go of Rosie's hand and rip it open, letting the pieces of bag fall on the floor. The gift turns out to be a piece of wood. A perfect oval framed by rough bark. And someone—Norm, I assume— has chiseled "Home Sweet Home" into the middle of it. My fingers trace the slightly crooked, burned-looking letters. It's absolutely beautiful.

"No," I say, laying the sign in the center of the table. I grab my parents' hands in each of mine and grip them as tightly as I can. "We aren't leaving. You deserve to stay, and you should make it work."

And so should I.

• • •

Walking to school the next day, I feel strangely calm. Maybe I've reached that acceptance phase—like those death row inmates who smile and wave as they head to their execution. Or maybe it's because I'm dressed the way I want to dress, in my lucky blue shirt, tiered skirt, and red galoshes (because it's been raining, and also because who cares?).

As I cross the lawn, students run up to me, greeting me and congratulating me on the dance. A couple of them are wearing auto mechanic–style jumpsuits; a few are in galoshes. One guy even has on a fuzzy pink vest over his T-shirt. And character-themed backpacks and lunch boxes are everywhere.

At first I'm stunned that people are being nice to me after I was so horrible to my friends. But then again, because it was the Helping Hands and not anybody with real power, probably no one else knows about it. Or cares.

That's so wrong.

"I'm voting for you," someone shouts.

"You're totally going to beat Caitlyn," yells someone else.

At first I have no idea what they're talking about. And then I remember: the whole homecoming-queen thingie. The elections are today.

Oh goody.

I head toward the front doors and see Miles and his pals in their usual spots. The minute he recognizes me, he comes right over and throws a possessive arm around my shoulders.

"Man, what the hell?" he says, pulling me off the walkway and onto a quiet section of the lawn. "I've been trying to get ahold of you. Do you, like, not have a phone or something? What the hell happened to you Saturday?"

"I wasn't feeling well and went home," I say, somewhat truthfully.

"You look better today," he murmurs, his finger tracing the neckline of my shirt.

"Stop," I say, pulling away. "Look, Miles. I'm sorry to be so weird, but this isn't happening. We're not together."

He rolls his eyes. "Oh man. Don't start this crap again."

"Seriously. I'm not playing a game." I want to be mad at him, but I can't. Not totally. After all, I messed with him too. Besides, I feel a little sorry for him. It's a total cliché, but it's true what they say about being lonely at the top. People don't see you as a real person.

"Come on," he says impatiently. "Just drop it already and be cool."

"You know, you were right at the coffee shop. When you said I wasn't being real."

"Hell, yeah. I'm always right." He grins and steps closer, restarting his overbearing charm.

I take a step backward. "But just because I'm not who I pretended to be doesn't mean I'm who you think I am."

"Huh?"

Okay. Point taken. Even I can't sort that one out.

"I mean . . ." I try to put it in his terms. "I'm *not cool.* I'm not your type. Don't waste your time on me."

He runs his hands through his hair. "You know, you're really starting to piss me off with this game of yours. If you keep it up, I just might decide you're not worth it and blow you off for good."

"Yes!" I've never been so happy to have a great-looking guy reject me. "You got it. Go with that thought!"

"But . . ." Miles is so shocked that I called his bluff he goes speechless.

"See you around." I give him a semicondescending pat on the arm and head into school, ready for whatever's next.

Instead of going to homeroom, everyone is supposed to report to the auditorium first for a special assembly.

As I'm carried along with the tide of students in the hall, Shanna suddenly appears beside me.

"Aren't you excited?" she asks, her big round eyes even bigger and rounder than usual.

"I guess. What is this thing, anyway?"

"The homecoming rally!" She gives a little toss of her head as if she can't believe my ignorance.

"Okay. So . . . what exactly happens?"

"Nothing really," she replies. "You just sit on the stage and smile and they introduce all the nominees for queen. That's all."

Oh. So this is why she looks extra-fluffy-and-fashionable today.

As we plod down the corridor, I see Hank and Frank just a few heads over. I instinctively raise my hand in a wave, but they look away. Meanwhile several nameless others are calling my name and wishing me luck.

"I bet you're going to win," Shanna says a little stiffly.

As we pass through the auditorium's open doors, I suddenly spot Jack. He's only a few yards away, near the stage, talking to Mrs. Pratt. He sees me and quickly looks away, shifting positions slightly so that his back is to me.

I feel a sudden tightness. Not the Stabbies—this is higher, more of a heart-and-lungs pain than a stomach pain. It occurs to me that I could describe the different sensations to Penny and see if she might have some explanation. Then I remember: she's probably not talking to me either.

Shanna, on the other hand, clearly thinks we're best buds. She grabs my arm and pulls me toward the stage. "Come on. We're supposed to be up there."

Sure enough, Caitlyn and the other girls are already present, perched as prettily as possible atop folding chairs. Caitlyn sees us approach and makes a little scoffing noise. Then she does her version of the hair-toss maneuver and exchanges glances with someone in the audience.

It's Sharla. She's sitting in the front row, looking

red-faced and pouty. As Shanna and I take our seats, she folds her arms across her chest, crosses her right leg over her left, and starts jiggling angrily.

I feel a little sorry for her and Caitlyn, just like I did for Miles. They're also dealing with a bunch of un-wanted change. Besides, Sharla is right that I don't be-long on the homecoming court. It's like I'm here under false pretenses.

If only she knew that I really don't want to be here. I'm tired of being in the spotlight. All these years and in all those schools, I've always tried hard to be one of the superpopular people. I thought they had it so easy. But in at least one way, they don't. They're always being watched. And if you know you're being watched, how can you be you?

Dr. Wohman steps up to the microphone and taps on it. "Please take your seats," he drones.

The noise falls to a dull roar and I hear a few shush-ing noises like gusts of steam. Someone in the back yells, "Go, Mag-*gie!*" and several people laugh. The squeezy feeling in my chest grows stronger.

"Today you will be voting on the queen of our home-coming celebrations," Dr. Wohman says as if he's read-ing off a card. "I would like to formally introduce each one of these young ladies and tell you a bit about them. First, we have Tenisha Lewis."

The crowd claps as a supercute girl with short black hair rises from her chair. She does a bouncy walk to the front of the stage and stands there, waving. Along with her short-skirt-and-sweater ensemble, she's wearing a pair of yellow duckie galoshes.

"Tenisha is one of our all-state gymnasts," Dr. Wohman says. Now he really is reading off a paper. "She's also a member of the French Club and the Austin Belles."

"That girl thinks she's so hot," Shanna says in a side whisper. "I heard she once did a movie. You know, one of *those* movies."

I clap politely, hoping no surprise registered on my face.

After Tenisha takes her chair, Dr. Wohman calls out, "Hannah Hirsh."

This time a tall, willowy girl struts up the stage and stands next to Dr. Wohman.

"Hannah represented Lakewood at the regional show-choir competition last year," Dr. Wohman goes on. "She's also a member of the drill team, Mu Alpha Theta, and the Austin Belles."

"Such a snob," Shanna mutters. "Her parents are, like, the richest of everyone in the school."

"Caitlyn Ward," Dr. Wohman announces after Hannah sits down.

Caitlyn sashays to the front to lukewarm applause. A couple of people even boo. It's such an obvious display of hostility that I feel really bad for her.

"Let's have none of that." Dr. Wohman shakes a pudgy finger at the audience. "Now, as you know, Caitlyn has been a cheerleader for four years here at Lakewood. She's also a member of the French Club, the Booster Club, and the Austin Belles."

More lackluster applause, and Caitlyn practically runs back to her seat. I look over at Shanna, waiting for her to make another snarky comment, but she doesn't. She's just sitting there with that wide-eyed blank look she always wore in her days as Caitlyn's silent accomplice.

"Shanna Applewhite," Dr. Wohman calls out.

Shanna rises somewhat shakily and walks downstage. As she nears Dr. Wohman, her foot hits the microphone cord and she stumbles a bit. A few people chuckle. Sharla practically hyperventilates with laughter. A deep strawberry pink seeps up Shanna's neck as Dr. Wohman rattles off her various clubs.

Oh no, oh no, oh no. *I'm next!*

Time seems to go all warpy as Shanna takes her seat. I see Dr. Wohman turn toward me and see him mouth my name. I'm sure he says it out loud, but I can't hear it with all the blood rushing into my head.

I get to my feet and do a wobbly walk to the front. My heart is beating so hard it's amazing I'm not ricocheting around the stage. Finally I take my place beside Dr. Wohman.

It's different up here. You can see everyone's eyes. Sharla is expending every ounce of energy to make the world's biggest frowny face at me. Off to the left, Miles is grinning and whispering with his buddies. I see Drip sulking in a seat near the middle. The twins are in the back, apparently studying their shoes. Carter is all jittery in his chair—staring at the ceiling, the floor, the people around him . . . anything but me. I don't see Jack anymore, but Mrs. Pratt is standing along the wall, watching me with a weighed-down expression.

And then I see Penny. She's near the front, not far from Sharla. My eyes must have passed over her a couple of times before I finally saw her. She's staring at me with her usual poker face, mouth partly open, eyes big and glistening. It hits me how pretty she is. Her perfect skin. The way wisps of hair curl around her cheeks and chin. How come people never notice it?

"Sugar Magnolia is a relatively new student in our school community," Dr. Wohman says. "She's a member of the Helping Hands Club."

"More dances!" someone yells.

I turn to Dr. Wohman, overcome with sudden inspiration. "Can I say a few words?" I ask.

Dr. Wohman looks taken aback. "Ah . . . well, I don't see why not." He moves away from the microphone and lets me step up to it.

"Hi," I say, a little too loudly. My voice echoes all over the auditorium. People sit forward in their chairs. "I just want to say that you shouldn't vote for me."

The audience laughs and claps, loving the joke. Only it isn't a joke.

"I'm serious," I go on. "Don't vote for me because you think I'm brave or cool or real. I'm not any of those things. I'm . . . I'm . . ." My voice cracks. "I'm a big loser."

More chuckles, but they sound nervous. People are exchanging baffled glances.

"I've been dressing weird and acting strange on purpose so that everyone would leave me alone . . . because I was scared. I thought if people stayed away, then no one could hurt me." I take a shuddery breath. The place is totally silent now. "If you really want to honor someone real, don't think of me. Think of my friend Penny, who makes casseroles for sick people and mows people's lawns for no reason but to help them out. Think of Mrs. Pratt, who treats every student fairly and even spends her free time helping less fortunate students. Think of . . . Drip." I pause, trying to think of her real name, but I can't. "She always tells it like it is and never takes crap off anyone—no matter who they are."

As soon as he hears the word "crap," Dr. Wohman snaps back into principal mode.

"Okay, that's enough," he says, trying to lead me away from the microphone. "Thank you for—"

"No! Let me finish!" I whine, shrugging off his hand. Now that I've started, I can't stop. I turn back to the audience and wag my finger at them the way Dr. Wohman did earlier. "You guys boo Caitlyn because you think she's so phony. Well, I'm an even bigger phony. I hurt all my friends on purpose." I'm really bawling now. My voice is high and rattly and my cheeks are a wet, sticky mess. "I was so sure they wouldn't stand by me, I blew them off first. I didn't even give them a chance."

My voice disintegrates into a series of squeaks. At this point my words are all globbing together, so nobody can even tell what I'm saying. I stare into the crowd. My vision is too blurred to make out individual faces, but it looks like all the students are shifting around and turning their heads so they don't have to look at me.

I glance over at Dr. Wohman. The anger has left his face; now he's just gazing at me in pity. I want to tell him "That's all," and maybe apologize, but all I can do is give him a helpless stare. The heavy, high-pressurized feeling has spread throughout my body, choking off any further speech.

Not that it matters. I'm done.

Slowly, I back away from the microphone and the restless, murmuring crowd. Instead of returning to my chair, I race down the side steps of the stage and out one of the doors into the empty, eerie corridor outside.

So that's it. I might be friendless and unpopular, but at least I told the truth.

And I've never been more real.

By lunchtime I'm pretty much back to normal. I've stopped crying and my ribs no longer feel like they're going to crack from the inside. A bizarre sense of peace has settled over me. I don't care what people think anymore—not really. It's like I've somehow moved beyond it all. High school just isn't the real world.

Strangely enough, I've finally gotten what I wanted. Everyone is avoiding me. A few people shoot me sympathetic gazes. Some openly point and mock, but most people won't even look at me. I passed Caitlyn in the hall and she didn't even sneer. She opened her mouth as if she wanted to say something, then seemed to change her mind and took off.

I have no idea how the homecoming vote went in first period—although I'm pretty positive I'm not going to win. Instead of circling one of the nominees, I wrote down Penny's name.

Yes, it was therapeutic to admit everything in front of the entire school, and yes, I'm mostly beyond caring. But as I pause at the entrance of the cafeteria, I can't help getting a little trembly. Now it's no longer my choice: I *have* to eat alone.

Snap, snap, snap. Heads look away as I weave around the tables, searching for an empty seat. As I stand there, turning this way and that, Miles walks up to me on his way out of the snack bar line.

"Man!" he says, pausing beside me so that we're shoulder to shoulder. "You really *are* a loser." He shakes his head and continues on to the Bippy table.

I feel a weird, twisty sort of relief. It can only be a good thing that Miles wants nothing more to do with me.

Finally I spot a place and sit down, eager to dig in to

Les's black bean salad after such a draining few hours. Two or three bites later, I feel the table shimmy. I look up and see Penny sit down across from me.

"They had hot dogs, but I got the chef salad instead," she says. "Do you know there are chemicals in hot dogs that make your cells mutate? Plus, the government allows a certain amount of rodent hairs."

A big happiness bubble is rising inside me, lifting my posture and making my eyes water. "Yeah," I say with a grin. "I think I heard something like that."

We eat in easy silence for a while.

"Penny?" I say, again noticing her pretty, Madame Alexander–doll face.

"Yeah?"

"Why did you sit down with me at lunch on my first day?"

Penny chews thoughtfully for a second. "Because . . . I thought you looked sad."

"Oh."

"But you don't look sad anymore."

I smile at her. "You're right. I'm not."

Epilogue: Starting Again

TIP: Be your flawed self and see what happens. . . .

"Ladies and gentlemen . . . this year's Lakewood High homecoming queen is . . ."

Come on, come on! I urge silently.

I'm standing on a football field with the other nominees, but I'm the only one being escorted by both my parents, instead of just my dad, and the only one in glittery space boots and a silver chiffon cocktail dress.

"Shanna Applewhite!" Dr. Wohman finally announces.

"Thank god," I mumble. Not that I was rooting for anyone in particular; I'm just glad it's over.

Shanna lets out a huge squeal and hugs her dad for a

long time. I'm happy for her. I think this might be good for her confidence.

"I'm sorry, butterfly," Rosie says, giving my shoulder a squeeze.

"I'm not," I mutter.

"You know"—Les looks down at me, and I see that his eyes are all misty—"you don't need a ribbon and crown to be beautiful."

"Thanks, Les."

The three of us walk off the field arm in arm, my boots leaving little pockmarks on the turf. We head for the section of bleachers where the Helping Hands are sitting together. The twins are holding up a homemade sign that reads Maggie for President, while Carter has one that says Come Home, Maggie! They clap as we approach.

"Aw, man! I know you don't care but I still wish you would have won," Drip grumbles. "These things are so rigged."

"I like how your dress sparkles," Penny says.

"Thanks." I glance around, hoping to spot Jack, but of course, he's not there. Even since the rest of the Helping Hands forgave me, Jack has kept up his big silent treatment. It still really hurts, but I don't want to ask too much of the Universe.

"Miss Dempsey!"

I spin around and see Mrs. Pratt standing behind me, wearing a crafty smile.

"Hi," I say. "I didn't know you'd be here."

"How could I not come root for you?" she says. "Besides, I remembered you saying your application deadlines were coming up and I wanted to give you this." She hands me an envelope. "Go ahead. Read it."

I open it and slide out the paper.

To Whom It May Concern, I read silently. *It is my great pleasure to recommend Sugar Magnolia Dempsey for your college. In my twenty-one years of teaching, I've never before seen so much growth in a young person. Miss Dempsey is the rare type of individual who's open to learning not just from books, but from life as well. . . .*

"Wow," I breathe. I've never felt so humbled and honored. This means more than any rhinestone tiara ever could. "Thanks. Thanks so much!" I throw my arms around her and give her a hug.

"You're welcome," she says with a chuckle. "Oh, are these your parents?"

"Hi, I'm Rosie."

"I'm Les."

"Gretchen," says Mrs. Pratt. "So nice to meet you."

As they start talking, I take a couple of steps back and read the rest of the letter. I feel proud and grateful and twirly with excitement. It's like the letter is a sort of magic ticket—an express pass to my future. Even though I'm not sure where I want to go to college anymore—the idea of going wherever Trevor goes is kind of silly now— it feels great to think my opportunities are open.

I'm so caught up in Mrs. Pratt's nice words that I

don't hear my name being called. Suddenly I become vaguely aware of a figure on the ground next to the bleachers.

"Maggie!" the figure shouts again.

I look over the railing and see flowers—white petals with red and gold centers—and Jack's head looming above them. My heart starts beating so fast I wouldn't be surprised if it burst out of me and started *boing*ing all over the football field.

"Hi," I call out. I quickly tromp down the steps toward him, scared he might disappear like a mirage.

I reach the mud-splattered concrete and stand in front of him. He seems real. My dream version of Jack probably wouldn't have his hair slicked back so neatly or a shaving nick on his jawline.

He notices me staring at the three-quart pot in his hands. "It's a magnolia," he says, bobbing his chin toward the blossoms.

"I know," I remark. "It's beautiful."

"It's for you. I figured you'd rather have something alive and with roots than something that will slowly die in a few days."

I smile. "You really aren't a Republican, are you?"

"Nope." He grins back at me. "And I'm not a Democrat either."

"So what are you then?"

"I'm me."

"I'm me too," I say. *"Finally."*

Jack's face goes all serious. "Listen, uh . . . I've been

doing some thinking and . . . I really want us to be friends."

"Oh." A little bit of the giddiness goes squelching out of me. "Friends, huh?"

"Yeah," he says, blowing out his breath. Maybe it's just that he's lugging around a tree, but he seems sort of weary. "I'm sorry. I'm just not ready for anything else," he goes on. "But I'd like for us to hang out. And maybe something can, you know, grow out of that. If not, at least we're friends."

I stare into one of the sapling's large blooms, thinking about what he's saying. He's right. Whatever happens, it should come naturally. Besides, there's plenty of time now that I'm staying here in Austin.

"Okay," I say, meeting his eye. "Friends."

He smiles and ducks his head, as if shy or relieved. Catching sight of his beeline part, I reach out and gingerly mess up his hair.

"I've always wanted to do that," I confess, lowering my hand once I've achieved the perfect disheveled look.

"Funny," he remarks. "I've always wanted to do this." Carefully holding the plant in his left arm, he reaches toward me and gently pushes all the stray hairs off my face, then finishes by smoothing each side with long, sweeping strokes. "There," he says.

We grin at each other for a moment, and I feel a little doddery in my boots. If this is friendship, it's a really special kind.

"Yoo-hoo! Doodle!" Rosie is waving down at me. "Are you ready to go? Oh! Hi, Jack!"

"Hi, Mrs. Dempsey."

"We're not staying for the game," I explain. "I invited the Helping Hands back to the apartment. We're going to dance on the roof and eat dead heads. Want to join us? It's what friends do."

"Um . . . that sort of depends. What are dead heads?"

"It's a snack this buddy of ours is bringing," I tell him. "Come on. I don't think I can carry that plant in these shoes, anyway."

"Sure," he says. "Hope I get to see more baby pictures."

By now Rosie and Les and the Helping Hands have descended the bleachers. Everyone grins at us knowingly.

"You coming with us, Sugar?" Les asks, shaking the keys to the Bumblebee.

"That's okay. I'll ride with Jack," I reply. "I know the way home."

Home. I love saying that. It makes me feel cozy and safe and part of something real.

Home sweet home.

About the Author

Jennifer Ziegler had no problems being unpopular in school. Her only major move was from the extreme chill of Anchorage, Alaska, to the muggy heat of central Texas when she was eight years old. She currently lives in Austin with her extremely patient husband, two hilarious children, and a new puppy.

Jennifer is also the author of *Alpha Dog*. Visit her online at www.jenniferziegler.net.